My Summer of Magic Moments

Caroline Roberts lives in the wonderful Northumberland countryside with her husband and credits the sandy beaches, castles and rolling hills around her as inspiration for her writing. She enjoys writing about relationships; stories of love, loss and family, which explore how beautiful and sometimes complex love can be. A slice of cake, a glass of bubbly and a cup of tea would make her day – preferably served with friends! She believes in striving for your dreams, which led her to a publishing deal after many years of writing. *My Summer of Magic Moments* is her fourth novel.

If you'd like to find out more about Caroline, visit her on Twitter, Facebook and her blog – she'd love to hear from you!

@_caroroberts
/CarolineRobertsAuthor
http://carolinerobertswriter.blogspot.co.uk

Also by Caroline Roberts

The Torn Up Marriage
The Cosy Teashop in the Castle
The Cosy Christmas Teashop

Caroline Roberts

My Summer of Magic Moments

Harper
impulse
we've got the love

Harper*Impulse* an imprint of
HarperCollins*Publishers*
The News Building
1 London Bridge Street
London SE1 9GF

www.harpercollins.co.uk

A Paperback Original 2017
3

A catalogue record for this book is available from the British Library

ISBN: 978-0-00-823627-4

This novel is entirely a work of fiction.
The names, characters and incidents portrayed in it are the work
of the author's imagination. Any resemblance to actual persons,
living or dead, events or localities is entirely coincidental.

Typeset in Minion by Palimpsest Book Production Ltd, Falkirk, Stirlingshire

Printed and bound by CPI Group (UK) Ltd, Croydon, CR0 4YY

MIX
Paper from
responsible sources
FSC™ C007454

FSC™ is a non-profit international organisation established to promote the
responsible management of the world's forests. Products carrying the FSC label
are independently certified to assure consumers that they come from forests
that are managed to meet the social, economic and ecological needs of present
and future generations, and other controlled sources.

Find out more about HarperCollins and the environment at
www.harpercollins.co.uk/green

For Heidi

'There are magical moments in every day. We just have to take the time to see them.'

Anonymous

Author Note

The inspiration for the magic moments idea in this book grew from me wanting the characters, especially Claire who goes through so much, to find joy again in the simple pleasures in life. As the book developed, I had the idea to make this a part of Claire's journalism work. As I wrote, I realized I didn't want it to be just *my* perceived magic moments that Claire might experience on her break away, but other people's too; these little gems of moments that we can all have, but sometimes forget to appreciate. So I asked friends, family, colleagues, looked at newspaper articles and also googled to find other people's magic moments to include in the book. The responses were so lovely and often very personal, so thank you to everyone who sent a moment to me; apologies that I couldn't quite fit them all into the narrative and chapter headings. They really have made the story all the more special.

I hope this book makes you think about what your magic moments might be, and appreciate them all the more when another comes your way.

Caroline x

1

A cup of tea and a stunning view

A thin veil of early morning pink-grey light was suspended above the sea. The colours reminded her of the inside of a pearlized shell, subtle and beautiful. She hugged the mug of tea between her hands. Up early again – six a.m. It was a regular occurrence after the nightmare of the past year. Her mind and thoughts veered between tumultuous and exhausted. She'd thought she might as well get up, make her first cup of the day. At least here she could sit and enjoy a calming sea view.

What a bloody journey it had been yesterday. Not the best start to what was meant to be a relaxing break. Her car had broken down two streets from 'home' – she used the word loosely these days – in Newcastle-upon-Tyne. She'd had to get it towed back to a garage, only to find out after much tutting and shaking of heads by men in oil-smeared boiler suits that it was never going to be fixed in an hour, or even a day, and that it was likely to cost a small fortune. So she'd had to take the metro to the main station, a train to Alnmouth, and then spend another bloody fortune – twenty-five quid no less – on a taxi to get to her idyllic cottage by the sea, which was meant to be somewhere near Bamburgh but seemed to be in the middle of nowhere.

The idyllic cottage itself left a lot to be desired. On unlocking the peeling white-painted front door, Claire had discovered a hallway of beige woodchip wallpaper with tell-tale bubbly patches of damp. She'd come to the kitchen next, which sported basic white MDF cabinets and a cooker that looked like it had come out of the ark. She hadn't dared to try and use it last night, settling for the sandwich she'd bought on the train and never eaten, and an apple she'd had in her bag.

She'd sat on the dark-brown velour sofa in the lounge area, staring at a clock that had stopped, possibly several years ago, on the mantelpiece over a real fireplace. Looking around at the matching brown armchair, whose seat cushion sagged heavily, a nest of 70s-style wooden tables and a couple of faded prints on the walls, she'd wondered where the hell she'd ended up. This was meant to be a relaxing holiday, a chance to chill-out. And she'd booked for a *whole three weeks*. It was cheap, admittedly, but she hadn't expected anything quite this basic.

She'd tried to cheer herself up. Yes, the place was a bit old-fashioned and in need of some TLC, but maybe she was just tired. She'd had an exasperating day, after all. She decided to have an early night, so she'd tucked herself up under a handmade patchwork quilt in her upstairs double room, and told herself it would all seem better in the morning.

In the light of a June morning, it still didn't look that promising! The whole place seemed tired, worn, and all the windows and ledges appeared to be a mass of rotten wood. The house was crumbling at the seams, and to top it all, after a hunt for the boiler and radiators to turn on against the morning chill, she'd realized it had no central heating. A cup of tea had been the only option, and now she thought she might as well head outside and get some fresh air and a sea view. She supposed she should be grateful that the balcony that led out from her upstairs bedroom was holding up.

Right, Claire Maxwell – enough moaning, you old tart. You're here to rest and recuperate. Her mind took on a school-marmish voice which sounded very like her mother's. No, they hadn't given her nearly a month off work to sit grumbling. This was the start of her new life, and she had no idea where it was going to take her. For now, it was sitting on a rickety wooden balcony on a Friday morning in June watching the sun rise over the North Sea. It was a place of calm, with a solitary gull swooping in the sky and a pair of black-and-white oystercatchers balanced on spindly legs dipping their orange beaks in the shallows.

A door slammed somewhere nearby, causing her balcony to wobble. She gripped her mug to prevent a spill. There were two stone cottages here, side by side, which fronted the beach – being isolated had been its appeal. Typical that the other was occupied, but it was the summer season. There was some guy coming out; he was probably here with his wife and a brood of noisy kids. The rest of them would be safely tucked up in bed for now, it being six a.m., but no doubt ready to shatter her peace in another hour or so.

Claire stared at the man; she had nothing better to do. He walked from his grassy square of garden straight out onto the beach. He was tall, broad-shouldered, with sandy-blond hair – quite handsome, actually – wearing flip-flops, a white T-shirt and red shorts. He looked in his thirties. He began to jog straight for the sea, stopping a couple of metres before he hit the waves to slip off his footwear. Then, in one swift movement, he pulled off his T-shirt, revealing a rather gorgeous toned and lightly tanned torso. Hey, things were looking up! Another swift motion and his shorts were off. Jeez, he wasn't wearing any Speedos beneath. The peachy whiteness of his firm buttocks and the muscular V of his back entranced her. He bent slightly to drop his clothes. Gulp. Claire leaned forward in her seat, her heart racing.

He continued his now-naked jog down to the sea. The rear view was gorgeous, athletic. Wow! Was this real? Had she guzzled way too many glasses of wine or something last night? Was this wishful thinking, a hallucinatory dream? She *really* didn't want to wake up from it if it was. She squeezed the mug in her hand – it was solid, painted a pukey-looking green colour, and the tea had a cooling milky look to it. This had to be real.

The guy reached the breaking waves, took a dive straight in, and there he was, bobbing up and down in the surf line. She watched him swim out to the calmer, deeper sea. He seemed a confident swimmer.

Ooh, then she realized he'd have to come back in, facing her in the buff with nuts and bolts and everything in full view. She should probably go discreetly back indoors, give him a bit of privacy.

And miss a view like that? Sod it. No! You didn't get the chance to see a gorgeous body like that often, if ever. Her ex certainly hadn't had a physique like this guy's. But what if he saw her? Sitting there gawking like a perv? She'd look a bit odd, wouldn't she – voyeuristic. But really, when was she going to get the chance to sneak a look at a body like that again? After all, she was here first. He shouldn't be flaunting himself like that if he didn't want a normal, warm-blooded woman looking at him.

She decided to shift her deckchair slightly back into the shadowy area of the balcony – he probably wouldn't notice her there – and sat back down, watching his head bobbing like a seal out at sea as she smiled to herself. Well then, it wasn't so quiet here, after all. And what was the harm, after everything she'd been through, allowing herself to watch a strong, healthy, rather handsome male?

Cancer had a way of doing that to you – putting things in perspective, making you realize just how precious life could be, that you needed to seize every moment – especially little magic moments like seeing a gorgeous man naked. Why not? Why not indeed.

So, still holding the dregs of her tea, she leaned back in her chair and took it all in: the sea rolling and gently crashing, the smell of salt in the air, the cry of a gull, the golden warmth of June sun breaking into another day. And she watched 'Adonis' reappear from the waves. First his shoulders, chest, the definition of his abs, his stomach. Ooh, what was about to be revealed next? . . . and . . . Oh blimey, a brown thatch of hair. And yes, it would be cold in the North Sea, but that was still impressive. Not a bad effort at all, Mr Adonis.

Right, now behave, Claire Maxwell – get a grip on yourself and go on inside.

But if you move now, he's bound to see you, her alter ego chipped in cheekily (this voice definitely not sounding like her mother). Her cheeks felt flushed and her heart was pumping. What if he saw her? That would make it very awkward if they met over the coming days and weeks. She could imagine the conversation:

'Hi, I'm Claire, your neighbour for three weeks.'

'Ah yes, I spotted you ogling my naked body . . . Do you make a habit of voyeurism?'

She shrank back in the chair. If she got up now, she was pretty sure he would see the movement from the balcony. Best to stay put.

He strolled towards his pile of clothes – whoa, stare, don't stare, gulp – slipped on his shorts, the T-shirt, the flip-flops, and shook his hair out, the action reminding her of a wet dog, then jogged back, seemingly oblivious to her presence.

Claire was left with a big grin creeping across her face.

2

'I have always been delighted at the prospect of a new day, a fresh try, one more start, with perhaps a bit of magic waiting somewhere behind the morning.'

J. B. Priestley

As well as her cottage falling apart, the hot water system left a lot to be desired. She'd gone inside to freshen up for the day, but had been seared, then iced, by a relic of an electric shower that was positioned above an avocado-green bath (more shitty green, she'd thought). The whole experience was like something out of a torture movie. She'd had to spring in and out of the piddling stream of water trying to time it right, and washing her hair had been a joke – half the suds were left in as she gave up and clambered out. At least there wasn't much hair to bother with at the moment: the curls only just growing back, giving her a pixie crop that her sister, Sally, said suited her – a gamine Audrey Hepburn look, apparently. Claire thought she was just trying to be nice.

As she towelled herself dry, she carefully dabbed the ridged scar that ran across her left breast. It didn't hurt much any more; just the odd weird pain now and again. But she didn't like to look at it. She was still trying to get used to the change in her body.

She moved to the bedroom. It was slightly better than the bathroom in decor: a pine double bed with blue-and-white patchwork bedding, a cream throw (granny's crocheted best), and a white-painted dressing table with mirror – an attempt at jaded seaside chic (or plain jaded), which roughly worked. The best part of the room was its French doors, which opened out onto the balcony overlooking the expanse of silver-gold sands and the little stream which wound down beside the two cottages and out to the shoreline.

Claire sat in her underwear on the dressing-table stool in front of the pine mirror. She had always been petite at five foot three, but was rather skinnier than she'd like to be after her illness. She smoothed on some moisturizer, brushed on mascara above her deep-brown eyes – it was great to have eyelashes again – and applied a slick of pale-pink gloss. She'd never been interested in wearing a lot of make-up, and today she wanted to feel the fresh air and sun on her skin. Then she dressed casually in a pale-pink T-shirt and denim shorts.

The first day of her holiday awaited her. She didn't have to go to work, she didn't have to get to hospital appointments. The world and this crazy run-down cottage were her oyster. She was determined to make the best of this escape time. What was she going to do with it? She decided to go for a walk along the beach to find the village of Bamburgh. It shouldn't be that far.

She headed left onto the sands from her beachside garden, a scrubby patch of grass with a battered wooden table and four chairs. As she strolled, she remembered childhood holidays spent in the area with her parents and older sister years ago. It was why she'd chosen this place – happy memories: salt and sand and shivers, warm-towelled hugs and eating yummy-drippy 99 Flake ice-cream cones from the Mr Whippy van that parked in the car park just above the dunes.

She began to feel that familiar tug in her chest. Her lovely dad wasn't here any more. He had died five years ago, bless him, a heart attack snatching him from his family at only sixty-two. She missed him so much, even now. How life changed. Her own illness had shaken up her life in ways she could never have imagined. She was close to her sister and mum; they'd been so supportive through her treatment. In fact, both had offered to come and stay during her break to keep her company, but she'd just wanted to be on her own, have a bit of time out, so she'd politely but firmly refused their well-intentioned offers.

She slipped off her deck shoes as the sand started creeping in around her ankles, and enjoyed the feel of warm, soft grains beneath her bare feet. The sun was climbing in the sky, sending glints of gold off the lapping waves. Dog walkers passed her, their charges dashing about with glee, tumbling with tennis balls, bounding into the sea, coming out matted and shaggy then shaking arcs of glittering water around them. She'd have liked a dog. They'd had Millie, an affectionate Labrador, when she was a child at home. She'd been part of the family. But Paul, her ex, had never been keen on having a pet, preferring a tidy house and order. Damn it – what was he doing creeping into her thoughts? Push those thoughts aside right now, she told herself. Bury all the hurt he caused in a great big hole in the sand.

Today was about her. And her life from now on. Onwards and upwards. She was going to have a look in the village, get some nice local provisions, then head back, make a salad or something for lunch, chop some veggies for soup, and later she intended to sit and chill in a chair in the garden in the sunshine, reading her latest book and generally pleasing herself. She hoped the family next door wouldn't appear noisily at that point. Oh well, she chided herself, she wouldn't be an old misery of a neighbour. Kids would be kids, and they were on a beach, after all – let them play. Oh yes, that was another thing Paul wasn't keen on: having children. It had never been 'the right time', or maybe, she mused wryly, she was just never the right person. The bastard.

The day stretched before her much as the beach did far ahead. She'd been wandering for a while. Exactly how far from her cottage was the village? She knew the towering castle set on the dunes marked the village area, but now she'd turned into the next crescent-shaped bay she *still* couldn't see it. It must be bloody miles away.

But she was here to relax, so strolling along the beach on a mild June morning was fine. She was in no hurry. To slip routine, work, the wearing rituals of chemotherapy, radiotherapy – was bliss. She'd made it through – she was a survivor. And she knew full well there were those who hadn't; she felt a tight knot in her throat just thinking about them, those lovely ladies she'd sat next to for their hour-long chemical shots in the bank of chemo chairs as if they were at some kind of weird hairdressers where they stole your hair instead of tended it. She didn't want to waste another day, though she didn't know yet what it was she really wanted. A rest and a bit of time out had been the only things she'd realized she'd needed for now.

One day at a time, Claire. Feel the sun on your skin.

Daylight, fresh air. The warmth of a cosy bed, be it a rickety one. Sip a cup of fragrant tea, a glass of chilled white wine or warming Merlot whilst looking out to sea. Hah, or even better, looking at a toned male torso. The memories of this morning's vision rose in her mind, making her smile.

A man's body. She hadn't felt a man's touch for a long time. Things had started to go wrong between her and her husband even before the cancer. And then afterwards, once she'd been given the 'all clear', she'd learnt how very wrong. Nothing like being kicked when you're down. But no, she wouldn't allow herself to dwell on that this morning. Today was about new starts, fresh hope and enjoying being alive. She'd think about the hunky swimming guy instead.

She picked her way over a cluster of rocks, the lime-green seaweed slimy under her bare feet. The stones, seemingly slick-black in colour, were, under closer inspection, riddled with navy and iron red. She remembered rock-pooling with her gran, dipping in those cane-stemmed fishing nets, trying to catch a shrimp or tiny silvery fish – they were fast, those ones, wriggly little numbers, nigh on impossible. It kept her and her big sister, Sally, entertained for hours. Gran sat watching them from her blanket on the dunes, a book in hand and a huge picnic of goodies stowed in the cool box. They'd stayed, the four of them, Gran, Mum, Sally and her, crammed into a caravan down the coast – five of them once Dad turned up after work. Fish and chips with lashings of salt and vinegar eaten from the newspaper wrapper as they sat on the harbour wall at Seahouses. She could almost smell them now – maybe it was just the salt in the sea air. Yes, she'd have to make a trip there. Happy days! When life was so simple.

The rhythm of her steps took over. Sometimes the sand was grainy, rough between her toes, then it was smooth, moulding to her feet. There were other footsteps in the sand too: shoe prints, paw prints, the tiny slats of a sea bird's feet, and a mild breeze rippled through the spiky dune grass. Claire sighed, stood for a moment and breathed in the fresh sea air. This was why she was here. It felt good to breathe, to walk, to be.

She turned another corner and there at last was Bamburgh Castle towering in the distance. It was a bit of a relief, to be honest: though she was enjoying the walk, she was beginning to tire. Her energy levels weren't yet back to normal 'AC' – after the chemo. Her cancer nurse had warned her that it could take up to a year to feel back to her old self, and it had only been five months so far.

The castle dominated the skyline, powerful and stunning, perched on its rock base in the dunes. She wondered how long it had been there, what it had been built for? She'd heard something about the Northumbrian kings centuries ago. She'd have to brush up on her history, find out more and do the castle tour one day. The stone of the castle walls was an unusual salmon-pink colour, unlike the cottage she was staying in and the others nearby, which were more honey-coloured with tones of flinty grey.

This part of the beach below the castle was busier, being nearer the village and the car park; there were families on a day out, children building sandcastles and splashing at the shoreline, a couple of young lads kicking a football about. She spotted a teenage girl tracing her initials in the sand with a stick, then adding a '4' and another set of initials with a big bold love heart around them. She smiled. Ah, the easy love and hope of youth. If only life and love were that simple. Claire knew only too well how the waves would come in and wash it all away soon enough.

A track led into the dunes from the beach. Claire decided to follow it, hoping to find a way through to the village. She'd need to buy some provisions to keep her going. Having come on the train in the end, she'd only brought some tea bags, coffee, a couple of apples and a pack of Jaffa cakes. She wound up and through the dunes, following the sandy pathway, spiky marram grass pricking at her bare legs. She sat to put her deck shoes back on, dusting her feet off, but she could still feel itchy grains of sand between her toes as she set off again – a hazard of beach life, she supposed. There was an opening, and she found herself coming out onto a cricket pitch at the far side of the castle. Pretty stone cottages lined the hill, clustering the quaint village green.

She was on a bit of a budget till next week's pay day now that much of her spending money had disappeared on a train and taxi fare, so she decided to head for the village stores and buy some vegetables to make a big pot of soup. As she was strolling up the hill, she spotted a small delicatessen, squeezed into a cottage front room by the looks of it, halfway up. Artisan loaves were looking enticingly at her from the window display. Maybe she could stretch to a gorgeous freshly baked loaf too. She went in, her mouth watering over a stone-baked rosemary and sea salt and a wholemeal with honey and pumpkin seeds. Decisions, decisions.

'Hello, pet. How can I help you?'

A short, middle-aged lady with grey-tinged auburn hair smiled from behind the counter.

Claire plumped for the wholemeal and asked for a pack of local butter to go with it.

The lady handed over her change. 'On your holidays?'

'Yes, got here last night.'

'Staying in the village?'

'Well, just along the road a bit, the cottages down by the beach. Farne View.'

'Oh, I see.' The woman's face seemed to drop, as though

she knew of it. But then she smiled encouragingly, adding, 'Well, I hope you have a lovely time.'

'Thanks. Do you know where I can get any vegetables? I fancy making some soup to go with your lovely bread.'

The lady told her that there was a greengrocer which stocked everything and more at the top of the village. She was to head for the gap in a red-brick wall. Claire set off, passing a butcher's. An aroma of freshly baked pies drew her in, as well as the window stacked with goodies and a counter laden with an array of fresh meats. She popped in, unable to resist a homemade steak pie which she decided she'd have for her lunch – the soup would take a while to make so that would do for supper. She also bought some rashers of bacon and a half-dozen eggs for another day. Then she headed for the long brick wall on the top side of the village green, following it until the gap and a sign appeared.

Whoa, this was very different to the Asda down the road from her semi-detached house in Gosforth. It looked more like a walled garden than a shop, yet was filled with all sorts of provisions: fresh herbs, fruit, vegetables. She filled a basket with carrots, a swede, parsnips, leeks and onions, a packet of stock cubes and some milk.

The carrier bag was laden, and, she realized too late, heavy. She'd have to walk all the way back with it. Why hadn't she thought to bring the rucksack she had at the cottage? She must remember she didn't have the same energy levels as she used to. Her body was still trying to find its way back to normality. She sometimes wondered if it ever would . . . Maybe it just needed time to find a *new* normal.

3

Jelly shoes, sunscreen, floppy hats and sandy sandwiches

It was a slow walk back from the village. Claire sat down on a rock to eat her pie, which was delicious: a crisply baked pastry shell, tender steak and moist gravy. Bliss. She guessed she was about halfway back now. She got up to set off again about fifteen minutes later and rebalanced her load, but her arms felt about four feet long. Her shoulders were searing by the time she got back to the cottage. So much for a pleasant stroll on the beach! She'd have to find out if there were any buses that went by the cottage next time she wanted more than a few items of shopping. The soup had better be worth it.

After a cup of tea to perk herself up, she began chopping the veggies with a half-blunt kitchen knife, the best of a bad bunch of kitchen utensils. Then, after finally working out how to use the hob on the ancient-looking gas stove, she fried the onion off in a little butter. She'd had to use a match to light the flame – luckily she'd found an old packet on the mantelpiece of the fireplace – cautiously poking it towards the hissing noise under the metal ring. She added the veg, a jug of stock and some seasoning; she'd even found some fresh thyme lurking in the flowerbed outside the front door and added a few sprigs for good measure. She gave it all a good stir, popped a lid on the pot, and turned the gas flame low. So that was supper sorted.

What to do with her time? She wished she'd bought a bottle of wine in the village now. Mind you, that would have been even more to carry. But yes, she could picture herself sitting out on the balcony with a glass of chilled Pinot Grigio – though funds were tight, she could have made the bottle last a couple of days. Oh well, another cup of tea would have to do.

She made her way upstairs and out onto the balcony, picking up her book on the way. She was drawn to the old wooden deckchair overlooking the beach and the sea; no naked swimmers this time unfortunately, just dog walkers and families. Two children were playing in the stream alongside the cottages that wound its way down to sea, trying in vain to dam it up with large pebbles they'd found nearby, paddling in the cool waters, splashing away happily. She wondered if they might be the children of Adonis next door. Watching them took Claire back to those days of jelly shoes, sunscreen, floppy hats, sandy sandwiches and ice cream. Childhood days when you didn't have a clue where life was going to take you, when you didn't even have to think about it.

It was peaceful here. Just what she'd needed. A sense of solitude, and yet there was life going on just outside your door, your beachfront garden, where you could join in if you wanted to, or opt out for a while. No deadlines, no work calls, no hospital appointments, not even texts pinging in, her phone off for now – the signal here seemed pretty poor anyhow. A place where you could just look at the view, breathe in the salt-sea air, and just be.

She finished her cup of tea, picked up her book and started to read, losing herself in the romantic comedy, glad to be in someone else's world for a while. The beach started to empty, the air began to cool a little, the light thinned to the white-gold of an early-summer evening.

Right, she'd better go check on that soup – didn't want it burning or sticking to the bottom of the pan. It was meant to be on a slow simmer, but who knew what that ramshackle cooker was capable of. She made her way to the kitchen and peeked under the lid – it should have been thick and the vegetables softened by now, but it was looking watery, with solid cubes. In fact, there was no heat or steam coming off it at all. She peered down at the ring. Nothing, no flame. She took the pan off and tried to relight the flame – nothing. Great. She was stuck in the middle of nowhere with a pan of raw veg for supper.

She fiddled with the knobs on the cooker. There was no hiss of gas coming through. She checked the electrics were on with a flick of the kitchen light switch, in case that was something to do with anything. An old strip light flickered into use, so that seemed to be all up and running. But as for the cooker, still nothing. She stood staring at it for a while, pondering, as her stomach started rumbling.

She went to find her phone. Standing on tiptoe by the window in the upstairs bedroom to get a single bar of signal, she dialled the number for the owner of the cottage, Mr Hedley, an elderly gentleman she'd spoken to when booking. She listened to the ringing tone. More ringing, no answer, not even an answerphone. Damn.

This seclusion wasn't all it was cut out to be. Who did you ask for help?

The neighbour. She wondered if he might still be there? She peered out of the front window and spotted his black 4x4 parked on the gravel driveway. It was worth a try – she didn't have many options left here.

Slipping on her deck shoes, she headed across the driveway to knock on his door. This cottage was larger than hers, and in a far better state of repair: the window-sills were freshly painted in white, unlike hers, which were crumbling with brown rot amidst flakes of peeling paint. A pretty pink rose climbed the wall beside the front door.

She knocked and waited. Nothing. She knocked again, louder this time, and banged the letterbox a few times; there didn't seem to be a doorbell. Damn, he must be out, maybe on a walk or something if the car was still there. She'd try later, and have to settle for bread and butter in the meanwhile. But just as she was about to turn away, she heard the scraping of a door inside, the sound of footsteps, and a shadow appeared behind the glass.

The front door inched open, 'Yes?'

It was the guy from the beach this morning.

'Oh . . . hi . . . I'm Claire . . . next door.' And all she could think of was his naked body in all its full and gorgeous glory. She felt the colour flushing up her neck, reddening her cheeks. 'Ah, uhm, the cooker.' Firm buttocks, muscular thighs. *Focus Claire.* Get a grip. 'It seems to be broken. I just wondered if you might be able to help at all?' She smiled hopefully.

He didn't smile back, just gave her a rather annoyed look, one eyebrow raised, as though he'd really rather not help. 'Ah, I see.' The house behind him seemed quiet, as though he was the only one there.

He wasn't exactly leaping to the rescue here. Despite his good looks and the cute sandy-blond curls, he seemed a bit odd, to be honest. No 'Nice to meet you' or 'Of course, I'll pop across and check it for you'. You'd think she'd just asked him to come over and clean out her toilets or something.

'I'd be really grateful if you could take a look. I have no other means of cooking,' she tried.

'Ah, okay . . . I suppose. Just give me five minutes.' He had a slight Scottish lilt. And with that he closed the door, leaving her standing on the step.

What was that all about?

Nice to meet you too! she thought and trudged back across the drive. *Charming!*

Hot bod, no personality – typical. Oh well, it wasn't as if she had any intention of getting to know her neighbour or anyone else in an intimate or even friendly fashion in any case. She supposed he would or would not appear later.

She'd just put the kettle on, thinking a cup of something might allay the hunger pangs, when she heard a crunching of the gravel outside, then a knock on her own door. She answered it. He was there. Tall, still not smiling, cool, green eyes fixed on hers.

'The cooker, you say? Gas?'

'Ah, yes. It's just not working at all. Like there's no gas coming through.'

He raised both eyebrows this time. There was a twitch of annoyance at the side of his mouth.

She lifted her brows in response, quizzically. 'What?'

'Have you checked your gas bottles?'

'Uhh . . .'

'You know, the big orange things just under your kitchen window. When they empty you need to change them.' His patience appeared to be thread thin. Trust her to get Mr Grumpy as a neighbour.

'No, I don't know anything about those.' It wasn't as if the property owner had left any useful instructions or anything for guests. How the hell was she meant to know?

'And I don't suppose you know how to change them either?'

Spot on there, matey. 'Nope.'

'Right, well I suppose I'd better show you then. Then you'll know how to do it yourself next time.' *And not bother me* was very clearly the next line, though unspoken.

They headed round to the side of the cottage outside the kitchen. Two large orange metal canisters stood propped under the window. Ah.

He lifted one easily; it seemed light. 'Empty.'

She felt a right idiot for not checking and not knowing anything about gas bottles. It just came piped out of the ground where she lived.

'Okay, so turn the switch here,' he continued. 'Then turn this valve on top until it clicks, like this.'

'Oh, okay.' She was nodding, trying to take it in.

He lifted the connection away from the bottle it had been on, shifted the empty canister out of the way and

27

dragged the other into position. 'Opposite way to fix on, screw valve back, flip switch to "on". Pretty simple, really.'

'Right, well, sorry to bother you and all that.' It had obviously been an inconvenience to him.

'And you'd better tell old Mr Hedley to get a new one in so you don't run out altogether next time.'

'Okay, will do. Thanks.'

He just nodded. 'Right, well, that's me done.' He turned and walked away, back to his tidy beach house, and closed his door. Back to his life. She wondered for a second what it was like, his life? It seemed like he might be there on his own after all. Then she put her thoughts aside. She had her own life to worry about. Her own hurts to heal. It seemed like her neighbour wouldn't be a nuisance with noise, at least. In fact, he suited her plans for peace and solitude very well.

4

A hot, bubbly bath

Awake again. The rickety bed creaked as she moved. Pitch black. There were no streetlights out here, just the sound of the rush and pull of the waves on the shore for company.

God, her left boob was uncomfortable. She must have shifted to lie front-down in her sleep and crushed it a bit. The scar was still tight sometimes, and then that weird taut pain nipped down her arm from the armpit. She wriggled her fingers, loosening them up.

She lay there thinking. She'd done it, made her escape to her cottage by the sea. Got away for a while. A chance to breathe again.

It felt like she'd been in limbo since the op and the chemo, the radiotherapy thereafter. She'd grown used to that new life of appointments, hospital visits – it had structured her days and become her norm. She'd become friendly with the nurses and the other patients, and in an odd kind of way she missed them. Even though it was for the best-ever reason that she could jump ship and leave that weird journey. It had felt strange trying to settle back into her old life, which had come as a surprise after longing for that day so much. Yet nothing seemed the same once she was back working at the newspaper, catching up with her lovely friends Andrea, Jo and the girls in the office. When they started chatting about which shoes to wear with which dress for their Friday night out, it felt like a world away from where she'd just been. She should have been leaping around with joy, but she just felt quiet inside, more thoughtful than she'd ever been. Yes, it *was* good getting back to work, but it was like the axis of her world had shifted.

She travelled back in her mind to the line-up of fake leather chairs, the chemo ward – sitting there with magazines and chit-chat, everyone's lines attached to a drip like something out of a sci-fi movie. The hour's wait, unnerving at first, but then you got used to it. She'd made it through . . . She felt tears prick behind her eyes. Others hadn't. Rebecca, Leanne . . . the friends she'd chatted with, looked forward to seeing on her weekly visit, a nod and a wave to their families as they passed, saying hello, goodbye. Talking, planning what they'd all be doing when they got out of this place. Bloody hell – some of them had never got out of that place, and she owed it to them to make the best of this life she'd been given back.

Claire had the feeling that change was about to happen, but she didn't know quite how yet, which way things were going to go. All she knew for sure was that she couldn't waste the rest of this life, this new chance.

Yes, she was beginning to find her feet, though life still seemed a little wobbly at the moment. She must hold on to the fact that she'd been given the all clear, or as clear as they could promise for now. And *for now* was a good enough place to start.

It was still dark outside – she could see from the crack in the curtains. It must be the early hours of the morning. She should try and get some more sleep, but her head was way too busy. She'd get up and make a cup of camomile tea.

Venturing downstairs, she popped the kettle on and waited for it to come to a boil in the cranky kitchen. After steeping the teabag, she took her mug through to the lounge. She didn't bother to put the light on. It was peaceful standing there just gazing out at the night sea, the silver flickers on the crests of waves under the light of a crescent moon. The warmth from the mug in her hands was calming.

She thought she saw a glimmer of light flick on, then off, possibly from the cottage next door? Maybe she wasn't the only one up at weird hours in the night. She'd put the light on in the kitchen – had that disturbed him? After all, it was three a.m. Oops, he might be an even grumpier neighbour tomorrow.

Claire woke up groggy after her restless night. Tea on the balcony time.

Huddled in her dressing gown, she went downstairs to the kitchen to put the kettle on. Crikey, even in summer it was chilly in this place. She hadn't spotted a radiator or any kind of electric heater yet, just the real fire in the lounge. Thank heavens she hadn't booked a winter break.

While the tea was brewing, she spotted a few tattered books on the kitchen shelf – recipe books; there was one on baking bread. She took it down and flicked through a few pages. She'd always been partial to a bit of armchair baking, watching the trials, tribulations and fabulous creations on *The Great British Bake Off*. Maybe she should give it a go. She had plenty of time on her hands. And that loaf from the deli yesterday was scrummy; she wondered if it was hard to make?

She took the book out with her. She enjoyed a cup of Earl Grey on her upstairs balcony in the rickety yet comfy deckchair. And pondered what to do with her break. How *was* she going to make the best of her time? A list started forming in her mind. Yes, she was meant to be relaxing, but she couldn't help being a 'to-do list' kind of girl. Hmm, the first thing she fancied was a hot, deep and very bubbly bath.

So, number 1: Soak in a hot, bubbly bath.

What next? Hmn, yes, number 2: Sip a glass of chilled white wine with the sun on her face, the sound of the sea, and a lovely view. Perfect. She just needed to go and buy the bottle of wine.

Number 3 (she was getting into the swing of this now): Watch the world go by for a while and hopefully listen to the sound of children's laughter – there were bound to be some kids on the beach at some point. That was always guaranteed to make you smile.

And if she was desperate for company later in the holiday, it would be lovely to invite her two small nephews up for the day. They always made her smile too. She remembered them finding her prosthetic bra insert when she'd stayed over at her sister's house after the mastectomy. She'd slept in her younger nephew Ollie's bedroom overnight, and he and Jack had spotted the mystery item lying on the bedside table the next morning. They'd been fascinated and had decided to use it as a Frisbee, chucking it around the room – she'd come back from the shower to find them mid-throw. Her sister, Sally, had been mortified and gave them a right telling-off, but Claire had seen the funny side – they were just kids playing. She'd ended up laughing until it made her sore.

Number 4: make some homemade bread. Yes, she'd have a go at that. So along with the wine she'd need to pick up some bread-making ingredients.

Number 5: watch that gorgeous (if grumpy) guy next door get naked again. She'd have to be alert early in the mornings, just in case. So, he might be a bit unsociable, but that didn't stop a girl wanting to take a look. But, there was no sign of Mr Gorgeous-but-Grumpy's toned naked butt on the beach this morning, though. Shame. Perhaps knowing that she was there next door had put him off. Bloody empty gas bottles. If she hadn't had to knock on his door, he might never have realized she was there, and the morning swims might have continued, brightening her day. She vowed to be alert during her stay in case, however.

Number 6: dance in the rain. She wasn't sure where that idea came from, but it seemed like a nice, carefree thing to do. When it next started to pour down (and, being Northumberland, that might not be long), she'd head out onto the sands and do a jig – just because she could.

Number 7 (she was on a roll now): make a new friend. Someone here in Bamburgh. The lady in the deli came to mind; she seemed nice and chatty.

Number 8: what else made life feel good? A cup of tea,

a glass of wine (already got that), cocktails. Hmm, yes, before all the treatments she'd been partial to the odd mojito in Bella's Bar with Andrea down at the quayside in Newcastle, but maybe not now. Sex on the beach, now where did that thought come from? But not the cocktail, oh no, the real deal. Wow! That would be pretty cool and extremely sexy – or gritty and sandy, but worth a try. But, that could prove difficult to achieve, since she was staying here on her own and indeed she didn't actually intend to have anything to do with men for quite some time. One day, maybe. Never say never. Her list could carry forward!

Number 9 wasn't forthcoming, so she decided to leave that and number 10 to be confirmed. There was no point wasting wishes till you knew what you wanted.

She wondered if there was a post-cancer wish fairy. Like a tooth fairy. You lost a boob and got a few wishes for it. *Wow*, how did her brain come up with this stuff?

Actually, thinking of her list, maybe she should be less selfish and wish everyone she loved or knew good health, bucketloads of happiness and some magic moments for themselves. That could be number 9 sorted after all.

She sipped her tea and leafed through the bread recipes; they didn't look too daunting, and the ingredients wouldn't be expensive. That was one thing she could definitely do today. And next – no time like the present – she'd take a leisurely bath.

She left the balcony and headed for the bathroom, where she turned the taps to full. At least there seemed to be plenty of hot water today. She poured in some of the Molton Brown bubble bath she'd saved from Christmas, removed her robe, trying not to look at her scars, and sank below the surface to chin level, bubbles of fragrant ginger-lily bursting lightly around her. Bliss. She should be *drinking* bubbles in here too, sipping a chilled glass of champagne – but the budget didn't stretch to that. Still, maybe she could pop along to the everything-and-more store in the village for that bottle of white wine for later. She'd be ticking off her wish list at a rate of knots!

She reached for the baking book, topped up the hot water and lost herself in a world of '00' flour, rosemary focaccia, and stone-baked crust. She emerged after forty minutes pale and prune-like, but relaxed and content.

Half an hour later, armed with rucksack and cagoule, she set off up the beach again. The clouds were gathering dramatically on the horizon, a shaft of grey cutting down to the sea where the rain was sheeting offshore; definitely a sunshine and showers kind of day. She'd head for the deli – they'd hopefully have the flour and yeast she needed. She could picture herself kneading away in the 1950s kitchen like Mary Berry. Actually, what she could *really* picture was herself imagining it was her husband's face she was slapping and pounding. Boomph. Just when she'd thought life might return to normality after all the treatments. Paul . . . That bombshell. She was still shaking from it. How hadn't she guessed? 'In sickness and in health . . .' He'd hung in there just because he'd felt sorry for her, only to dump it on her like a shedload of shit, right at the moment that should have been the happy ending.

Okay, enough of feeling sorry for herself. She wasn't going down that route. Stop all negative images, right there. She was here for peace and quiet, not violent thoughts. But maybe a bit of dough beating would be good therapy.

The beach was quieter today; the weather was keeping people away. There were some hardy anoraked holidaymakers and dog walkers about, and one stoical family camped out with windbreaks.

After a forty-five minute stroll, she reached the village. At the deli she was greeted with a warm smile by the same lady. Today she was wearing a cheerful vintage-style flowery apron.

'Hello, pet – back again then?'

'Yes – the loaf I bought here yesterday was gorgeous. I've been inspired to try and have a go at baking some bread myself. I'm after flour and some yeast if you have it?'

'Oh, marvellous. How exciting. I just love home baking. I do all the artisan loaves here myself.'

'Wow, that's impressive. So you created the wholemeal honey loaf?'

'Well, yes I did, and thank you. Right well, you say you've never baked before, so I'd suggest trying something simple for starters.'

'Absolutely. I've found a recipe in an old cookbook for a basic bloomer.'

'Sounds as good as any to start with, my lovely. First things first, you'll need some strong 00 bread flour. Do you want to make white or wholemeal?'

'I'll start with a basic white.'

'For yeast I'd recommend the dried sachets. They're as good as anything and easier to work with. Oil – do you have any oil, just to work the dough? Olive or sunflower?'

'Sunflower.'

'And salt?'

'I think there's some back at the cottage.' She'd spotted a Saxa pot lurking in a kitchen cupboard. Mind you, the packaging looked like something her gran had had when Claire was a kid. 'Actually, it's probably been there since the 70s, so yes please, I'll take some salt too.'

'Okay.' The lady busied herself at the shelves at the back of the store, gathering the goods. 'Where was it you said you were staying?'

'The Hedley cottage, away along the beach. It's called Farne View.'

She turned, her eyebrows arching up. 'Ah yes, I do know

of it.' Her lip twitched; the cottage's reputation must precede it. 'And you're okay there?' She looked sceptical.

'Yes, it's fine. A bit basic, but fine.'

'Right, well, I'm Lynda, by the way. Nice to meet you.' She wiped the flour from her palms onto her apron, then offered her hand over the countertop.

'Claire. I'm staying for a few weeks, so I'm sure I'll be back in.'

'Great. I look forward to seeing you, Claire. Have a lovely stay. And good luck with the bread. You'll have to pop in and tell me how it works out.'

'Hah, yes – and no doubt next time I'll be coming back to buy one of yours!'

'You never know, you might just have the knack for it. You might be a natural.'

'I'll see.' She wasn't so sure. Though she loved to watch other people baking, it had never been her thing so far. A few half-risen cupcakes had been her highlight.

She settled up and headed out just as a young mum and toddler were coming in.

'Thanks. Bye, Lynda.'

'Bye, my lovely.'

It was nice chatting to the locals. And, Lynda seemed really genuine and friendly. At least not everyone was grumpy round here.

* * *

Right, how difficult could this bread-making malarkey be then?

Firstly, she'd need some kitchen scales. Would there even be any kitchen scales here? After a full investigation of the cupboards, she found an ancient set made of black painted metal that had the proper individual weights on one side and a scoop balanced on the other. Boy, they were heavy to lift out. Luckily the old cookbook was in imperial measures as all she had were pounds and ounces for weights. She needed a pound of the strong flour, and she guessed at a sachet of the yeast as the recipe stated half an ounce of fresh. Some oil – she'd use sunflower; it said vegetable, but that would be fine. She then measured out the water she needed from the tap into a glass jug.

Okay, here goes. Everything went in at once, apparently. Oops, but not all of the water; she quickly stopped pouring. '*Mix to a firm dough,*' she read. Her hands went in and were soon covered up to her wrists in soft, gloopy paste. This was *sooo* messy. It reminded her of Play-Doh from when she was a kid, but even that stuff hadn't been half as mucky as this. This was more like something you'd fill cracks in the walls with. Actually, it might just come in handy for the cottage – stick the old walls back together where they'd begun to crumble.

'*Push with the heel of your hand and fold back in.*' She had to keep oiling the work surface as the dough kept sticking to it, but gradually it started to become firmer, more elastic. She was meant to do this for ten minutes. That hadn't sounded bad, but after five minutes her hand was aching and the mix didn't seem anywhere near bouncy and smooth like it was supposed to be. Smooth? Knobbly and falling apart was more like it. She kept going. Push out and roll in. At least the rhythm of kneading was taking her mind off things. After a while it appeared to be rolling as one piece and felt springy under her palm. Eleven minutes; that would do. Next she had to put it in an oiled bowl. She covered the dough with a tea towel as directed and left it on the side.

She felt less like Mary Berry and more like the contender who gets chucked out in the first round. Or more likely one of the ones who never actually made it as far as the Bake Off tent.

The deed was done, the bread was left to rise. The recipe said it needed at least an hour and a half for this stage. Time to pour herself a nice chilled glass of the Pinot Grigio she'd picked up from the all-in-one store after visiting the deli, and sit outside. The clouds had dispersed after a short, sharp shower and – wonderfully – the sun was back out. Claire found a fusty-looking wine glass in a kitchen cupboard, gave it a wash and then took the bottle from the fridge and unscrewed the lid. The smell was fragrant and fruity; she poured herself a medium-sized glass.

She went outside and sat on one of the wooden put-me-up chairs at the little wonky table in her small patch of scabby-grassed garden. Looking out across the sea with its breezy, choppy waves glinting in the sunlight, she took a long, slow sip of her wine. Apples and herbs and vanilla hit her all at once. Wow, it was great to taste properly again. The chemo had dulled every sense, diminishing her taste buds, but gradually they were coming back. She wouldn't drink too much alcohol, of course, wary of abusing her body that had already been through so much. But a little of what you fancied . . .

She'd taken her phone out with her – hopeful, considering the poor signal; but within a few moments a text beeped through.

It was her sister, Sally. *How's it going, Clairebo? x* A nickname struck up between them over a penchant for Haribo sweets.

Fine, all good x, she texted back. Short and sweet. She'd try and ring her later, walk up a dune and catch a better signal.

Sure? Sally bounced back. Protective about her little sis as always.

Of course. Just chilling here. Enjoying the sea view.

Not bored of your own company yet then?

No, I'm not that bad company am I?

Nah, course not. How's the cottage? Cute?

Hah. Claire gave a wry grin. Thank God Sal couldn't

see it falling apart behind her. *Quirky* was the most honest answer she was going to give.

Thinking of coming down to see you for the day next Saturday. Okay with you?

Bang went her solitude. But hey, they'd always got on, even if her sister could be a bit bossy at times; that seemed to be par for the course with older sisters. And Sal had always looked out for her, had been a good shoulder to lean on throughout her cancer treatment.

Yes, that'd be nice. I'll ring you in the week. Tell you how to find the cottage.

Great.

Mark and the kids fine?, Claire tapped in.

Yeah, all good here. See you soon x

See you next week! x

So she'd be getting a visitor.

An hour passed. Claire went back in to sneak a look at her creation. The dough had doubled at least, so she must have done something right. She then thought she'd better turn on the oven at that point. Gas Mark 6, the recipe said – this gas stuff was so unfamiliar; her oven at home was electric and in Celsius. She turned the knob, then realized there was also an ignition button, pushed at it with the cooker door open so she could see what was happening, and watched a blue flame run along the back of the oven. All seemed fine.

Half an hour later she was back inside kneading the

dough again. She'd thought it would be ready to go in the oven at this stage, but on rereading the recipe she realized it needed a further hour of 'proving' after she'd done a bit more kneading and shaped it into an oval-styled bloomer. Blimey. All this for one loaf of bread. It had better be worth it. She could have walked to the deli and back a couple of times by the time it would be ready and picked up something probably a lot more yummy from Lynda's artisan bread basket.

Finally the loaf was ready to go into the oven with a dusting of flour on the top. It would be ready in thirty minutes, apparently. She checked her watch. It was four hours since she'd started. Oh my.

Half an hour later, she opened the oven door cautiously . . . *Here goes.* The loaf looked rather pale. She took it out, but it didn't feel quite right under her touch. Should it be bouncier, crispier? She hazarded a guess that it wasn't quite done and popped it back in for ten minutes. It was smelling lovely, there was nothing quite like the scent of freshly baked bread. Maybe some things were worth waiting for.

The bloomer finally came out looking golden and generally the right kind of shape. She ought to let it cool, but the fresh-baked smell kept drawing her back to the kitchen. She couldn't wait any longer and was soon slathering butter onto a just-cut slice. Hmm, pretty good. It was tasty – maybe a touch on the doughy side, but not at all bad for a first attempt. It would go well with the rest of the soup for supper, or perhaps make a scrummy bacon sandwich.

As evening approached after a long, relaxed afternoon with her book, she sat out on the deckchair on her first-floor balcony watching shades of bold pink and peach diffuse the sky over a sunset sea. With her second glass of chilled white wine to hand, she sat quite still, listening to the rhythmic ebb and flow of the waves lapping the shore. A pair of black-and-white terns swooped steadily across the bay, then headed inland over the dunes to roost.

She'd popped a cardigan on over her T-shirt. It was a balmy evening nonetheless, calm and still. It was beautiful here, so very peaceful; the solitude restful. Yes, she'd enjoy seeing her sister at the end of next week, but for now this was what she needed. In fact, despite the run-down state of the cottage, this was just about perfect.

The next morning, Claire was up early again. She wandered out onto the bedroom's balcony to greet the day and spotted the six a.m. pile of clothes – a little further up the beach this time. Her heart gave a little leap. Damn, she must have missed him going out. But hey, she was definitely going to settle down on the deckchair for the view on his way back in. Her cup of tea could wait.

Of course he was much further away from the cottages

this time, probably being cautious now he knew there was someone next door. She sat watching for a while, and then there he was, swimming towards the shore and rising out of the water, tall, toned, dripping in salt water and stark-bollock-naked yet again. Oh yes, *what* a body. It felt like her guilty secret – lurking in the shadows of her balcony admiring the 'sea view'. But she just couldn't resist. Even if he was a grumpy-ass, she didn't have to speak with him to admire his fit physique.

She had a pretty chilled-out day after that. She toasted some of her homemade bloomer for breakfast with butter and strawberry jam – scrummy. She spent a pleasant couple of hours reading, and then went for a leisurely stroll, in the opposite direction from Bamburgh this time, enjoying the views towards Seahouses and the Farne Islands. She dipped her feet in the cool North Sea and let the breaking waves froth over them, rising up to her shins.

She heard the engine of a car revving close by that evening, a scrunch of gravel, and then there were no lights on next door after that, so he must have gone home. It was Sunday. He might well be a weekender, she mused. She really was on her own in that little cluster of cottages now.

It seemed very quiet and dark that night: the woodwork creaking in the wind, a rattle of the window frame, a loose gutter flapping, and that was about it. She snuggled down under her duvet, wondering if he owned the house next door, if he might be back next weekend, or if he had just been on holiday himself and that was the last she'd ever see of him.

5

*Fish and chips with lashings of salt and vinegar, a 99
Flake ice cream, and a harbour view*

Her days settled into their own rhythm: waking, walking,
reading. It was wonderful not having a schedule, or deadlines, or anyone else to please. If she wanted to lie in, she
could, though that didn't seem to happen – she was still
waking up very early. If she wanted to go back to bed
with her book in the afternoon, she could. If she wanted
to bathe at three a.m., she could – in fact she did just
that one night. She could walk, run, sing, dance along to
her iPod, bake, wander around naked (she didn't actually
feel like doing that, but she *could*). She could do nothing,
do anything – within reason; no car and little money was
a bit of a hold-back. There was a golden beach, an expanse
of sky, and a bucketload of time. It was totally up to her.

The first week of her holiday passed by. She'd walked back to the village again on the Wednesday, chatting to Lynda in the deli, buying some wholemeal flour for her next baking adventure, and some gorgeous local cheese and pâté. She'd also picked up some 'Bamburgh Bangers' from the butchers and made herself an epic sandwich with her own fresh bread, sausages and fried onions – the taste was amazing!

Her favourite spot of an evening was out on the grassy patch of her garden, where she watched the last of the beachgoers drift home, the sea birds pottering about the shoreline until it was time to roost, the changing light, a melting of peach and gold turning the sky into soft, watercolour shades after the bold acrylic colours of the day as she sat on a deckchair with her book and a glass of Pinot Grigio, a cardie slung around her shoulders as dusk crept in. It didn't get really dark till half past ten.

It had been a good first week: and she was certainly enjoying her time out, and she was beginning to relax for the first time in ages. Being on her own was working out well.

Her sister's car rolled into the gravel driveway at ten o'clock sharp on Saturday morning. Claire had felt a touch of trepidation the night before; they got on well enough, but she knew Sally would take control of the weekend – it was just her way. There had also been a midweek phone call. 'You've got a spare room there, haven't you?' And the Saturday day visit had become a nightover, and in fact a weekend break. She hadn't dared admit to Sally what state the cottage was in. She desperately hoped it would stay sunny and they'd be able to spend most of the time outdoors. Her sister was bringing her car, so having transport would be a bonus, anyhow.

'Hi, Claire.'

Sally eased out of her BMW saloon with a broad smile, bearing a bunch of sunny peach and yellow carnations. Her sister was taller than her, her hair a richer shade of brunette than Claire's which fell in a groomed sweep to her shoulders. At thirty-three, she was three years older than Claire. She was wearing her trademark beige chinos with a pink stripy blouse. She was definitely of the 'Yummy Mummy' brigade, and Claire always felt slightly scruffy and uncoordinated beside her. She gave Claire a big hug, took her overnight case out of the boot, and strode towards the cottage door, as always moving swiftly and with confidence.

'You're looking good, sis,' she said authoritatively.

'Ah, you're just saying that.'

'No, course not. It's the hair.'

'What, you mean I've got some now?'

'Well, yes. That short crop, though. Suits you. I think I said last time it has a kind of an Audrey Hepburn look about it. Anne Hathaway, even.'

'Thanks.' Claire's voice was timid. It had been a long time since she'd felt anywhere near to looking good. She remembered it well, that gutting feeling seven months ago when her hair began to fall out. Oh yes, having your hair coming out in clumps, you realize how pointless it's been worrying for all those years since your teens about whether it's too curly, too mousy or too dark.

'Right, well what's the plan of action?'

Claire hadn't really got her head past making them some coffee and possibly taking a stroll on the beach. 'Coffee?' She smiled. 'We can sit out in the garden facing the sea.' She needed to get her sister out of the house quickly before she could make too close an inspection of the accommodation. 'It's just instant, I'm afraid.' She knew Sally would rather have freshly ground coffee in a cafetière, which actually would have been rather nice, but with the last-minute travel arrangements, there was only so much she could pack, and she hadn't thought to buy some in the village.

As they sat overlooking the beach, watching the distant rolling waves – the tide out this morning – they began to reminisce.

'Hey, do you remember being here with Gran and Mum in the school summer holidays?' Sal started.

'Yeah. I think it was those holidays that inspired me to come and stay over this way.'

'Crammed into that little caravan. That twin bedroom we had was tiny. We were nearly face to face as we slept.'

'Yeah, and when you snored it was literally in my face.'
'*I never snored.*'

Claire raised her eyebrows. 'And then Dad used to come up at the weekends,' she continued.

'Yeah. Dad.' They both went quiet, thinking of him, memories slamming into both their minds. That tall, solid man, whose hair had turned from a rich dark brown to white over the years, who'd watched all their netball matches, taken them swimming, played rounders on the beach, given them ice creams, new shoes, wedding dresses, love and support.

Claire felt that familiar knot in her throat. 'Bless him.' They both sighed.

When he'd died, Claire was about to take her journalism finals after going back to college as a mature student. He'd never got to see her graduation. That was five years ago now. She still missed him so much. His big Dad bear hugs and down-to-earth advice. But sometimes, even now, when times got tough, she'd hear his voice in her head: 'Come on, Claire, you can do it – show them what you're made of, love.'

In a way she was glad that he hadn't had to see her go through all the cancer stuff. But his hugs would have helped her through it all.

'Yes,' Claire resumed. 'And he used to turn up after work at that caravan on a Friday, still in his jacket and tie, laden with sweets. Mum used to go mad, saying they'd ruin our teeth. Then he'd take us all out to that little harbour place for fish and chips.'

'Oh, and those fish and chips,' Sal took up. 'They were the best ever. Fresh from the newspaper, sitting down on the harbour wall. The seagulls used to go crazy for the scraps.'

'And remember that one that pooped on Mum's head!' Claire grinned. It had ruined her mum's hairdo, and she'd been livid at the time.

They laughed, sharing memories of a happy childhood.

'That was Seahouses, wasn't it? That's just down the road,' Claire added.

'We could go there for some lunch,' Sal suggested. 'What do you reckon?'

'Now that sounds like a good idea.' Hot crispy batter, flaky white fish, vinegar, salt, crispy chips. Mmmm.

Sally took a sip of coffee, 'Yep, it's a plan. My treat.'

The two sisters sat on the stone harbour wall, each with a plastic carton resting on their knees. The nostalgic days of wrapping the fish and chips in recycled newspaper were no more. Still, the smell was delicious, and the taste was damn good. They'd put plenty of salt and vinegar on. How come fish-shop salt and vinegar always tasted better than that at home? They dived in with their little wooden forks, breaking off bits of crispy batter and chunks of juicy cod. It was one of the best meals Claire had had in ages.

'So, how are you doing really, sis? Enjoying the break?'

'Yeah, it's been a nice week. And I'm okay,' Claire replied, chip poised in mid-air.

'Good to hear it. It's been a pretty tough time for you.'

'Suppose so.' Claire was swinging her legs against the harbour wall like she used to as a kid.

'Listen to you, making light of it. You've been amazing, you know. Dealing with everything you've had to. Getting through that shitty cancer. All the treatment.'

'Well I didn't have a lot of choice in it all, did I? But I'm feeling much better than I have in ages. Getting back to fitness too.'

'Good for you . . . Look, Claire, I'm not very good at this stuff, and I never said it at the time, but I really wanted to say . . . I'm proud of you.'

Sal *never* came out with soppy stuff like this. She was a 'pull your socks up and get on with it' kind of girl. Claire found herself getting all emotional. The next chip got jammed in her throat. She gulped. Sniffed. Looked up at the skyline, then across at the boats bobbing in the harbour.

'Wonder if there are any dishy fishermen around?' Sal broke the tension.

'Hmm, a nice lifeboat man might do. All hunky and heroic,' Claire rejoined.

'Yeah, and he wouldn't stink of fish all day. Good thinking.'

They laughed, tucking back into the last of their chips, Claire scraping up all the crispy fragments at the bottom.

'Thanks,' said Claire. *For the fish and chips. For being a great sister. For everything.*

'You are so welcome. Come on, let's head back. We'll stop off for a bottle or two of wine to take back on the way.'

They were about to turn right to cross into the cottage's driveway from the main road when a black 4x4 made the turn in front of them from the left. Claire recognized the sandy-blond hair of her neighbour. Her stomach gave a weird flutter.

They had to drive past his vehicle to get to their parking bay outside Farne View. He got out of the car at the same time as them. He still wasn't smiling. He was dressed in dark jeans and a blue checked shirt, open at the neck. Claire had forgotten just how tall and broad-shouldered he was. She looked across to say a brief 'Hello', just as Sally was giving her an intrigued raised-eyebrow, mouthing, '*Who* is that?'

'Neighbour,' Claire mouthed back. Her sister wouldn't be so excited had she actually spoken to him.

Mr Grumpy did actually manage a 'Hello' and a curt nod back, but Claire caught that hint of annoyance lingering across his brow. It felt very much like they were invading his space.

As soon as they got through the door, Sal blurted out, 'Who the hell is that hunk next door? You didn't mention any dishy neighbours on the phone. No wonder you were hesitant about me coming down. Wanted to keep him all to yourself, hey? No need for any lifeboat men now.' She winked exaggeratedly. 'Of course, being a married woman and all that, I'd stand back graciously. He'd be all yours.'

'Hah, he's a right misery, to be honest. Met him last weekend. Looks can be deceiving, I tell you. I had to get some help with changing a gas bottle – you'd have thought I'd asked him to lick the toilets out.'

Sal had a weird look on her face. 'Hmm, I'm just picturing him licking . . . '

'Enough! Stop it, you crazy woman.' Even with No. 8 The Cocktail Zone on her list, the reality of sex seemed so far out of Claire's world right now, she felt uncomfortable just thinking about it. She might as well declare her body a sex-free zone and be done with it. It would be one less thing to worry about.

Sally ventured up to the spare room to drop her case, which she'd left in the hall earlier. Claire waited nervously, then heard the squeal. Her sister shouted down the staircase.

'Have you *seen* that bed . . . and the mattress? What the hell kind of place is this? Ugh! I wouldn't be surprised if it has bed bugs or lice or something. Thank God I had the sense to bring my own mattress protector and fresh linen –' She appeared at the kitchen door. 'How the hell do you sleep here at night, Clairebo? It's pretty run-down, isn't it? Not what I was expecting at all.'

'It's a bit basic, yeah.'

'*Basic*? That's complimentary. It's a bloody shack. I daren't tell Mum – she'd be here in a shot, turfing you out and booking you into the nearest four-star hotel.'

'Don't you mention a thing.' Claire shot her sister a sharp look. 'I like it here. It's quirky.'

'Hah, you can say that again.'

'Well, while it's dry, let's get out and stretch our legs,' Claire soothed. 'The beach here is amazing.' A walk would de-stress Sally, hopefully, and get them both out of the cottage for a while. And later, with all the food and wine she'd kindly bought, and wouldn't take a penny for, at the Co-op back in Seahouses, her sister would be nice and snoozy by the time bedtime arrived and would have forgotten the stains on the mattress. She could hope for a miracle.

As they passed next door's garden, Claire was sure she could hear what sounded like a large dog barking from the house. Hmm, she hadn't heard or seen a dog there last weekend. She put the thought to the back of her mind as she and her sister strolled along the shoreline, soon taking off their shoes and paddling in the shallows. Claire couldn't resist a splashing session – taking the two of them right back to the days of sibling fun-fighting.

Both ended up laughing and rather damp from the waist down. No matter – the sun was warm and they'd dry in no time.

'It's nice to see you smiling again.' Sally touched her arm.

'Nice to *be* smiling again. See, told you – I'm fine. And even if the house is a bit ramshackle, it seems to be doing me some good.'

'Maybe it is,' Sal had to concede.

At the end of the day, supper eaten and cleared away, they sat out on the balcony taking in the evening sun with the last of the red wine. Claire had produced a supper of local cheese and her third attempt at homemade bread – a white bloomer with a rosemary and sea-salt crust, cold meats, juicy tomatoes, olives (a bit of an Italian theme going on), with a bottle of Chianti. Now the pair of them sat chatting easily. Claire's concerns about her sister's intrusion on her hideaway time had eased. It was actually really nice. They were beginning to rediscover that close sisterly bond they'd had as teenagers, which had somehow slipped into the middle distance when husbands and children and other diversions were around. She'd forgotten quite how well they did get on when it was just the two of them.

Halfway down the second bottle of red now, Sal having had the bulk of it, they were sat out on the balcony wrapped in duvets they'd brought out from their bedrooms. 'I know it's hurt like hell, Clairebo, but I think that prick of a husband of yours leaving isn't such a bad thing. Not in the long run.'

Well that was pretty blunt. Claire stared at her. Sal had never warmed to her husband Paul from the start (correction: ex-husband, as of eight weeks) – there had always been a frostiness between them. Not that they'd ever had an argument, or that anything in particular had happened; it was just that they were almost *too* polite when they had to meet – there was a coolness that hadn't changed over time.

'You *are* better off without him, you know,' she continued.

It was still a little raw, even though Claire knew that it was probably the truth. 'The less said about him the better,' she muttered. How did you just forget six years of marriage? All those good times as well as the bad. She went quiet for a while.

'You're probably right,' she conceded after a pause.

She remembered how it had happened. She'd been given the good news from the oncologist after a follow-up scan, that there was no further evidence of cancer, and was so relieved. It was the week afterwards, that was all, when she was back at home looking forward to the future, *their* future. He'd just come out with it. Told her that he'd been seeing someone else, that it had started before her diagnosis. He couldn't have left her like that. So all the while, all through the op, the chemo, the radiotherapy, the first months of recovery, they'd been living a lie. His staunch, loving support had been merely duty, a cover for his guilt. She'd found the energy, from sheer rage probably, to throw a suitcase at him and told him to get out. He had, swiftly, with a couple of overnight bags and his ticket to a new life and new lover.

Claire stayed quiet.

'Sorry, I shouldn't have said anything, Claire . . . but I just want you to be happy. You *can* be happy again.'

'I know. I'm not rushing into anything, though. I mean man-wise. I wouldn't say no to a bit of happiness.' Claire laughed, a little too loudly. 'It's okay, Sal. It's probably best out in the open. And thanks for coming up, sis. It's nice that you're here.'

'Hey, no worries. It's great to see you, and in fact it's been lovely just to have a night away from the madhouse of my family. A bit of head space, you know. I love 'em to bits, don't get me wrong, but every now and then you just need a bit of time out from the demands of "Mummy, I need a poo, Mummy, I'm hungry, Mummy, I'm thirsty, Mummy, where's my football kit?"' She took a sip of her wine. 'And the best? "Sal, if you're tired, can I at least have a hand job?"' The red wine was obviously loosening her reserve.

Claire laughed. 'I wonder how he's coping?'

'What, Mark? He'll be fine. He's got hands of his own, you know.' Sally giggled.

'I mean with the boys.'

'Ah, he'll be okay. He's pretty good with them, and it'll do him good to spend some more time with them. *And* he'll appreciate me even more when I come back, hopefully. They were heading off to the cinema this evening, latest Disney movie and a pizza supper. I'll give them a call in the morning. It's a bit late now.'

'You'll be lucky to get any signal anyhow.'

'Ah, I see.'

Claire had never had that – a family of her own. Even with all the stresses of family life, Sally was happy – her children were her everything. You could see it written all over her face. Paul had never wanted children. That had seemed okay at first, when she was young and idolized him – they were fine as a couple. He had his engineering business, his busy life, the foreign holidays together; children would just get in the way. But she'd always wondered in a little hide-and-seek corner of her thoughts whether he might change his mind one day. A part of her had hoped he would.

'Hey, do you realize it's nearly midnight, Bo? Time for bed, methinks. Oh Jeez, have I really got to get into that fleapit now?'

'It's either that or a lumpy sofa.'

'Christ, the things I do for you, sis. If I'm itching in the morning, you're in for it, I can tell you.' She half grinned, half shrugged, resigned to her fate. 'If *I* ever need a getaway break, I won't be coming here, that's for sure. It's going to be five stars in the Maldives.'

'Great. If you need some company . . .' Claire grinned.

'Come on, then, let's do this thing.' Sal stood up.

The pair of them waddled in from the balcony in their duvets, looking an odd sight. They brushed their teeth, sharing the little floorboard-creaking bathroom. Then Sal headed off to her room. 'Here goes.'

'Night, Sal. Thanks again for coming.'

'My pleasure, hun.' There was a slight pause. 'Except for the grotty bed.'

Claire heard a creaking as her sister ventured in. Heard the click of the light switch, the blink into darkness. She lay down in her own bed, settling onto her pillow with a sigh and a warm feeling of love for her sibling. Then, unable to resist pulling out an old saying of their gran's, she perched up on one elbow and shouted across the landing, 'Night, night, sleep tight. Hope the bed bugs don't bite.'

'Bitch,' was launched back. But she knew Sal was grinning too.

It was the best night's sleep she'd had in ages. Claire squinted her eyes to try and gauge the time. Gone ten o'clock! She could hear someone shuffling about downstairs, the sound of a kettle bubbling to a boil. Ah, a cup of tea, that would be good. She tried to sit up and felt like she'd been hammered all over during the night.

Hammered was certainly something to do with it, she winced, trying to pull a leg out of bed. Oh, good God, she hadn't had a hangover in years. Through all the cancer treatment she'd steered clear of alcohol, thinking her body had enough to deal with. Obviously her tolerance levels had plummeted – she hadn't had much more than two glasses. Okay, so maybe they were large glasses. Now she realized she'd probably been a bit stupid, but she'd been enjoying herself, had lost track.

She summoned the energy to creep downstairs, to find Sal in the kitchen popping teabags into mugs.

'Hey, you – I was going to bring one up to you.' Her sister looked amazingly bright-eyed and breezy.

Claire slumped onto a kitchen chair, leant her arms on the table and placed her head in her hands.

'Paracetamol, hun?'

'Yes please.'

'No worries, always keep some in my handbag.'

Thank God her sister was so organized. 'Ta.' She raised her head a little, trying to avoid any sudden movements as things seemed to be slamming around in her brain.

Sally passed her a large glass of water and placed two painkillers in her palm. Her tongue seemed to seize up as she popped them in and tried to swallow, her throat constricting around them. She gulped down a couple of glugs of water to shift them. Now she remembered why she didn't normally drink much.

'Been up long?' she rallied, trying to make conversation. She didn't want to waste the limited time she had with her sister.

'Since about three a.m., *itching*.'

'Nooo!'

'Just kidding, Clairebo! Had you there, though. No, I've only been up about half an hour myself. Been sitting looking at the view. Not a bad spot you've got here. I can just picture it all done up, a nice white-and-blue beach theme going on. All distressed furniture and shabby chic instead of just shabby.' Sal passed her a steaming mug of tea.

'Hmm.' Yes, she could picture that too, like something out of *Homes & Gardens*, all beachside chic. Her sister had always had an eye for design – her own house was gorgeously furnished and decorated.

Claire then wondered what, or more precisely *who* her sister had been watching out on the beach. It would hopefully have been too late for Grumpy-Gorgeous's early-morning swim. That was a little gem she liked to think she could keep to herself.

'That guy next door was out jogging with his dog.'

Was she some kind of mind-reader?

'Oh, right.' She tried to sound cool. 'What kind of dog has he got?'

'Labrador. Black one.' Pause. 'He's quite dishy, isn't he?'

'What, the dog?'

'Hah, very funny. Your neighbour.'

'Hmm, not bad. I told you he's a right grumpy thing, though.'

'He certainly is. I had to nip and get something from the car as he was coming back in. He wasn't very chatty, I must say. He's called Ed, apparently. That's about all I found out. The dog's cute, though. She was far more friendly.'

'I wouldn't mind a dog myself one day.' Claire was glad to move the conversation on.

'Me too – a spaniel or something. Though our house is mad enough at the best of times. Can't quite imagine a dog in the mix at the moment. Maybe when the boys are older, then they could help walk it.'

Claire sipped her tea, hoping the painkillers would kick in soon, but it was kind of soothing letting her sister chatter on. She just nodded now and then, with an occasional 'Ah-huh', until finally her head began to clear, though it was still fragile. 'Think I might head up for a shower.'

She felt somewhat revived by the splashing of warm water and zingy blast of shower gel.

Half an hour later they were strolling down the beach, heading towards Bamburgh, where they spent a very pleasant hour in the courtyard garden of the Copper Kettle tearooms with a pot of Earl Grey and some very scrummy slices of lemon drizzle cake.

'So what are your plans for the rest of your break?'

'Well, not too much, to be honest. It's been so nice just to have time on my side, a book to hand and a gorgeous sea view.'

'Hmn, that does sound rather lovely. But isn't it a bit *too* quiet? A bit lonely?'

'Not really. That was the whole idea behind coming away – to have some space, some time out for a bit. I'll manage, I'm sure. My own company's not that bad. Anyway, I'll have to start thinking about the next feature for my column soon, so that'll keep me busy. Em's filling in for me for two weeks, but I need to send something in to the newspaper for the next week. I can't be out of the loop too long, especially now I'm finding my feet again back at the *Herald* after all that time off sick. I'm just waiting for inspiration to strike.'

'I'm sure you'll come up with something, Claire. Your blogs were brilliant all through the cancer stuff. Really honest and inspiring. You didn't get voted the North-East Columnist of the Year for nothing.'

'No, I suppose not . . . Thanks. I was doing it more for me, though, to be honest. It just happened to be popular.'

'Well, you're very talented. And at least something good came out of it all. I'm sure you helped a lot of other people going through something similar, and their families too.'

'Yeah, writing it down definitely helped. Verbal therapy, I think.'

'You see. A true journalist at heart.'

Later that afternoon, Sal was popping her overnight case into the boot of her car. They'd spent the day chatting, taking a long leisurely walk on the beach, and had a picnic lunch of bread, cheese and fruit in the garden.

'Right, I suppose I'd better be setting off,' she announced cheerily. 'Back to reality and all that.'

Reality? Normality? Claire didn't know what that was any more. Her life had taken so many unexpected turns of late. She waved her sister off, watched the rear of her car swing out onto the main road, and felt her heart sink a little. As she turned back in through the door of the cottage, she recognized a niggling feeling of loneliness creeping over her. Her sister was right. Her cottage escape, her haven – okay, more hovel than haven – suddenly seemed a little *too* quiet and remote. Perhaps it was just that they'd had such a lovely time reconnecting over the last two days.

She'd thought she didn't need anyone. She was wrong.

6

Laughing in the rain

Claire rattled around the cottage the next morning, then decided she might as well bake some bread. It would keep her busy and provide her with something tasty for lunch. Lynda from the deli had lent her one of her baking books for inspiration, and she perused it over a cup of tea on the balcony, deciding on a sea-salt-and-rosemary-topped sourdough.

She was soon in the kitchen measuring and mixing, then pounding and kneading the dough. As she worked away, she thought what a lovely couple of days it had been with Sally. Magic moments spent with her sister, she smiled to herself, picturing how daft they must have looked huddled like teenagers in their nightclothes and duvets on the balcony at midnight. The rush and pull of the waves sounded even louder in the dark when you couldn't really see them. You just caught glimpses of the odd crested sparkle in the moonlight. The pair of them sat there drinking mellow red wine, and chatting.

As she pushed the heel of her hand into the dough once more, a light-bulb thought pinged in her mind. *Magic moments.* She'd been looking for inspiration for something to write about for her column. Her job as a journalist wasn't going to go far if she sat doing nothing for weeks on a beach. She'd brought her laptop, and had been waiting for the right article to form in her mind. With the recent split from her husband, her soul had felt battered and bruised; she'd been struggling to find any creativity in there at all lately. But yes, magic moments – we all needed those. What made life good, special? Not winning the lottery or being given a heap of cash – there were many miserable millionaires around, and money didn't keep anyone healthy. But the simple things . . . things everyone could have or do: be with family, friends, a smile from a stranger, watch a gorgeous male swim naked – *hey, stop it*; that image just wouldn't shift from her brain – laugh until your sides ache, eat warm, soft bread straight from the oven, preferably with a big blob of melting butter.

Her dough was probably kneaded enough, she realized, so she set it on a dish and popped it into the hot-water-tank cupboard to rise, that being the only truly warm place in the house. She tidied up, washed her breakfast things and the mixing bowl, wiped down the floured surfaces and cleared the kitchen. She put the oven on to warm, read for a little while, then went back to check on the dough, which had doubled in size. She then shaped it and scored the top with three slashes as the recipe instructed, which apparently allowed it to rise and cook without splitting. Then she put it in to bake. It wasn't long before the smell of freshly baked bread filled the cottage, making her mouth water. She peeked in the oven: the loaf looked golden brown, well risen with a crusty top. She set it on the side to cool.

Outside, the clouds were breaking into cauliflower-shaped cushions. She decided to take a stroll. The forecast on the radio had said heavy showers, but if she managed to get out between them, it might just clear her head and shake off that lingering, empty feeling that had crept up on her. Sal would be home again, back with her brood, catching cuddles from her two boys, a hug with her husband. She'd be sleeping with some-body's arms around her tonight. Claire could only be happy for her, but the small tear in her own heart had begun to gape.

She walked about a mile at a leisurely pace, going the opposite way from Bamburgh and nearing the rocks at the far end of the long sandy beach that marked the start of the harbour town of Seahouses.

At the far end of the beach, she turned to head back to the cottage again. Oh. The sky this way was a very different story. She hadn't noticed the dark, heavy clouds brewing behind her. She'd better get a move on. Rain was definitely on its way, and by the look of the gunmetal-coloured shaft sheeting from the sky out to sea, it wouldn't be too long in coming. The sky was menacingly beautiful. The skies here were so different from the cityscapes of home. So big. It sounded silly, but they were. Panoramic. You felt the power of the elements, saw the weather as it formed.

She began a marching pace, striding across damp golden sand, leaving firm footprints. The beach was quieter today; the forecast had no doubt put the tourists off. There was a lone dog walker further up the bay with a couple of terriers scooting about beside her. And then another figure, moving quite fast, jogging towards her. It seemed familiar. Tall, male, broad shoulders, long athletic legs. Mr Grumpy-Gorgeous – clothed and jogging now: he certainly liked to keep fit. Well, he was certainly fit, in all meanings of the word. She laughed to herself. Felt a little glow of anticipation as he approached, though she wasn't even sure if he would raise a smile, let alone speak to her. Would he even recognize her?

Closer now, she could see the taut muscles pumping in his legs, the sweat on his brow, his hair curling damply with sweat. As he neared she could hear his heavy breathing. He was pushing quite a pace. She realized she must have been staring – oops. He managed a small stiff wave of acknowledgement as he passed. Claire gave a brief neighbourly wave back.

She walked on. Big flat plops of rain started. She'd better hurry up. She couldn't even see the cottages from here – there was still another headland before their bay. The plops were getting heavier, starting to soak her top.

Footsteps pounded up behind her. 'Fancy a jog? I think we're about to get a soaking.'

My God, he'd spoken. And that might even be a glimmer of a smile across his lips.

'Okay.' She was stunned, by both him and the turn in the weather. Why was she saying okay? She hated running. But it was bloody bucketing it down now. It was as if someone had just turned the volume up on the rain – you could almost hear the gear change, and then thud, thud, thud, droplets all over. It was even pitting the sand.

'I can't go very fast, mind.'

They trotted off, keeping time, Ed obviously slowing to match her pace.

'Typical English summer, hey,' she quipped.

'Yes. I'd much rather a good soaking than sitting in the garden with a glass of chilled Sauvignon,' he answered.

She glanced across. He might be the weird type who would actually enjoy this. But there was a stray smile across his lips, which were actually rather luscious. He looked so much nicer when he smiled.

'You should do that more often.' Shit, the words were out before she'd had time to think.

'What?' He stared across at her.

She might as well carry it through now. 'Smile. It suits you.'

'Ah.' He was silent for a few seconds.

Oops, that would teach her. Engage brain before mouth. 'Um, do you . . . run a lot?' she asked, trying to get the conversation back on track, though it was getting hard to speak and run at the same time. And the rain was actually pounding them now: there were little trickles streaming off her hair, running into her eyes and down the bridge of her nose.

It wasn't the best conversation starter, but running was a better subject than swimming. *Now why did she have to go and think of that?* The image of him naked was making her feel all hot – she'd be blushing, for sure, though the rain would hopefully hide it.

A crack and a boom shook the air around them. She felt the vibration through her body. Wow! Lightning flashed across the sky out at sea. A sheet of solid rain shifted across the waves. A summer storm. She was absolutely soaked to the skin now. She looked across at him, his damp curly hair now scattering drips as he moved, his running top wet and tight to the muscles on his chest.

It made her laugh out loud, how drenched they were. How small they seemed against the power of the elements.

'Like this, do you?' He had a quizzical look on his face.

'Yeah, I think I do. Like I'm really alive.'

A frown creased his brow; she saw him take a sharp breath.

He ran a little faster, moving ahead of her.

The cottages were in sight now. She finally caught up with him at her garden gate. 'You okay?'

'Yeah . . . I'm fine . . . if wet.' He managed a wry, somewhat enigmatic smile.

'Do you want to come in?' Whoa, she hadn't planned to ask him in. The words had just come out. Yet again. Oh well, in for a penny, in for a pound. 'You could warm up with a cup of coffee or something. I have dry towels.'

He stood looking thoughtful. They were getting wetter by the second.

'Sometime today might be nice,' Claire prompted.

'Ah, yes, okay. Thanks.'

She unbolted the door. A cold draught hit her.

'God, it's freezing in here,' he said. 'Old Hedley's never bothered putting central heating in yet, then?'

'Nope, sorry.'

They wandered through, dripping a trail to the lounge.

'Aha. I could light the fire for you.' He'd spotted the grate, the real fire.

She hadn't used it yet.

'Oh, okay. Great.'

'Do you have any newspaper, some matches?'

There was a stack of logs and some kindling piled by the wall next to the hearth. She nipped out to the kitchen to grab a two-day-old paper she'd got ready for recycling, and collected the matches she used to light the hob.

'You must freeze to death in this place.' He was huddled by the unlit hearth.

'Hah, glad it's summer, that's all I can say. But I wouldn't know where to start with lighting a real fire, to be honest.'

'Well.' He looked up at her, taking the newspaper and giving a small grin. 'Watch and learn.'

He started rolling tight batons of paper, loading them into the grate. She liked watching him work – intent on his task with his back to her, broad shoulders, arm muscles working away. She realized she was staring, but hey, he'd asked her to watch! She was rather enjoying observing him doing his fire-lighting man thing. She didn't mind being looked after in this instance. But all too soon, the cold began seeping into her bones. She left him to his fire lighting and went upstairs, fetching two big towels out of the bathroom and wrapping hers around her. That was a bit better. She handed him one as she got back to the lounge.

'Thanks.' He placed it round his shoulders.

'I've got some soup left over. Are you hungry? It will only take a few minutes to heat up, and I made fresh bread this morning. It's the least I can do . . . warm us up.' *And what was the most she could do?* Out of the blue, she suddenly visualized lots of other naughty things they could do, involving duvets and warm bare skin. Blimey, where had that come from? Her mind hadn't veered that way in an age, her body even longer.

He lit a match. Flames began to slowly lick at the paper and the stack of sticks in the hearth.

'So that's what I could smell from across this way this morning. Homemade bread.'

The fire began crackling around the kindling and paper, its glow already beginning to take the chill off the room. She headed to the kitchen, taking the matches with her, and lit the stove to warm the soup. She cut slices of soft, crusty bread and spread it thickly with butter. Within five minutes, she was bringing it all back in on a tray.

'Good dry logs,' he commented.

The fire was now flaming gold and orange, its warmth starting to thaw the room. She handed him a mug of vegetable soup, passed the bread, then sat down beside him cross-legged on the floor, but her jeans were sodden and getting cold, clinging roughly to her legs. Damn, she should have changed them when she was upstairs, but she didn't want to move away from this lovely fire, the warm mug of soup. She put her mug down and stood up, pausing for a second. Oh, sod it, they were coming off. She wrapped the towel around her waist, then undid the button and zip.

'Hope you don't mind, but these jeans are soaking wet still.'

'Doesn't worry me.' He took a gulp of soup, his eyes crinkling with amusement.

She slid the jeans down and off. Ah, that was so much better. She could thaw out properly now. The towel covered her knees at least.

'Better?' He was smiling. He seemed surprisingly relaxed. It was as if the real Ed was finally showing through.

'Better.' She took back her mug of soup and sipped, beginning to warm both inside and out.

So here she was, sitting in her cottage by a roaring log fire with an undoubtedly attractive man, who was dressed in a towel, jogging shirt and shorts, whilst she had on only pants, bra and a long-sleeved T-shirt under her towel. Weirdly, it felt okay.

He dunked thick chunks of bread into his mug. 'This is really good.'

'Thanks.'

'So you know how to light a fire now?'

'Yep. You learn something new every day.'

'Indeed.' He sipped. 'You'll need that life skill in here. It's a bloody wreck of a place. Don't know how you've lasted so long, to be honest. Had you down for a few days max at the start.'

'Ah, did you now? I'm made of hardier stuff than that.'

'Yes, I can tell.'

Was that a hint of admiration in his tone? Bloody hell! What had happened to Mr Grumpy? Had he gone and got a personality transplant over the weekend, or had the rain washed away his ill humour?

As he leaned across to put another log on the fire, his foot brushed hers, sending little electrical pulses through her. She wasn't wearing any trousers, her sensible head reminded her. Thank God she'd shaved her legs this morning. She'd better go and get some dry clothes on as soon as. She didn't know quite what had come over her; she wouldn't normally strip off her trousers in front of a man she scarcely knew. But she was just getting warm again, enjoying his company, and didn't want to move quite yet. Didn't want to go upstairs and break the spell.

When he settled back down, his foot lay there touching her own.

'This is cosy,' he said, matter of fact.

'Ah-hah,' she agreed. A tense feeling came over her. Anticipation?

He held her gaze for a second or two, then smiled. God, he had a lovely smile – nice white teeth, soft lips, a suggestion of manly stubble on his upper lip and chin. Why on earth had he kept that smile hidden? Maybe he had a lot of pressures at work, came here to get away from it all. It took him a while to wind down, obviously, considering how cool he'd been the last few times they'd met.

'What do you do for a living?' Claire piped up.

'I'm an architect. I have a practice in Edinburgh.'

'Ah, interesting. Designing buildings and the like, then.'

'Yes, I do all sorts, but the bread-and-butter stuff is the smaller work, like house extensions, new builds. Often where they want something unique. What about you?'

'Journalist. I work for the local press down in Newcastle. It's pretty low-key, but I love it, most of the time. You get to meet lots of different people.'

'Sounds interesting.'

'Sometimes it can be. But other times I'm raking about looking for stories, interviewing people about their pet dogs or the latest parking rises. It's not all glamour and paparazzi, especially not in North Tyneside.'

'Is this just a holiday for you, then?'

'Yes . . .' She faltered. 'I – I've taken a bit of leave . . .' She didn't want to start going into the reasons why. And he was polite enough not to ask further. 'It's a great place here – the beach and everything,' she clarified, in case he thought she was some kind of nutter who loved living in a hovel.

'Yes,' he answered, then went quiet. He seemed to be thinking.

It felt odd that they were huddled in towels with only centimetres between them. The fire was crackling away, giving a golden glow, throwing out its heat now. He turned to her. Stared at her seriously, intently. She held his gaze, noticing the green of his eyes, the tiny flecks of yellow close to the pupil, but then had to look down. There was something too intense about it.

When she looked up again, his face was closer to hers. The whole atmosphere in the room had changed. And suddenly this moment felt like it was where they were both meant to be. No time for thinking – she moved her mouth to meet his. Gentle at first, then hungry. His lips tasted salty from the bread, from the sweat from his run.

They were kissing harder, passionately. She kneeled up, wanting to feel him nearer, pressing her chest against his. This contact, this sensuality, was so powerful. She had been on her own for so long in her world of fear and illness and betrayal. But hey, was this really happening? Stuff like this didn't happen to her, Claire Maxwell – this was like some movie scene. *Don't overthink it . . . Go with it Claire*, a little voice cheered her on.

His lips were still on hers, his hands stroking through her hair, tugging sensually, and then she felt his strong arms around her back, closing her towards him. Her towel fell away, though she was still wearing her damp top. Her inner tension began to melt. She felt safe in his arms. Nothing mattered but this kiss. Unexpected, yet so natural. So needed. Two people caught in a storm.

And this was *so* turning her on, the warmth flowing right down to her thighs. Wow, she hadn't felt like this in such a long time. His erection matched her desire – she could feel him hard, nudging against her hip.

Oh God – she couldn't just . . . could she? She'd been with her husband for six years, and had had only a couple of boyfriends before that. She'd never had a one-night stand. And she didn't really know this guy. She knew he was fit and had the body of a god, had seen his taut thighs, muscled chest, and boy, so much more. Was that enough of a reason? *Hell, yes, what are you waiting for?* something shouted inside. He was kissing her neck now. Ohhh, that felt so good.

But could he be some kind of Jekyll and Hyde character? She'd certainly witnessed the grumpy side. And now all this passion. He could be an axe murderer or anything. Who'd chopped up all those logs for kindling? He might have killed his ex and escaped down here, hiding from the police. This could be his hideout. Bloody hell, she'd been watching far too many suspense dramas.

Perhaps he was just a hot-blooded, passionate man, who was sometimes reserved . . . until you got to know him, and then he let loose. Oh bloody hell woman. *Go, go, go.* This had been a long time coming.

She tugged at his T-shirt, his towel having dropped off ages ago. Oh my, what a chest. Gorgeous – just as lovely close up. She ran her hand over it, all defined muscle and a few sexy blond hairs. Then he was slipping out of his shorts, just boxers now – sporty black ones, tight. She hardly dared look at the contours, but sneaked a peek. Wow. David Beckham eat your heart out.

Kissing once more. His tongue warm and deliciously probing.

His hands on her top, pulling it up over her head. Oh God, down to bra and panties.

Reality hit. *Shit, her scar* – he'd be moving to undo the clasp of her bra at any moment. What would he think? If she forewarned him, that would surely kill the moment, but if she didn't, just seeing what he was going to see would strike the passion dead immediately. And she couldn't bear to see his face, the horror that might show there. *Shit, shit, shit.* Maybe she could ask him to leave the bra on. She pulled back.

He looked at her. Put his head in his hands, then started rubbing his forehead roughly. 'Fuck. Fuck . . . Look, I'm sorry. I can't do this.' *His* voice.

Suddenly he was up scrabbling for his shirt, his shorts, running for the door. Surely he couldn't have read her thoughts, known what was there beneath her bra. She watched the back of him dashing down the hall, then heard the slam of the door. Like he couldn't get away fast enough.

Her desire unravelled within seconds, leaving her confused and frustrated.

What the hell was going on?

* * *

After the rainstorm and the near-miss lovemaking, everything had seemed rather surreal. *So*, she'd had a gorgeous man down to his boxer shorts in her living room by a roaring log fire . . . and then he'd gone and run off.

Oh, sweet Jesus, as if her life wasn't complicated enough. Okay, so he may have sensed her unease, her fear of revealing her damaged breast, her scars? Perhaps he was telepathic or something. Or she was beginning to look freaked out without realizing it.

But there seemed to be more to it than that . . . something within him too. Something that he shielded behind that grumpy mask. She was sure it was a mask; she'd seen another side to him today, a glimpse of the person he once was, or could be again. Perhaps she wasn't the only one who had storms, secrets, scars.

Claire settled down with a cup of tea by the fire; she'd kept it going by piling on more logs throughout the afternoon and it was giving out some welcome heat. The rain kept billowing, tapping on the windows. Staying in was the only option. She'd keep warm and cosy, get back to the safety of her latest read – a romantic novel with a touch of humour. Best let the relationship stuff remain safely on the page and in her mind.

She'd already texted her sister, her mum and Andrea, her friend and fellow journalist at the *Herald*, wanting some contact with the outside world. Sal sent a reply that she was *Back to bedlam with the boys. Mark being far worse than the children!* Claire could picture them all in their red-brick semi in Gosforth, a tumble of love. Sal had told her they had loads on, and wouldn't manage to squeeze in a beach trip as a family, but she'd go and visit them soon herself. She remembered how great her nephews had been when she was in hospital, full of curious questions: 'Auntie Claire, what's that funny hat thing?' – it was the cooler to try and save her hair. And 'How big is the needle thing they need to stick in your arm? Is it massive?' Claire hadn't minded; everyone else was wondering the same things yet being far too polite and bland with *How are you?* and *Is it all going okay?* She had often felt like saying, 'Oh yes, bloody marvellous having needles stuck in you, bits cut out of you, and your hair falling out. Fan-bloody-tastic.' But they were only trying to be kind. The boys had been a welcome relief, bringing with them bold-ness and chocolates and laughter.

Later, in her bedroom, she lay thinking by the light of the bedside lamp.

What would he have seen, Ed? If they'd gone that step further. Would it have been so bad? She hadn't looked directly at her scar in months, hadn't really wanted to after that initial shock in the hospital ward. She had lived with it, got on with it, got dressed and covered it up every day, but hadn't really thought too much about it until today. Until someone else was going to have to see it too, and it scared her. His likely reaction. Maybe it was a blessing he'd run when he did, because he may well have wanted to seconds later. Would his face have dropped, along with her bra? Would he have tried to rally but bottled out and left, making polite excuses?

What would he have seen?

She took a long, slow breath. The low lighting of the bedside lamp in the room was just enough, the daylight still a soft grey through the window: long June shadows, late nights. She got up and stood before the full-length mirror.

She pulled her sweatshirt off over her head. Her comfy washed-out bra – that on its own might have been enough to put him off, she mused wryly. Her breast shape looked okay so far, with the bra on – she'd chosen a reconstruction soon after the initial op, back to her original 34C. The V of her cleavage looked fairly normal.

She reached her hand up to her left cup and felt through the material, the faint ridge of the scar under her touch. Closed her eyes a second, reached behind for the clasp of her bra. Held her breath. Released it. Dropped the off-white material down to the floor. Stared. Hadn't expected the tears that startled her eyes and misted the image for a second. Wiped them away. Focused. She had to see what he would see.

Her throat tightened and she gulped back a small sob. The scar still had the power to hurt her, but not as much as before.

They hadn't been able to save the nipple; it often caused more problems trying to keep it, they said. So there was a breast shape with a bold reddish-purple scar line horizontally across it and little stitch indentations at right angles to it. A bit like ruler markings. She ran her forefinger along it, felt each delicate ridge. It didn't hurt to touch any more; if anything, it wasn't as sensitive as before the op. It only felt uncomfortable when she forgot and lay down on it, flat on her stomach. The lack of nipple looked odd. Could anyone find her attractive now? She thought back to all those stupid teenage doubts: Were her breasts big enough? Had they got a slight droop? And, oh my God, panic – a rogue hair around the nipple, the tiniest blondest hair ever. What the hell had she been thinking back then? What on earth had there ever been to worry about? It was laughable now. She'd like to give her teenage self a good shake.

She felt crushed, confused, yes. But she was here. Others hadn't made it. Was it selfish to be thinking this way? The faces of those friends on the chemotherapy ward who hadn't got through appeared in her mind. A lump lodged in her throat. This was her battle scar. And she was alive to see it. She must hold on to that. She was a survivor. She couldn't waste her life worrying about a missing nipple, a ridge of scarred flesh.

This was her now. This was Claire Maxwell. She had to accept it. And she could. Her fear was how someone else, a man, a lover, might feel about it. She felt such a deep yearning to be held, to be loved again. Not just by her mum, her sister, her friends, precious though that support was, but by a man. She longed to get lost in someone else's touch, have wonderful, gasp-out-loud, satisfying sex. It had been such a long time. Having Ed so near today had shaken up her world.

They were so close, *so close* to having sex – just about naked, for fuck's sake. And he had *run away*. Her shoulders starting shaking as she pictured the pair of them. She began giggling at the bizarreness of the situation, and her bare breasts began jiggling. Life was bloody bonkers, whichever way you looked at it. But then the tears flowed. For her scars, her fears, for her lost friends, for the patients she hadn't known, the ones facing their nightmare journey right now, and the ones that cancer had stolen from their families.

She wrapped herself up in her cosy dressing gown, went to the bedroom window and stood looking out at the half moon. Dusk was closing in around it now. There were glints of silver on the sea.

A ping of light arced across her garden. An upstairs room lit up next door. She thought she could hear the echoes of music, something classical, lyrical. What was he doing? What was he thinking? Was he looking out at the sea too?

The world was as big as a moonlit sky, as small as a grain of sand; it was crazy, it could hurt, it was beautiful. You could get lost in it.

Two lonely lights, side by side.

7

The smell of freshly baked bread

After the mortifying events of the previous day, Claire just wanted a quiet, normal kind of Tuesday. She pottered around the cottage as the weather was still unsettled, but managed a short stroll on the beach between showers, dipping her toes in the sea, sharing the shoreline with a couple of gulls, quite happy to watch the world go by.

On Wednesday, she spent time in the sea-view garden. The sun had decided to make a comeback and prove it was summer after all. She really must crack on with the editorial piece for next week's *Herald*, she mused. She was features editor; she had a good following. The stories of her battle with cancer had inspired others, but she didn't want to dwell on that any more. Her writing needed a new direction, something to cheer people up.

She sat thinking for a while, and then the thoughts flowed. She realized that what she wanted to write about was those simple things in life that make you happy; the conversation she'd had with her sister had stayed in her mind. She opened a Word document on her laptop and found herself planning her first 'Magic Moments' article.

She paused, considering what moments should be on her own list, then began typing:

1. A sea view and sunshine on your face.
2. Time spent with family. *(She remembered how lovely the weekend had been with her sister.)*
3. Tea and cake with friends. *(Yes, she'd arrange that with Andrea and the girls when she got back.)*
4. Hearing the sound of children's laughter. *(Visit to her nephews asap.)*
5. A hot, deep, bubbly bath. *(Another one tonight!)*
6. Losing yourself in a great book. *(This afternoon!)*
7. A hug. *(In her darkest moments during the cancer treatment when words were no longer enough, a hug had said it all, made her feel safe, comforted. And hugs could be happy too. Aw – she'd need to find someone . . . She'd definitely be getting one from her mum on her return home . . . did that count? What she'd really imagined was a strong man's arms around her. Thought removed – that*

was veering way too near to Ed territory, and look where that had ended up.) Hmm . . . what next?

8. A chilled glass of wine on a summer's day. *(Ready to pour at your leisure, madam.)*
9. The smell of freshly baked bread, closely followed by its taste, just out of the oven.
10. Doing something to help someone else.

She'd keep an eye on how she could help others. It always made you feel better. More connected, somehow. She might do something for a cancer charity, or offer to get the old lady next door's shopping for her. Or take her a nice freshly baked loaf – why not? She could continue her baking back home, for sure.

She decided to leave out her aspirations for sex on the beach and the naked-swimmer viewing sessions – for now. It might trigger all manner of weird and wonderful suggestions in her mailbag and cause uproar at the family-styled newspaper.

She wrote a short intro about how she was inspired to write the article, and briefly mentioned her break away to provide some background. At the bottom of the column she'd ask her readers to send in their own magic moments. It would be lovely to see what made other people happy, if there were things that united everyone or special, funny or unusual moments.

Claire felt pretty sure this would make a lovely column.

And it would be nice to have something positive to say – a change from all that sad and scary news. She just hoped her boss, David, would feel the same once he'd read her proposal. He always insisted that bad news sold more papers – how often did you see a cheery headline?

She finished the article and reread it, tweaking a few words here and there; an hour passed quickly. She'd take another look later; it was always better to take a break from a piece of writing and go back to it with a fresh mind. There was always some daft typo or clumsy phrase lurking in there, ready to catch you out.

The next morning, she decided to walk into the village, thinking that the fresh air and exercise would do her good. From the puffy white clouds above, it looked as though the weather had settled again, though it was still rather cool for June. She'd had another flick through Lynda's cookbook last night, and fancied trying out some flatbreads. She could buy a fresh chicken to cook and some salad to go with them.

The walk along the beach was calming – the sounds of the sea, soft sand between her bare toes. She strolled, carrying her plimsolls in one hand. On the second bay, an elderly silver-haired chap was striding towards her. She'd seen him several times this holiday. He walked with an old-fashioned wooden stick, but at a good pace; it seemed like he did this stretch of beach often.

'Morning, lass.'

'Morning.' Claire smiled back.

'I've seen you lots of times now, haven't I? You staying here?' He paused.

'Yes, at the cottage there in the next bay, Farne View.'

'Ah yes. Having a nice time?'

'I am, yes. It's lovely here.'

'Grand, isn't it? You won't get a better beach than this one in the whole world, I reckon. The name's Peter, by the way.' He held out a slightly wizened welcoming hand.

Claire took it and gave it a firm shake. 'Nice to meet you, Peter. I'm Claire.'

'Well, enjoy your walk, Claire, lass. Maybe see you again.'

'Possibly, but I'm away home at the end of next week. Back to reality.'

'Ah well. I'm the lucky one that lives here. You'll have to come back sometime, mind.'

'Yes, that would be nice.' *Would she ever come back?* Or would life just take over? She'd be busy at work and getting on with life; would Bamburgh and her cranky cottage just drift away to a special place in her heart, never to be seen again?

'Nice to meet you, lassie. Well then, I'll be on my way.' And off he jauntily strode, leaving steady footprints in the sand.

Claire set off once more. It was good to feel her energy levels returning. She could walk much faster than at the start of her stay, and didn't need to take a break or sit on the rocks for a breather. Though it was still nice to pause, to take in the stunning view – today an azure sky with puffs of white cloud, circling gulls, the metallic shifting-grey of the sea breaking into white foam at the shore and transformed into crystal droplets as a dog shook its fur. She watched a father and toddler son digging a big sandcastle, heads bent down, intent on their task. Beach life.

When she reached Lynda's deli she was feeling altogether more relaxed. Ready to put the mini crisis with Ed behind her and make sure she enjoyed the last week of her stay.

'Hello, petal. How's life in your cottage by the beach going?' Lynda smiled from behind the counter.

'Fine. No, it's good. I'm feeling so much more relaxed than when I got here. Stronger.'

'That's great. I hope you don't mind me asking, but have you been ill, pet?'

'Yes. Yes, I have. Some months ago now. I've just got through breast cancer treatment.' She didn't mind opening up with Lynda, who seemed genuinely friendly, such a warm person.

'I see. I'm sorry if I sound nosy, but my cousin's just been through it – last year. There was something about you that made me wonder. So you're all clear now?'

'Yes, thank goodness.'

'That's good news.'

'And your cousin?'

'Yes, good news for her too. Thank heavens. She has two teenage daughters. It was a tough time for her. I'm sure for you too. Those treatments take it right out of you, don't they?'

'Yep, they can do, Lynda . . . But like I say, I'm feeling so much better now.'

'That's the main thing.' She smiled. 'So, how can I help you today, or did you just fancy a chat?'

As well as some provisions to put in the fridge, Claire ordered some strong white bread flour and yeast, and some sesame seeds, dried thyme and marjoram for the top of her next bread creation.

'Mmm, that sounds interesting. What kind of bread are you planning on making today, then?'

'Maneesh.'

Lynda looked blank. 'And what's that when it's at home then?'

'Hah, it was in that book you lent me. A Middle Eastern-style flatbread.'

'Very fancy – sounds delicious. When will it be ready? What time shall I pop in?' She grinned cheekily.

'Actually, you're very welcome to pop in.' *Some company might be really nice.* 'If you have a few spare minutes on your way home, or something, call in for some coffee if you like.'

'Hmm, sounds like a good idea . . . And I get to sample these baking delights?'

'Of course.'

She felt comfortable with Lynda, even though she must be a good twenty years older than her.

'You're on, pet. That would be lovely. I'll call in after closing time for a quick cuppa. I have to pass the end of your driveway, anyway. I live just on the edge of Seahouses. It's old Hedley's cottage, isn't it?'

'Yep, that's the one.'

As Lynda was measuring out the ingredients, Claire spotted a familiar black vehicle parked just across the road. *Guess who?* Her insides gave a weird flip. Bugger. Oh well, she'd hang around in here for a little while longer; there were no other customers in yet.

'Has it been busy here?' she asked.

'Not too bad. Whit week was pretty hectic because of the school holidays, but now the children are all back, it's settled down a bit.'

'How long have you been here in the deli?'

'Oh, about ten years now, pet. It was always my dream. I used to be a receptionist at a funeral directors, believe it or not. It was fine, I liked the job, met some nice people. The relatives, I mean.'

Claire smiled, picturing Lynda chatting away to the corpses. She could imagine her being pleasant and friendly on reception – she had a lovely manner for dealing with the bereaved.

'I just wanted to run my own business,' she continued,

'and it had to be a deli. All that lovely food, and the chance to bake my own bread. I'd been baking away at home for years, trying out all sorts of recipes, and bread was what I loved creating the most. When I saw this place up for rent, that was it – I knew it was my ideal shop. The deli in the cottage on the corner. And Bamburgh is such a beautiful village, with plenty of tourists to keep a little business like this going. It's perfect for me. I've never looked back.'

'That's great. It must be wonderful to achieve your dream like that. It's a gorgeous shop.'

'Thank you.'

The car was still there across the way, but there was no sign of Ed. A family came in for ice creams, oohing and ahhing over the delicious flavours. It was getting a little crowded, and Lynda was now busy scooping and serving. Claire should slip away, go to the butcher and get the chicken to roast for her dinner. That was all she had left to do, and then she could get off back down to the beach.

'See you later, Lynda. And remember to pop in if you have time on the way home. You'll be very welcome.'

'Will do. See you later.'

Claire walked up the pavement beside the row of stone cottages, and was just heading into the butcher's shop when *boomph*, she bumped into someone coming out. Shit! Ed.

Her cheeks blasted pink with embarrassment. Thanks, Fate.

'Ah . . . sorry,' he started, as she was saying, 'Oops, sorry.'

He looked as mortified as she imagined she did.

They took two steps away from the door together, then one forward together in a sort of get-me-out-of-here dance. Then he stopped and looked right at her. 'Look . . . I'm really sorry about the other day.'

'Ah,' was all she could muster. This was excruciating.

'I mean . . . It shouldn't . . . '

'Have happened?' she blurted out. She might as well help him out.

'Well . . . maybe . . . yes. No.' He paused, looking down for a second.

Ground, swallow me whole right now.

'Not like that . . . I just . . . I mean, I shouldn't have dragged you into anything.'

As far as she was concerned, there hadn't been much dragging going on. But it was obvious he needed a get-out clause. 'It's okay. I get it. It should never have happened. So shall we try our best to forget it ever did?'

He looked relieved.

Could she forget the image of him in his black boxers with his erection tightly packed, ready for action, by the roaring log fire? Ah brain, stop it for God's sake. He was right in front of her on the pavement. She felt the burn of embarrassment flush up her neck, right to her cheeks.

'Right, well,' she coughed.

'Right,' he echoed.

She had to get out of here – this was *so* awkward. 'Okay, well then, I'd better be off.' All bright and breezy. She realized she sounded very jolly-hockey-sticks.

'Yeah, okay. No hard feelings, I hope.'

Gulp! Why did he have to mention the word *hard*?

'No, of course not.' Her voice came out a little squeaky.

'Good.'

Thank God she only had another week to go. Then that would be it. No longer having to live next door to grumpy-gorgeous Ed. No chance of bumping into him in the locality. No more embarrassing scenes like this.

Ed walked away, back to his jeep. Okay, so she really felt the need for cream cakes or something now. She'd go and get some chocolate chips for brioche. Back to Lynda's deli, then. She stood for a second, unable to help herself as she watched Ed duck into his vehicle and drive off.

Then she headed back into the shop.

'Back already?' Lynda said, smiling. 'Keeps himself to himself, that one.' She'd obviously caught the focus of Claire's gaze. 'Nice-looking, mind. Your neighbour down at the cottage, isn't he?'

Of course everybody would know everybody in a place like this.

'Hmm. We don't have a lot to do with each other.'
Well she was never going to tell her the truth, was she.

It was easier said than done, the forgetting all about it
part. For some weird reason, despite his grumpiness and
his running out on her semi-naked at the crucial moment,
she still couldn't help thinking about him.

The oven was on, set to gas mark 8, one mark above
the recipe. Claire had got the measure of the cooker now.
The thermostat must be a bit out, but she'd finally sussed
it.

She put the flour in a large bowl, added the salt and
sugar to one side and the yeast to the other, then started
adding olive oil and some water. She began mixing as the
recipe stated, using the fingers of one hand, which was
a bit tricky, not to mention messy. But gradually it started
forming a dough. As it became soft and stretchy, she was
able to shape it into a smooth ball. She had to leave it to
rise, apparently, for an hour until it doubled in size, so
she headed out into the beachside garden to sit with a
glass of Pinot Grigio and her book.

The hour soon passed and she was back in the kitchen
following the next stage of the recipe, trying to 'fold back
the dough on itself', as the recipe said, 'until all the air
was knocked out' – how on earth did you tell? She cut
the mix into three clumps and rolled each of them into
a large flat circle. Her baking trays were ready, lined with

parchment, and she'd already got the topping mix made up in a bowl – a gorgeous combination of sesame seeds and herbs with olive oil – which she spread over the surface of each disc.

The oven seemed to be hot enough and ready to go, so in they went. She checked her watch. They needed fifteen minutes, that was all. Ten minutes later the smell was delicious. She couldn't wait to open the oven door and see what they looked like, but she held off for a few more minutes, not wanting to spoil them with her curiosity and a cool draught of air. Of course the old oven didn't have a glass window, so it was a matter of guesswork as to whether they were the right colour yet.

Time was up. She put on her oven gloves to open the door and reach for them, and was delighted to find them a beautiful golden colour with a touch of toasty-brown at the edges. Perfect. She hoped they'd taste as good as they looked. She'd bought some humus to dip the bread into, plus some garlic-stuffed olives at Lynda's earlier (one advantage of being on your own, meant you didn't have to worry about garlic breath!) and she'd have them with a salad for supper later. She left the flatbreads to cool on the side on the wire rack from the grill.

A while later, there was a knock on the door. Luckily Claire happened to be inside the house, or she might have missed it. For one mad moment she thought it might be Ed coming back to explain . . . or to carry on where he left off, *gulp*. But then she remembered having invited Lynda and glanced at her watch. It was five fifteen. That fitted. It was surely Lynda. She felt a slight stab of disappointment.

But there on the step was her new friend, bearing a wide smile and a scrummy-looking packet of biscuits with a wrapped-up chunk of something.

'Hello, lovely. Darling Blue, the cheese you like. It's near its best-before date – you may as well have it.'

'Aw, thanks, Lynda, but you really didn't have to bring anything. Those biscuits look delightful, though.' She read the label – strawberries and clotted cream shortbread. Yum.

'The house smells gorgeous. What have you been baking? Did you have a go at that bread? The Manic or whatever it was.'

'Maneesh.'

'I knew it was something like that.'

'It looks good. Let's hope it tastes good too.'

'I'm sure it will.'

They walked through the hallway into the kitchen. Lynda eyed the decor. 'It's a bit old-fashioned in here, isn't it?' She was obviously trying to be polite.

Claire laughed. 'You could say that. Rack and ruin also comes to mind. Don't worry, I'm getting used to it.'

'Well, the bread looks wonderful, anyhow.'

'Thanks. I've finally got the measure of that oven. It's been a nightmare, but I've sussed its wicked ways, and its thermostat to be precise.'

'Good for you.'

'Do you happen to know much about the cottage, Lynda? Its background?' Claire was curious. 'Has Mr Hedley ever lived here himself?'

'No, no. He has a place on a farm about three miles away. He inherited Farne View from an elderly aunt. It had been empty for years.'

That figured.

'She had to go into a care home, bless her. She was a lovely old lady. She'd just got too frail to look after herself, and Hedley never used to help her much. She didn't have any children of her own, so the place stood empty. When she died, he got the cottage in the will. Never did anything with it, mind.'

'Oh, I see.'

'Then he decided to make it into a holiday cottage. We all had a chuckle down at the village at that. Yes, it's a nice spot, but *really*?'

'Hah, and then I got to stay in it!'

'To be honest, I was surprised when I heard that's where you were. Ah, she was a lovely old lady, though – Evelyn was her name. Must have lived here forty years, at least. She struggled to keep the place up when she was here on her own. Her husband had died a long time back.

She tried her best. Used to walk into the village most days, then get the bus back with her shopping, even into her eighties. Until it all got too much.'

Claire could picture her tootling about in here. All the cookbooks and utensils in the kitchen had been left as they were. It was probably even her salt pot lurking in the cupboard. It all made sense now. The old-fashioned quilt and crocheted blanket upstairs. It had no doubt been very much the same when she was here.

The old house must miss her.

'We have no idea, down in the village, why he hasn't sold it off. Especially if he's not going to bother to look after it. We think he's holding out for a property developer or mogul to come along and offer him a million for it. Just because it's got a nice sea view. He'll be waiting a while.'

Claire gave a wry smile. In a weird way, she was glad that Mr Hedley hadn't sold it off, glad that she'd had the chance to stay here. She'd grown fond of the old cottage and its foibles. And in fact, as they walked out to her beach-garden, in her heart she knew this really was a million-pound view – perhaps more when it had a certain naked swimmer in it.

'Well, what can I get for you, Lynda? Cup of tea? Coffee? Or shall we try some of my just-made Maneesh bread with a bowl of your olives and a glass of wine? We can sit outside if you're happy with that.' The sun was glinting gold over the sea. It would be nice to be out in the garden.

'Option three, definitely. Just a small glass for me, though, as I need to drive home.'

'That's fine. I'll just pop back in and fetch it. Take a seat and make yourself comfortable.'

They settled themselves onto the wooden chairs on the back patch of lawn, with some slices of the flatbread, a small bowl of olives and the hummus dip spread out on the table. In the late-afternoon sun it felt very Mediterranean and slightly decadent.

'Mmm, this bread is definitely as good as it looks,' said Lynda as she broke into it. 'So you *are* a natural at it, after all. I might have to start making some of this Manic stuff for the shop. It's a lovely summer bread. I bet it would go down well with the holiday makers.'

'Yes, I bet it would.'

'Wow. What a view there is from here.'

'Absolutely. I can be on the beach in seconds for a walk if I want, or I can just sit and watch the world go by. It's lovely.'

'Yes, I can see the charm in it. I didn't realize it was such a pretty spot – you can't tell from the road.'

'It has its plus points.' Claire smiled.

'As long as the weather stays fair, I suppose. Maybe not so much fun here on a wet day.'

Hah, Ed sprang to mind again. The last wet day was certainly full of fun and games. 'No,' was all she said.

They chatted about the deli and about Claire's plans

for the last week of her stay, and she mentioned her job as a journalist, outlining her idea for her latest column.

'By the way, Lynda, what's your magic moment? As in, what special thing would make your day, however big or small?'

'Oh, now let me think . . . Well, then, I get a lovely feeling when someone comes back into the shop to tell me how wonderful something they've bought there has been, especially when it's something I've made myself, like the breads. That's special. You get a real sense of pride.'

Claire was nodding.

'Oh, and of course when I get my daughter back home for a while, or if we meet up for tea and cake or something. We can natter on for ages. She's doing well, our Evie. She's a teacher down in Gateshead. Lives down that way now, so I only get to see her every few weeks. It's lovely to see your children grown-up and happy, making their own way. But it's nice to have them back home for a while as well. You give them wings, but you hope they'll fly back home sometimes too.' She gave a warm smile.

Claire wondered if she would ever have that experience: having a child, watching them grow, helping them make their way in the world. Her heart gave a small squeeze. It might be a bit of a miracle after all her body had been through. That and the fact that she didn't have a man on the scene.

'That's nice, Lynda. It sounds like a lovely relationship you have with your daughter.'

'Yeah, we get on well. I'm very lucky.'

They chatted some more. Claire told her about her family back in Newcastle and Lynda mentioned her husband Steve, who worked on a farm just inland from Seahouses.

An hour soon passed.

'Right, well, petal, I'd better set myself away. Our Steve will be waiting for me by now, and no doubt wondering what's happening with his supper. Thanks for the glass of wine, and that bread of yours was delicious. It's been so lovely to chat.'

'You're very welcome. I've enjoyed chatting too.'

'Well, have a good last week, and be sure to pop into the shop before you head off away again.'

Claire walked Lynda back through the cottage to the front step, where the middle-aged lady gave her a warm hug.

'Bye, petal.'

'Bye.'

The house felt rather empty after she'd gone.

Later that night Claire found she wasn't angry with Ed any more. She just remembered his smile, how nice it was to see it, the little crinkles at the sides of his eyes, the way his grey-green irises lit up. She pictured his mouth. He had good teeth, white, just one slightly crooked one – the second tooth along at the top and even that was kind of cute. Nice lips too. And his kiss – that was pretty damn lovely. She sighed. Her head was full of him, and her body missed the promise of his touch. Damn it.

8

Magical . . . sea, sand, towers, knights and castles
                                    Anonymous, about Bamburgh

The next morning, Claire stood crumbling butter onto
a dough mix, then gently pushing the dough and butter
together with the heel of her hand as she followed the
recipe for chocolate brioche. Something sweet and
comforting – that was what she needed. In less than a
week she would be going home. *Home.* That word felt
hollow. Back to her old life, anyhow, or elements of it. It
would be lovely to see her friends and family, of course,
but not so easy to be back in the marital house, the
red-brick semi-detached one she'd been so excited to
move into six years ago. The one with the 'For Sale' sign
outside. The one she couldn't wait to leave.

With a line-up of brioche buns in the oven, she went

out and sat in the seaside garden. She looked across a calm, sparkling sea to a summer-blue sky, the sun warmer today, prickling her bare arms with heat. You really could get all seasons here in one day. For all the ups and downs of her stay, she loved this quirky cottage and its amazing sea views, the storms and the sunshine. Where you could sit and watch the world go by, or join in with the children paddling and go dip your feet in the rushing waves.

Sitting there with the warmth of the sun on her skin and the salt-tang of a pleasant breeze, watching the sea glint and roll and hearing its rush and pull was pretty magical. She thought back to how much she'd enjoyed last weekend with Sally, how they'd got closer again, reconnected. Laughing and chatting over a glass of chilled wine with someone you loved, be it a sister, friend or lover . . . that was magical too.

A lover, hah . . . she wasn't doing so well in those stakes. But the touch of a lover could be *so very special* when it was right. She sighed, remembering how it had felt all those years ago with Paul right back at the very beginning. And then Ed. Well, to start with, that day in the rain, anyhow. She could still feel the intense burn of his kiss. The warmth of his strong arms around her. It had been rather wonderful while it lasted. And, it had left her wanting more, which wasn't a great scenario considering the circumstances. Best to leave that one well alone.

Oh well, she might one day find a lover who wouldn't

run away from the scene, or wouldn't marry her and then run off with another woman six years later, just as she was given the all-clear from cancer. She could still believe in the magic of love, couldn't she? Life *was* going to be good again, wasn't it? She was just finding her feet at the moment.

She checked her watch – fifteen minutes had flown by. She ran back to the kitchen to retrieve the brioches just in time. They'd reached a deep-golden colour, the dark chocolate beginning to ooze from the sides. She left the batch on the side to cool, but couldn't resist taking one to eat straight away. She popped the kettle on for a fresh cup of tea.

Settling back into her wobbly chair, mug of tea on the little table beside her, she dunked a chunk of still-warm brioche into it and took a buttery, chocolatey bite. Delicious! Suddenly she felt truly alive, every sense tingling. She could smell, taste, touch, hear, see . . . She could breathe, and walk, and run, and swim – if she wanted to. She had made it through, and she was determined not to take life for granted ever again.

She decided to check over her 'Magic Moments' article that she had written yesterday, and send it off to the paper asap. She felt encouraged that her boss had replied to her email asking her to send him the finished article so he could take a look and consider it. They'd already had two weeks with the guest journalist hosting her column. Next week *she'd be back* (just like good old Arnold Schwarzenegger) and she needed to return with a bang. She had no intention of losing her features slot, or her job. She loved writing, and she sure as hell needed the money right now. Once the mortgage was taken out of the house sale, what was left – and then halved – would be eaten up as a deposit on a new flat, and then after that all the bills would be hers alone. It was a daunting thought, but she'd manage somehow. She felt ready. And 'a place of her own' had rather a nice ring to it. She licked the chocolate off her fingers and went inside to get her laptop.

Claire was determined not to waste the last two days of her holiday. Yes, she'd come with the aim of getting lots of rest and recuperation, and she'd had plenty of that; but she felt she wanted to discover a little more about this amazing place with its traditional Northumberland stone-cottage village and the most stunning castle dominating the dunes. In fact, that would be the perfect place to start this morning – a tour of the castle. She'd seen it was open to the public. It would be great to see it from the inside, as well as the out.

She went up for a quick shower – another cool one, water on the blink *again* – then got dressed in pale-pink cropped chinos and a T-shirt and packed a hoodie into her rucksack along with a bottle of water, an apple and a book.

She walked along the beach. The sands were damp and flat today – the tide was still out. After half an hour, she took the path through the dunes and headed for the road that wound its way up the side of the mount the imposing castle was based on. It appeared to be the only way in.

An ancient stone entrance tower with a horseshoe-shaped arch greeted her, but it had a heavy wooden gate across it. Claire checked the sign: she'd set off so sharp, the castle hadn't yet opened. She had twenty minutes to wait until ten a.m., so she wandered back down and found a spot in the dunes where she could look out to sea, watch the waves and the world go by and read her book. It was pleasant there. An azure-blue day, with only the odd puff of cloud out on the horizon. She kicked her shoes off, used her sweatshirt as a rug to sit on, and made herself comfortable.

The time soon passed, and after half an hour she set off once more. A straggle of tourists were now at the gatehouse, and she queued up to pay her entrance fee and buy a guidebook, to discover some of the historic background to this amazing place.

As she walked through the cool shade of the arch, it felt like stepping back in time. It was far bigger within the high stone walls than she'd imagined. Roads and grassy areas as well as many impressive stone buildings, all intact, spread before her. This was no ruined castle. On the way to the tallest of the buildings, she paused to climb some intriguing stone steps and peered over the protective wall and out across the sweep of dunes and golden bay. The view almost took her breath away: the Holy Island of Lindisfarne away to the north, the panorama of sea and sands leading out to a gently rolling North Sea, and away to the south she could just about make out her cottage nestled in the distance, and, further down the coastline, at the far end of the bay, the roofs of the harbour town of Seahouses, where she had sat eating fish and chips with Sally.

The guidebook said the grand stone tower, which was central to the castle site, was the Keep, the oldest remaining part of the castle, built way back in 1164. It was a massive square structure with an interesting bottle-shaped door that apparently let horsemen ride in at a gallop whilst still mounted. Her mind's eye conjured up a knight in his spurs, clad in a gleaming suit of armour. Inside the tower, she found that as well as many armaments, there were impressive but bulky shiny metal suits on display. How on earth the soldiers walked, let alone did battle in them, was a mystery.

The whole castle captivated her. The King's Hall was a fabulous, spacious wood-panelled room where ceremonies and grand parties had taken place. The display of porcelain dinnerware was impressive enough to vouch for a host of royal celebrations. Kings had owned the castle and stayed here for over twelve hundred years, until it was sold into private ownership in the 1600s – the current owners being the Armstrongs. Parts of the castle were now let as private apartments, she read. Wow, imagine this being your family home! It was a far cry from her semi in Gosforth.

Claire spent over two hours touring the site, losing herself in the past, in awe of the dramatic, beautiful fortress and its historic residents. She realized she felt hungry and spotted a welcome sign for the Clock Tower Tea Rooms.

Sitting at a table by the tall leaded windows with a cup of Earl Grey tea and a deliciously moist slice of Victoria sponge, she dipped into the guidebook once more. The castle hadn't been built on the sandy dunes at all, but on an outcrop of volcanic whinstone. The Anglo-Saxons, the Vikings, William the Conqueror and many more had all experienced this place. There must have been so many battles, so much bloodshed, and centuries of love and loss within these walls.

After a happy and interesting three hours, Claire headed out of the castle grounds, with a last glimpse at the glorious panoramic coastal view, trying to soak it all into her memory, then headed back to the dunes to sit once more in a sunny, sheltered spot with her book.

She must have relaxed so much that she dozed off, wakening to the sound of a gull and a warm glow of sun that made her skin feel a little tight on her cheeks. She was thirsty. Taking a sip of water from her bottle, which had warmed in her bag, she thought she'd pop to the village.

The deli was crammed full with a family choosing ice creams and a further couple waiting to be served. Claire waved cheerily through the window at Lynda, who smiled back at her as she passed a creamy, vanilla-filled cornet over the counter. She decided she'd pop in and see her friend tomorrow on her last full day. She hadn't tried the local pubs at all yet, having been a little reticent about venturing in on her own, but she suddenly found she fancied a long, cool drink. Why not . . . why not indeed?

There were two hotels in the village, both with bars – one at the top of the main street, the other at the base, near the castle. In the middle, just past the deli, was a more traditional-looking pub, aptly named the Castle Inn. Claire pushed open the heavy wooden door and went inside. It had wood panelling to halfway up the wall, and was hung with old paintings and photographs of the area. It had a cosy feel, with real fireplaces and a welcoming wooden bar area.

'And what can I get you?' the middle-aged barman asked warmly.

'Hmm.' She fancied trying something a bit different, maybe something local. 'Do you have any local drinks? Anything you can recommend?'

'Well, there's an Alnwick rum, or there's a Northumberland

gin called Hepple, unless you're a beer drinker – in which case we have lots of real ale.'

Claire couldn't quite imagine herself sitting there with a pint. 'The gin sounds perfect . . . with some tonic, please.' A long cooling drink was just what she needed.

'Ice and a slice?'

'Yes, please.'

She watched him pour the gin and add cubed ice and a slice of lime, then pour the tonic, which bubbled down over it all. Fizzy, long and cool – perfect.

She took it over to a corner table near the fireplace, which, it being summer, wasn't lit, and took a slow sip. Magic. It tasted herbal, almost perfumed – truly refreshing. She settled down with her guidebook, delving into the history of Bamburgh Castle once more.

'Hey, haven't I seen you here before?' A voice startled her.

A man with dark wavy hair, who looked in his mid-twenties, was standing right next to her table.

'Ah, I don't think so. This is the first time I've been in.'

'Ah well, maybe it's from the beach, then . . . Do you surf?'

'Nope.'

'But I have seen you on the beach, yeah?'

'Maybe. I've been walking there most days.'

'That's it. I knew it. I'm not one to forget a pretty face.'

Claire felt herself blush. The guy was tanned, fairly

good-looking, and years younger than her. But although it was flattering, all she really wanted to do was sit quietly and read her guidebook. She knew there was a reason she didn't venture into pubs on her own. She lifted her book pointedly.

'I hire out the surf boards. You might have seen my van,' he continued.

Ah, yes come to think of it, that was something she'd spotted in the beach car park. She nodded.

'You here on holiday, then?' He was persistent, she had to give him credit for that.

'Yep, and it's nearly the end of it.' No chance of getting to know me more, was the subtext. The book was still perched before her.

'Right-o. Live far away?'

She held back a sigh. 'Newcastle, Gosforth area.'

'Busy down there.'

'Ah-hah.'

'Tried that for a while – city life – but I'm *way* happier up here. Space, fresh air, catching the waves.' He mimed a surfing action.

She couldn't help but smile. He was probably only making conversation, after all, not about to kidnap her. She needed to lighten up a bit.

'Right, well, I'll leave you in peace. Have a good trip back to the metropolis.'

'Thanks. And nice to meet you.'

'You too.'

With that he gave her a friendly wink and went back to chatting to his mate at the bar.

Claire resumed her reading for a while, finished her G&T, and thought it time to head back to the cottage. It was gone four o'clock already. Dipping into the ladies' loos before she left, she saw that her face was slightly red – a touch of sunburn from her nap in the dunes, no doubt. Oh well, she'd go back with some colour in her cheeks, at least, and a host of warm, Bamburgh memories.

9

Lying on your back watching the clouds drift by

It was the last day of her holiday, and Claire woke with a strange sinking feeling in her tummy.

She got up early and sat for a while on her balcony with a soothing cup of Earl Grey, watching the sun arc up over the sea. No sign of any early-morning swimmers by the looks of it, so she wasn't going to get a last glance of Ed, not even from a distance. Oh well.

After a breakfast of strong coffee and buttered toast and jam, she took a stroll along the beach and popped into the deli to buy some local pâté and cheese for lunch and to say her farewells to Lynda.

'Hi, Lynda – I'm after some of your gorgeous pâté and that blue cheese I had last time. I also need a gift to take home for my nephews, sweets or the like. Any suggestions?'

'Well, the Lindisfarne fudge is always popular.'

'Sounds great.' Claire looked through the flavours and chose a traditional and a chocolate pack, as well as a bag of local choc-dipped cinder toffee.

'When do you have to head back, petal?'

'Tomorrow.' Claire gave a frown. 'Today's my last day.'

'Well, where did those three weeks go?'

'I know. Too fast. But I'm kind of looking forward to getting back too.' She'd missed her family and friends, and even work to some extent. And it would be lovely to catch up with her nephews over the weekend.

'You take good care of yourself, pet. And you know where I am if you ever come back this way. You'll always be welcome to call in, whether or not you're wanting to buy anything.' She smiled warmly.

'Thank you,' said Claire.

And with that, Lynda came out from behind the counter and gave her a big hug, which made Claire's eyes mist up.

'Now keep in touch, petal, and come back soon,' the older lady requested with a smile.

'Will do,' was Claire's response. A promise she hoped to keep.

The weird ache in her tummy reappeared as she walked back down the beach. She took her picnic to a sheltered spot in the dunes, about halfway back to the cottage, and took out of the bag the delicious cheese, pâté and juicy tomatoes along with a poppy-seed bread roll. Afterwards, she found herself watching the sky – it was amazing how relaxing it could be lying on your back in a sand dune watching clouds drift by, their shapes ever varied. She discovered a shark's fin and a teddy bear within the first five minutes, moulded from heaps of cumulus.

Later that afternoon, Claire braved her swimming costume and took a full-body dip in the North Sea – it had to be done before she left. It was bloody freezing so she only lasted about five minutes, doing a few strokes of front crawl before running shivering back up to the cottage, wishing she'd left a big towel ready down by the shoreline for herself! She was so cold she had to have a warm bath to thaw herself out. God knows what Ed got out of his dawn swim – he must be some kind of masochist.

There had been no further sign of Ed since she'd bumped into him outside the butcher's shop those few days ago. His car had been in the driveway that evening, but by the time she was up and about the next morning, it had gone. There was no one pottering about in the other garden that afternoon, and that evening there were no lights on. Perhaps he'd headed back to Edinburgh and was lying low, mortified after the runaway sex. It was probably just as well. There was no use torturing herself with the sight of him.

Once she'd warmed up, she decided to go back out

for a walk on the beach and find a spot where her phone got a signal, have a chat with her mum, and let her know when she'd be back tomorrow. She perched herself on a hump of grassy sand with an elevated view across the bay and dialled. Her mum sounded delighted to hear from her, said she was so looking forward to seeing her, which made Claire feel much better about heading home. She had her family there. After being on her own for three weeks, though that had been very intentional, she had felt an aching pull of loneliness and she realized how lonely her mother must feel sometimes since the loss of her husband. How they all missed Dad. She wished she could chat to him now. Feel his big strong arms around her.

Claire listened to her mother chatting on about life in suburban Newcastle, smiling as she heard the latest gossip from the crescent: that Mrs Jones's daughter (number 7) had got a First Class Honours in her Chemistry degree, how wonderful, and that little Joe from next door had fallen off his bike and knocked his two front teeth out, the poor little mite – the dentist had managed to pop them back in – hopefully they'd hold; his mother had had the sense of mind to put them in milk, got him to hold the cup with them in and drove him straight to the clinic. It was nice to hear her mother's voice chattering on and to listen to tales about other people. The focus had been on herself and her illness for far too long.

'Well, I'd better go, Mum. Lovely to chat. You take care, and I'll see you tomorrow.'

'I can't wait, love. Why don't I come and pick you up from the station? It's no bother. And you can tell me all about your holiday.'

'Oh yes, of course.' *Well, a limited account anyway.* 'Thanks.'

As she sat outside that evening watching sunset colours fade over a calm sea, Claire thought about all the things she'd done on her holiday: ankle-dipping as well as her full-on plunge in the cold North Sea, eating fish and chips and Mr. Whippy ice cream on the harbour wall at Seahouses, watching families bustling about and life go by, finding Lynda and the deli, the amazing castle, hot bubbly baths, a cool bed for one. She'd loved the silence, seagull cries, the shusshh of the waves, children giggling, shouting, barking.

No one reappeared next door that evening. Maybe it was all for the good, how it was meant to be. Some things were better left alone.

And then, after a surprisingly peaceful night's sleep, it was Friday morning, time to go home, or back, which-ever it was. She packed up her belongings and gave the cottage a good clean, ready to catch the eleven-fifteen bus that passed the end of the cottage driveway. She'd found out the bus times that linked with the station;

finances were tight enough without having to catch a taxi all that way again.

So there she was, standing on the roadside looking back over her shoulder at the two cottages with a strange mix of emotions. Getting away here had definitely done her a lot of good. It was a glorious place. The long stretch of beach with its golden sands, the ever-changing skies and sea, and the stunning castle and quaint village by the bay. She'd made a lovely new friend in Lynda. She'd learnt how to bake. She'd reconnected with her sister. And she'd grown to love the quirky little cottage behind her, even though it was falling apart. Bamburgh had stolen a little of her heart.

But all that stuff with Ed had left her confused. If it was just a one-night stand that didn't quite happen, then she was a grown-up, she could cope with it. But after his car had gone, when she realized that she might never see him again, he was still there nagging away in her heart. *Why?*

She'd been through enough – she didn't need complications, or Jekyll and Hyde men in her life who ran away from her scars – okay, so he hadn't *quite* got to see them, but had he sensed something? So, she'd made an acquaintance of some unfathomable guy called Ed next door, who had the body of an Adonis . . . ooh my, she'd never forget watching him strip off to swim that first morning. That was etched on her brain forever. She'd store that in a little place in her mind for safekeeping. But now it was time to go. To leave it all behind.

The bus approached, she waved for it to stop, grabbed her rucksack and small suitcase and mounted the steps. She took a window seat on her own a few rows back, and watched the two cottages roll into the distance.

10

An hour's respite from the mayhem of the city, tucked away in a coffee shop with a good book and a whopping piece of cake!

Charlotte, London

'Hello, darling!' Her mum Jane swept her into a perfumed hug under the red-brick arches of Newcastle-upon-Tyne's railway station. She was dressed smartly in beige chinos and a white blouse, her hair styled in its usual grey-blonde bob. Then she stood back, eyeing her daughter up and down swiftly as mothers do: the two-second scan of health and mind-set. It was usually a pretty good gauge. 'You're looking well, Claire. The sea air and break must have done you some good.'

'Yes, I think it has.'

'Your sister mentioned it wasn't the most luxurious

131

of cottages.' She raised her neatly plucked grey eyebrows.

Understatement of the year. Claire smiled. 'It was fine. It had a lovely view.' She decided to stick with the positives.

'Now then, I've got a lasagne made ready to pop in the oven if you'd like to come back to mine for a couple of hours. We could have a nice catch-up and some early supper.'

'Yes, that would be lovely. Thanks, Mum.'

So, that was it – she was swept up under her mother's wing and driven back to her rather plush semi-detached in Jesmond for an afternoon of tea and chat, and a warming, tasty supper. Her mother was a good cook, and it was lovely to be looked after for a while.

It was eight o'clock by the time her mum dropped her off at her own house in Gosforth. The 'For Sale' sign looked stark in the small square of her front garden. She was back to her home that was no longer *home*.

'Do you want me to come in?' Her mum seemed to sense her unease.

'No, I'm fine, Mum. I'm actually quite tired, so I'll just get my bags in, probably set off a load in the washing machine and have an early night. Thanks again for a lovely meal.'

'Well, you know you're always welcome. And I'll see you soon.'

'Yes, will do. And thanks for picking me up from the station.'

'Oh, Sally mentioned something about Sunday lunch, if you're interested. A little get-together before you head back to work on Monday.'

'Hmm, sounds good.' Sally's roasts were legendary. 'Are you all trying to feed me up or something?'

'Absolutely.' Her mum smiled. 'Well, see you soon.' Her Audi car gave a little rev, and started to moved forwards. She waved out of the car window as she drove off.

Claire found her house keys, walked up the black-and-white tiled pathway to the front door and turned the lock. It felt chilly and so very empty as she walked over the threshold. Too quiet. The contrast with earlier times struck her forcefully. A year or so ago, Paul would be in watching TV, or trying to cook something basic, if she was late home from work. His culinary skills had never got much past a rather tasteless chilli con carne or heating up a frozen pizza and tossing a bag of salad into a bowl. But at least he tried to do his bit in the house, and he was a dab hand with a hoover.

She thought back to when they'd moved in. The first few years of their marriage had been lovely, exciting times. Learning all those new things about each other, from his favourite coffee brand, Nescafe – nothing too fancy – to the way his fingers felt as they traced her inner thigh. The house seemed all the more quiet somehow, having once known a happy marriage there. They *had* been happy. But so much had changed. *They* had changed. Though the wallpaper, the carpets, the curtains they had once chosen together remained the same, piece by piece her old life had been chipped away.

On Saturday morning, as Claire sat in her kitchen with a cup of tea trying to get used to being back, her mobile buzzed into action.

'Hi, Andrea.' She'd spotted the caller name. Her ally from the *Herald*.

'Hey, are you back yet?'

'Yep, just yesterday.'

'Fab. Do you fancy coffee and cake over at Café 9 this aft? We have some serious catching up to do.'

'I might be tempted. When are you thinking?'

'Two-ish? Danny's out playing football today – he'll be a couple of hours at least. Time for us to put the world to rights. I'm dying to hear all about your holiday.'

'Okay, sounds great.' Far better than packing up boxes on her own.

'Meet you there then.'

'Yep, okay. Thanks. See you later.'

It was just a short walk from the house to the café, a favourite haunt of theirs. They did the most amazing chocolate fudge cake, served hot or cold, with cream or ice cream – fantastic at any time of year. They'd often met there in the good times between chemo sessions when her appetite and energy levels were back; by then she was well ready for chat and cake and it was a relief to do something normal. To talk about normal girlie things. Claire had been intending to phone her friend for a chat that evening, but meeting up in person would be even better.

The corner table by the window – there she was with a big grin, dark-brown hair flicked out somewhat chaotically yet trendily from her face, her trademark bright-red lipstick, and two cappuccinos, their usual, before her.

She stood up and gave Claire a kiss on the cheek.

'Hey you, you look great. Are you fancying cake?'

'Sounds good to me.'

'Chocolate fudge,' they both added at the same time.

'I'll go, you keep the table,' Claire said.

It was busy there, a Saturday afternoon, always popular with the students in the area, as well as a couple of young mums with buggies and a kindly-looking elderly couple nestled with their teapot and scones at a table at the rear.

'Hey, Claire. Haven't seen you in a while, hen. You been okay?' The café owner smiled from behind the counter that was laden with scrummy cakes and bakes. Many people in her everyday life knew of her illness – the bald head and headscarves of the past year had given the game away, if they hadn't already read her column and online blog.

'Yeah, I'm fine, Helen. Just had a lovely break away.'

'Well good for you, pet. You look well on it, I must say. Now then, what can I fetch you two? Don't tell me . . . chocolate fudge?'

'Has to be, it's divine. You make the best. Two slices, please.'

'I'll bring them over.'

'Thank you.'

Claire settled down next to Andrea at *their* window table. It was great for people-watching as well as chatting. They'd had some fun times viewing and occasionally scoring the passers-by (when Andrea was young, free and single, often rating men on looks, and butts in particular), the level of seating being perfect for a sneaky glance.

Claire took a sip of hot cappuccino. 'Ah, bliss . . . Well, how's good old work been?'

'Not too bad. Missed you though, chick. That bloody dragon Julia's been lurking around. "*Helping out*". She's been desperate to snag your column for her latest protégée, Lisa, who's also been trying to bag your desk, perching her skinny bum in your seat. I soon moved her on, don't you worry. Imagine working opposite that pair every day.'

'Well, I'm back now. She didn't get offered my column, did she?'

'No, no worries there – David's not that stupid. He let Emma use the column for her health and fitness article for two weeks. It worked well.'

'That's good to hear. I'm looking forward to getting back.'

'I really liked your "Magic Moments" article. David let me have a look over it. That's such a fab idea. Wish I'd thought of it. It goes out on Monday.'

'Wow, it does? That's great. I wasn't sure he'd go for it. Well, I just hope it strikes a chord. Being away made me realize how important those simple things are. And everyone will have their own take on it, too.'

'True. Talking of being away, how was it? You look really great, by the way. You have a tan and everything.'

'Hah! More like windburn! But yeah, there were a good few days this last week when I managed to sunbathe a bit. It was lovely . . . just what I needed.'

'Oh yes, sun, sea, sand and se—'

'None of that, I'm afraid.' Claire laughed a little too loudly.

'Are you sure about that?' Andrea eyed her curiously. 'What about that guy you texted me about?'

'*I* mentioned nothing. You were trying to wheedle something out of me that never happened.'

Andrea raised her eyebrows, unconvinced. 'You're blushing.'

Ah, shit – she was never any good at lying. Even though nothing sexual had actually happened, a whole lot more had. She felt the heat rise up her neck. She'd have to say something or Andrea would carry on digging for information, for sure. 'A near miss, that's all. Well, maybe a lucky escape.'

'I knew it. You can't lie to save your life, Claire Maxwell.'

'Well, that's not such a bad trait to have.' Though it sometimes made life rather awkward.

'I bet he was hot.'

'Not bad.'

'A surfer-dude type? All Aussie-toned muscle.'

'Now you're getting carried away. Shush.' She could feel the heat in her cheeks. Damn. 'Anyway, enough about me. How're things with you and Danny?' Time to divert the conversation. He and Andrea had been living together for a year now.

'Yeah . . . it's good. We're getting on really well. We give each other enough space to live our lives, you know, be our own people, which I like. But then when we do get it together, wow. Boy, that man is good in bed.'

A couple of male students looked up from the table next to them. Andrea just laughed and gave them a cheeky grin. The cute one with dark curly hair winked back at her.

'Spare me the details, per-lease.' Whereas Claire tended to keep things to herself, Andrea relished sharing every snippet of information. Sometimes Claire just didn't want to go that far – the images were *way* too private. But she smiled at her friend. At least someone was loved-up and happy.

After a pleasant hour and a half, Andrea said she'd better be heading off; she had some shopping to do and had promised to visit her mother.

'See you at work on Monday, hun.'

'Yes! It'll feel a bit weird, but I'm excited about going back too.'

'Good. You don't want to go all Robinson Crusoe on me and decide to live like a recluse in a cave on the Northumbrian coast or something?'

'I don't think so, Andrea. It was just a holiday by the sea.'

As she said it, she realized she was missing it already, that glorious view, the rickety, weirdly charming cottage. But she had missed her work and her friends too.

The house felt quiet. She made a simple supper of scrambled eggs and grilled tomatoes – after all that cake, she thought she'd better have something light and healthy. She put the telly on for company as she tootled around, thinking about what she might pack up next. Maybe her book collection, or she might sort through her journalism papers, the textbooks from uni, the many newspapers and cuttings she'd kept over the years, some of which were her own articles that had made her proud, often telling of someone's bravery, talents, kindness. She loved finding out about those kinds of things – meeting interesting people and being able to tell someone's story that might never have been heard otherwise. She was a feel-good reporter at heart, even though a lot of the time the news she had to deliver was heart-wrenching.

A text pinged through from her sister: *Coming for lunch tomorrow? Roast beef at 2pm if you fancy x*

Thanks, that'd be great xx

Welcome home!

Home. That word sounded so very hollow.

Thanks sis. See you tomorrow x

'Pass, Auntie Claire. Pass!'

She scuffled a shot across the back garden to Jack, her nephew, who was making a dash alongside the flowerbeds. His younger brother readied himself on the goal line, which was an imaginary zone between the apple tree to the left and his jumper, which had been thrown down on the ground about three metres away. She envied the endless energy of their youth. All the world was their playground. So innocent for now, but lessons they would have to learn along the way awaited them.

'Great pass!' Jack was definitely being polite. Playing football in plimsolls was not the easiest. She might end up breaking a toe at this rate, the ball was that solid.

Ollie was anxiously awaiting the shot, knees bent, body braced. Jack thundered the ball inside the apple tree, nearly taking his brother out and flattening a delphinium in the process. Oops, Sal would be none too pleased.

'He shoots, he scores!' He started running circles of the garden in a victory salute to himself. Ollie's shoulders slumped as he went off into the flowerbed to retrieve the ball.

'Right, you lot,' Mark bellowed down the garden. 'In you come and wash your hands ready for lunch.'

Claire felt like she was six, being called back by her dad. But she looked up and obediently made the move to go in. In fact, she realized her tummy was rumbling. Mark's voice softened as he gave her a smile. 'That order was for the boys, not you, Claire.'

'Well, it's good to know lunch is ready. And I probably ought to wash my hands too. I'm all footballed out.'

'Thanks for entertaining them.'

'No worries, they're good fun.'

'Thanks, Auntie Claire,' the boys called as they raced past her into the house.

Roast beef, huge crispy Yorkshire puddings, a stack of roast veggies and lashings of rich gravy – Sal's roasts were amazing.

There was nothing quite like a Sunday lunch with the family gathered round. It was like being wrapped in a warm, delicious blanket. Claire listened to the buzz of chatter. The boys talked about their latest Xbox games, the Newcastle score yesterday – at which Mark just groaned – and her mum asked Jack about the football team he played for on the weekends. Ollie was going camping with the Scouts the following weekend, and told how he was really looking forward to that – they were going to be allowed to make a fire from scratch with no matches. Bear Grylls was going to have nothing on them by the sounds of it – and there were general 'mmms' and comments on how lovely the food was. Claire felt absolutely full by the end of the meal, travelling from starving to pleasantly stuffed in precisely ten minutes.

After a short sit-down with a cup of tea, Claire offered to do the washing-up. She soon found herself in the kitchen with Mark, who started clearing the surfaces. They both stacked the dishwasher, then Mark began rinsing the messier pans in the sink. Claire took up the tea towel.

'So, how was your break?'

'Good, thanks. I loved the beach and the village there. It was really beautiful.'

'Yeah, went that way a lot when I was a child. We used to have a cottage inland, a bit nearer to Wooler. My parents were into hiking and biking, that kind of thing. I used to wish we could go to Disneyland or somewhere like that instead at the time. But I do remember it being beautiful.'

'Yes.' She could picture the long stretch of sandy bay . . . the dunes . . . her little cottage beside the sea.

And she wondered if *he'd* be there now. It was a Sunday, the weekend. Did he get there most weeks?

'Back to work tomorrow?' Mark pulled her back from her reverie.

'Oh . . . yes. I'm looking forward to it. I needed the break, but now I've recharged the batteries, I'm ready to go back.'

'Working on anything in particular at the moment?'

'Well yeah, the cancer blog came to a natural end. A happy one, thank God. But whilst I was away I got inspired . . . Actually, it was something Sally said that got me thinking, so the new column's going to be about "Magic Moments". You know, those contented moments in life – often the simplest things – that make you truly happy.'

'Sounds good. Interesting.'

'What would yours be? Your magic moment?' She picked up a baking tray to dry.

He popped some knives and forks into the rack as he took a few seconds to think.

'Hmm. My family . . . the boys, the daft things they do and say sometimes that just make you grin. Like the other night when we'd just had our supper, Ollie shot off his seat, ran past and then let out a huge fart that stopped him in his tracks. He turned to us and said, "Sorry, that was my bottom saying thank you for the food." We tried so hard not to laugh. We couldn't help it, though – we just cracked up at that.'

Claire grinned. That might be a good comical one for her blog. The things children say and do. It would be lovely to be able to mention plenty of different people's special moments in her column. She'd have to ask Sally and her mum what theirs would be.

'And things like an ice-cold beer from the fridge on a hot day,' he continued. 'Spending time with Sal, just the two of us, like old times.'

'You big romantic, you. I'm glad to hear the beer came first.' Claire gave a wry smile.

'Don't let on about that one. Mental slip, that was all.' He grinned back.

The very first 'Magic Moments' article was going to be out tomorrow, in the Monday edition of the *Herald*. She felt anxious, a butterfly flutter in her stomach, hoping it would go down well. Next week she would hopefully be hearing about her readers' own magic moments if it had struck a chord with them. The idea could evolve, perhaps into something special. She so hoped her regulars would like it. And her boss. It would be thrown out pretty swiftly otherwise, and she'd have to come up with something else, and quick, if her article didn't attract much interest.

She'd been away a long while on this holiday, even though it was much needed, and all those on-off times with the treatments she'd had over the past year. She felt she needed to prove herself all over again. Would people still like her stories? The way she wrote? When she got back tomorrow, she'd settle back into the team and really focus on her work. Her boss, David, had been more than patient and understanding so far, but she was all too aware there were other ambitious journalists ready and waiting to jump into her shoes. Her nerves began to bite.

11

'Magic is believing in yourself. If you can do that, you can make anything happen.'
                                     Johann Wolfgang von Goethe

'Claire, we need to talk. I tried you earlier.'

The phone had started ringing as soon as she got in the door. She recognized the voice on the phone immediately. Paul. For a split second she had hoped it might be Ed, that he'd tracked her down, but there was no soft Scottish lilt, and of course he wouldn't have her phone number or any idea of where she lived. Silly moo.

'Oh . . . okay.' She supposed they'd have to talk things through. Discuss the practical things you have to when you split up a marriage, a home, a life together, taking it apart piece by piece. The Lego marriage model – the one he'd smashed up that day he'd told her that he'd been seeing someone else, that he had just stayed to support her through the cancer, but now he was moving out. Yes, there were still lots of pieces of that Lego still hanging around, to put back in the box, ready to trip her up. Or maybe they were there ready to make something else with.

'We've got a buyer interested in the house.' His tone was matter-of-fact.

'Oh.' So soon.

'They looked round while you were away.'

'I see . . .' The estate agent had spare keys. Claire wasn't sure how she felt. There was a strange queasiness in her gut. Yes, she knew it was up for sale. And it hadn't all been good at the house; her illness, the shock of his betrayal, but it hadn't been all bad either. They'd had their happy times, their early years together, and it had been their home, her home. And where would she go?

'They want to come back for a second look. They're wondering if they can come round this evening – they haven't got time in the week. Are you in? Shall I tell the estate agent that's okay.'

She felt a bit numb.

'Claire?'

'Yes. That's okay. I'll be here.'

'Claire? Are you all right?'

He *so* didn't have the right to ask that question any more, to pretend to care about her.

'Yes, I'm fine,' she said firmly.

A couple in their thirties were looking round her home. It felt weird as she pointed out the features and benefits of the location and the nearby amenities, let them peer into the dishwasher, open up the boiler cupboard, wander through the master bedroom. It was as if she was opening up her heart too, but as she politely closed the door on them, it also felt like a release. She had known it would have to happen – she couldn't afford to buy Paul out. She'd only be rattling around here – too many rooms, too many memories. If the house went, it would force her move on too, physically as well as emotionally. She'd have no choice, and with half the money, she'd be able to put down a deposit on something smaller of her own. She could see it working out fine. Paul wasn't coming back, and she didn't want him to.

After they'd gone, she made herself a mug of strong tea and sat on the sofa gazing out at the small back garden, fenced in, neat with shrubs, and wished she was on that balcony back at Bamburgh beach looking out across the bold North Sea. Her thoughts crept back to Ed and his kiss and that crazy stormy afternoon when they'd been so close to making love. Well, okay, having sex. It was stupid to think the love word came into the equation.

Damn, though. Even if it had just been the once, a one-night stand, it would have been great to know his body, to know what it felt like to be in his arms. If only she hadn't panicked. If only she still had a normal pair of unscarred breasts for him to see and touch, and the two of them had carried on being drawn into a bubble of love. All right, lust then. Now, that would've been nice. *For one night only, Mr Ed* . . . Shit, she didn't even know his surname. No matter. This was a one-night-only fantasy, remember.

She finished her tea and decided to pack up some more boxes. She might as well get organized in case that couple liked the house and put an offer in. She concentrated on finding things she wouldn't be needing in the near future: old DVDs, CDs, spare bedding, towels. You didn't need an awful lot for one. She sectioned off a pile of Paul's things, most of which had gone with him already, and anything that looked a little old, or worn, or she just hadn't used for a long time she put into the bin or the charity pile. It felt quite therapeutic.

12

Friendship

Walking back into the three-storey, brick-built, Newcastle-upon-Tyne newspaper offices, which were on a side road two blocks from the main shopping area of Northumberland Street, had felt strange. It was as though she'd been away far longer than three weeks. It was probably the cumulative effect of the past year's illness, her treatments, time off for surgery, for chemo. Nothing had been normal for quite some time now. She craved normality now – she just wanted her life back how it was, though she knew it would never be quite the same. Such was life – a journey, a forwards leap, sometimes a slow crawl or a few steps backwards. This morning she was ready to leap.

That didn't stop her feeling a little nervous as she mounted the steps she'd been up hundreds of times before. Would she still be able to do her job well? Would her new 'Magic Moments' idea for her column go down okay, or would the boss think it weak or boring? What would the reader response to her new column be?

She was greeted by 'Hello's, 'Hi's and smiles as she walked through to her desk. She waved at Jo and Emma, friends as much as work colleagues, and felt boosted by their grins. There was no sign of Andrea across the way at her desk area yet. Then Claire spotted a lovely large pink daisy-like flower – gerberas she thought they were called – a single happy bloom in a bright-pink pot that looked suspiciously like Andrea's pen pot. An envelope was propped next to it saying 'Welcome Back', and next to that there was a pink-iced cupcake with tiny sugar flowers on the top. How pretty.

She was opening the card when a head popped up over the partition screen – dark-brown hair jutting out at quirky angles and kind blue eyes that were smiling. Andrea gave her a grin just as Claire read, 'Welcome back, gorgeous girl! Missed you! Xx.' Andrea had signed the card, as well as many of her colleagues.

'Aw, thank you, Andrea. That's so lovely. What a great welcome back. Mind you, I've only been away three weeks.'

'I know, I know. But I missed you . . . and these guys missed you too.' There were nods and smiles from all around the open-plan office.

Claire mouthed a 'thank you' across the room and made a thumbs-up sign.

She settled back into her work contentedly that week. It was good to be amongst friends and colleagues again, doing research, taking interviews over the phone or going out and about in person. She loved not only meeting different people, telling their stories, but also the writing, the editing, the buzz and sometimes panic of the deadline, the excitement of seeing her article in print and online. Best of all, the first 'Magic Moments' article was getting some great feedback, thank heavens. She'd already had several emails in, mostly positive, and the newspaper Facebook page had run a link to the website version of her article and had received over twenty comments so far. '*Loved it! Really cheered me up and made me think of what's important in life.*' '*The best things in life really are free. A laugh, a smile, a hug, a friend. Thanks Claire for reminding us all of this.*' And another: '*My magical place is at my family's favourite picnic spot – we call it the brick yard but it's the most beautiful place in the world – next to a babbling brook, toes dipped in the freezing water, the smell of wild garlic in the air mixing with wood smoke and the sounds of laughter – soul at rest, imagination running wild.*' There were several more that made her smile – and one downer: '*Found this so boring! My magic moment would be winning the lottery – and I'd blow it all on a huge party, holidays, a yacht, and a mansion.*' She wondered if the guy responding had ever read her cancer blog; none of that would be much help to him if he got it, unless he was paying for hotel-style accommodation in a private hospital wing with a fancy menu for meals. She scolded herself for being a misery. But then, she bantered back to herself – it might be harsh, but it was true.

As the weeks passed, the rhythm of her working days pulled her back to a new normality. This was it. Life on her own, post-cancer. The bustle of the morning bus commute into the city centre (it was never worth taking the car; parking cost a small fortune). Time spent with friends and family after work or at the weekends, chatting over tea, cake or a glass of wine – all these things felt lovely. And she was slowly getting used to the quiet times in the house by herself. Somehow it had been easier, quite pleasant, actually, when she'd been away on her own by the sea, but here, in a house bought for two, it didn't quite work in the same way. Oh well, it would be sold soon enough.

One weekend she decided to bake herself some bread, then realized she still had Lynda's recipe book. She'd have to post it back – after copying out her favourite recipes. Or, maybe, just maybe, she could nip back up to Bamburgh for a day trip. That might be nice. It wasn't that far – about an hour in the car – but she felt she needed to find her feet a bit better back in Newcastle first. It was a little too raw, the memories of that break still tugging at her emotions in a strange way. She seemed to be missing her cottage a little too much, and heading back any time soon wouldn't help matters.

Coffee-break time. Claire was making the hot drinks for the colleagues in her desk zone. The kettle bubbled to a boil as she scooped out Nescafé granules into the mugs. A rather grubby collection overall, she noted – some of them looked like they'd been hanging around since the 70s. Except for Andrea's, which was bright pink and had *Journalist – will work for cupcakes* written on it. Claire's mug said *Keep Calm, I'm a Journalist* in white on a plain red background. Paul had bought it for her a couple of Christmases ago. She'd never really liked it that much, to be honest. She might go and buy herself a pretty Cath Kidston one.

'Coffee, one sugar, dash of milk.' Andrea appeared in the small kitchen behind her.

'I know that much – I've been making you coffee for years.'

'I know. Just trying to sneak five minutes away from my desk and Dragon Julia's deadline. It's creative space time. If I read that same article over once more, I swear my head will explode.' She grinned. 'Anyway, I've been planning. You need a night out.'

'I do?'

'Yes, absolutely. Now you're back and fit and well, it's time to hit the town like we used to. You, me and the girls. What do you say?'

'Ah, I'm not so sure . . . I haven't been out like that in so long. I'd feel ancient.'

'Na-dah, I'm not buying that. I miss my bestie. And you are in *serious* need of a night out, girl. Tonic for the soul.'

'But I can't do all that seven or eight cocktails in a go any more. My body's been through enough.'

'Understood. *So*, you can have a couple of lovely glasses of wine, and when we hit the mojitos, you can have some of those great mocktails they do. Problem solved. And I'm not thinking of clubbing as such, even I feel a bit old for that now. Just a few really nice cocktail bars and we can have a dance down at Bella's Bar too. It'll be great. I'll even find a chair and a knee-blanket for you, if you'd like.'

Claire swiped at her friend with a tea towel. It was beginning to sound quite appealing. And it wasn't the knee-blanket that had swung it.

'We could even invite Gary from the Sports section . . .'

'Now that's taking things too far.'

Andrea was convinced that Gary from Sports had a crush on Claire and was determined to matchmake. He seemed a nice enough chap, to be fair, but he wasn't someone Claire had ever imagined a date with. And working relationships? Not a good thing.

'I'll cancel on you if you ask him. You said a *girls'* night.'

'So that means you're up for it, then. Great.'

'Okay. Yes. Take me out.' She laughed. She really was coming back to life.

'You are going to have *so* much fun!'

Claire wasn't quite sure if that was a promise or a threat, but she was smiling as she handed the mug of coffee over.

13

Cocktails, high heels and dancing on the tables

Time to drink champagne and dance on the tables.

Well, it wasn't quite champagne *yet*. But the bottle of chilled rosé they were sharing between them, as their group of five sat outside the Pitcher & Piano bar down on the quayside, was going down rather well. The coloured lights looked so pretty as they shifted hues on the Millennium Bridge joining the Newcastle and Gateshead sides of the River Tyne. The wonderful Baltic Gallery building and the snail-shaped silver dome of the Sage were just across the river, and they also had a view down to the iconic Tyne Bridge, with the smaller Swing Bridge just along from it. The arc of the river. The rippling reflections of evening sky and bold orange street lights. What could be better.

Andrea had been right. It was about time she came out and let her hair down, at least what hair had regrown so far! This was a nice way to start – sitting outside on a warm, sultry evening – which you could never quite count on up in the North East – chatting away with her friends. Along with Andrea, Jo and Emma from work was her close friend Lou, who'd been with her through thick and thin since Sixth Form. This team had been her support group as well as her lovely family, through the ups and downs of her cancer treatment, having been good friends before that time. They were here for her now, too. The best kind of therapy.

'Tell me more about this seaside cottage of yours,' Emma said.

'Yes, it was like you'd sneaked off to be a hermit for a while,' Lou added.

'Hah, it was pretty ramshackle to say the least. We're not talking glamorous residence or even shabby chic.'

They laughed.

'But you know what, I really loved it. Just waking up to that view . . .' Damn, why had she started talking about that? Now she'd conjured up the derobing of Ed. She really didn't want to mention him, so she continued, 'Watching the sun rising over the sea. And then the beach. It would be empty, just me and the view, and then it would gradually start filling with dog walkers and families. You could people-watch to your heart's content.'

'Nothing like the view from Café 9, I bet.' Andrea was thinking about their butt-rating sessions.

Hah, if only she knew!

'Dog walkers, that sounds exciting. Weren't there any handsome life guards or anything?' Emma chipped in.

'Nope, sorry to disappoint. It's not that kind of beach. Just wide stretches of unmanned sand.'

'What about Hot Guy next door?' Andrea blurted out.

Claire grimaced. She should have known Andrea would do this. She'd been trying so hard not to mention him, knowing they'd be onto this snippet of information like a flock of vultures.

'Ah, now that sounds more interesting.'

'Tell all.'

Bugger. 'Not much to tell, I'm afraid, ladies.'

'Ah, come on, you've got to give us more than that,' Lou coaxed.

'Okay . . . yes he was quite good-looking.'

'And?'

'How old? Hair colour? Physique?'

'Is this twenty questions or what?'

'We need details, Claire.'

'Thirtyish. Dark blond. Broad shoulders, kind of a swimmer's torso, I suppose.'

'Fit then.'

'Yes, I suppose he was,' she admitted. 'And *nothing* happened.'

'Shame. Not even a kiss?'

Claire felt herself heating up. Damn – the telltale red blush would be creeping over her cheeks for sure.

'Hah – I knew it,' Andrea ploughed in. 'I knew you'd had a sneaky kiss. Well, good for you. But stop guarding these secrets . . . we need full information, Miss Maxwell. We're your friends, and we have a right to know these things.'

They all laughed.

'Okay, well that's enough about my very limited love life. What's happening with you lot?'

'I'm married with kids,' said Jo. 'Not much love life going on at all.' She laughed.

'Ah, don't spoil it, we want to believe you're still all passionate and loved-up.'

Jo was the only one with a family in their group. 'Too tired most of the time. It's been so good to have a night off, I have to confess. Not that I don't adore them, of course.'

'Things are looking up for me,' Lou said shyly.

'Hey, you never said. New man on the scene?' Claire was intrigued.

'Yep.' A grin spread across her pretty face. 'As of last month. We met at the gym, believe it or not, over the water cooler. He has the most gorgeous blue eyes.'

'So did Hannibal Lecter,' Andrea quipped.

'Shut up, you. He's really nice. Works for an engineering company.'

'So,' Jo asked, 'have you had a date yet?'

'Yep. Three, in fact. It's going really well.'

'You dark horse.' Claire smiled.

'I just wanted to see how it was going before I told anyone.'

'Sounds like it's going more than well. Bloody great, in fact,' said Jo.

'Good for you, Lou,' Andrea commented.

They all knew Lou had had her share of man troubles in the past. Her engagement had been called off when her fiancé had made a bid for freedom, setting off *on his own* for a world tour just a few months before the wedding date. It was lovely to hear her sounding happy again.

'And lovely ladies, you will be pleased to know that life with Danny is still a-maz-ing. Footballers' thighs really are to be recommended.'

'I suppose he's got good pace on the ball, too,' Claire added, dead-pan.

Andrea nearly choked on her wine and the five of them creased into a heap of giggles.

'I think it's time to move on to the next venue, ladies,' Andrea said when she'd recovered. 'Anyone ready for a boogie? Who's up for Bella's Bar?'

They wandered along the quayside, linking arms, slightly wobbly in their stilettos. Blame it on the shoes, not the booze! They ordered a round of cocktails (and a mocktail for Claire) at the bar, then got into conversation with a group of cute guys who were on a work's night out. And then they danced. And danced. At one point, Andrea got up on the table, though the barman quickly came across and got her down, probably worried about a health and safety incident.

Now past one a.m., they were sitting chatting in a booth over a final nightcap. Claire was on the fizzy water by now.

'So what's on for everyone next, then? What are our plans, our schemes and dreams for the coming few months?' Andrea had posed the question.

'To achieve more than four hours' sleep in one stretch,' Jo ventured with a wry smile.

'See how it goes with my water-cooler man. And I'd love to get a promotion at work. I've been covering for a colleague who's been on sick leave, being head of department. And I've just heard she might not be coming back. I've really enjoyed it, and I seem to have done okay. It would be great if I could get the role.'

'That would be brilliant, Lou. Best of luck. And keep us posted – on man and job!' Claire gave her a hug as they sat side-by-side.

'What about you, Claire?'

'I want to do well at work, too. The "Magic Moments" column seems to be gathering momentum. And I'll be getting my own place soon, so that'll be exciting. A new page. But I feel like I want to do something else, something new. Even if it's a hobby.' She paused, gathering her thoughts. 'The cancer, the treatment, took all my energy and time. It sounds weird, but it kept me busy, filled my life somehow, the routine of chemo, hospitals. Maybe I could do something that links with that. I feel like I want to give something back, find a way to help people. All those other people facing it now. Something for charity, maybe.' It was becoming clearer in her mind as she talked.

'Like a Race for Life or something,' Emma suggested.

'That's it! That's perfect. I could raise money for Cancer Research and get fitter in the process.'

'I'll do it with you,' Lou said. 'I like going to the gym anyhow. And I'd like to try proper running.'

'Count me in too,' Andrea added, much to Claire's surprise. Andrea hated physical exercise – except for anything that took place in the bedroom, that is.

'Is that just the cocktails talking?' Claire questioned as her eyebrows shot up.

'Now don't give me that look. I'm *really* up for it. After all you've been through, and all those other people. It won't hurt me to run about for half an hour or so.' She made it sound easy.

'So you'll be up for a training run tomorrow morning, then?'

It was Andrea's turn to raise an eyebrow. 'Can we skip

to Sunday?' she pleaded, thoughts of her impending hangover in mind, no doubt.

'Okay, I'll grant you that. Right, we'll meet at mine at ten on Sunday morning for our first mile.'

'Yep. We're on,' Andrea agreed, adding, 'God, you're going to be such a slave-driver, Claire. I can see it now.'

'That's fine,' said Lou.

'And we'll support on the day,' Emma and Jo said, smiling. Jo added, 'In fact, I'll give you twenty quid right now to start the fundraising.'

'You don't have to do that yet.'

'I'd like to. And then there's no backing out for you lot. You'll *have* to sign up tomorrow . . . including you, Andrea. It'll be worth twenty quid to see you run.'

They laughed, except for Andrea, who pulled a face at her workmate.

'What are you going to call yourselves? You'll need a team name.'

'Hmm, suppose we will.'

Claire looked up at the neon sign above the bar just at that moment. 'Bella's Babes has a nice ring to it.'

'Yes, Bella's Babes it is!'

They chinked their glasses together. So, it was a night of cocktails, champagne, dancing on the tables and the newly founded Bella's Babes were all systems go for their first charity run.

14

'Don't miss a single sparkly moment.'

Anonymous

'Oh my God, I'm going to die,' Andrea gasped.

They had reached half a mile on their first jog and Andrea was clinging onto a brick wall beside the pavement for a breather. Just a breath, in fact, would be good. Claire's chest was feeling tight and she'd been glad of a reason to stop, and although Lou hadn't complained, she was standing there looking a bit pale too. This was harder than any of them had bargained for.

'How come I can walk for miles, but when I run it's like my lungs are being compressed and my leg muscles turn to lead?' Claire questioned.

'No idea.' Andrea pulled a face.

'Shall we walk a bit, at least keep moving?' said Lou, ever sensible.

'That's probably a good idea,' Claire agreed.

Andrea looked as though she wanted to slide down onto the pavement whether or not it had dog wee or spat-out chewing gum on it. 'Okay,' she managed bravely, peeling her fingers away from her support.

They walked on, heading for the open common land where the cattle grazed, believe it or not, right in the middle of the city.

'Watch out for the cows,' Andrea commented, 'or we might have to run again, and I honestly don't think I could do it. I'd just be trampled over by hooves and have to surrender. That wouldn't do the charity cause any good at all, would it?'

'Don't worry,' Lou grinned. 'They see joggers and walkers all the time round here. I don't think they're that bothered to be honest.'

'Weird why they're here, isn't it?' Andrea remarked.

'Must be some kind of ancient right over the land. The right to graze cattle in the middle of Newcastle City,' Lou mused.

'Right, come on then, girls.' Claire tried to rally Bella's Babes. 'It's just half a mile back. We'll walk fast, then try a little jog at the end.'

'Aaagh, I knew you'd be a slave driver, Claire Maxwell.'

'No pain, no gain! Just imagine all the extra stamina

you'll have for your sexual athletics with Danny once you're fit!'

'Hah, and in the meanwhile I'll not be able to walk let alone get into the missionary position.'

They laughed a little and then managed to put on a pacy walk to the end of the Town Moor. They agreed to jog again once they got back to the pavements of Gosforth. It would help their street cred if they looked like they were running at that point, or so they hoped. Though Claire's and Andrea's bedraggled appearance and wobbly legs – Lou still looked fresh, believe it or not – as they got back to Claire's street probably gave the game away!

15

A kitten to curl up with

Buzzzz. She was knuckle-deep in dough again, having decided to have another dabble at bread baking. She was making a couple of ciabatta loaves, one of which she was going to give to Sal as a thank-you for having her over so much recently. Damn the doorbell.

Claire hastily rinsed her hands and headed down the hall to open the door. It was Paul. It seemed a bit odd seeing him standing there on the doorstep. It was still half his house, after all, but she had to admit it was more polite than just barging in. That would have definitely annoyed her.

'Hi.' He seemed slightly awkward.

'Hi. Come on in . . . You okay?'

'Yep, fine. And how are you keeping?'

'Good, thanks.'

It was a little dance in polite words, masking the pain and hurt they had been through in the past months. The truth of what had happened between them was better laid to rest, but they would both always know.

He was still on the step. 'Come on through.'

He followed her to the kitchen. She wasn't quite sure why he'd come. She smiled. He looked like he'd put on a bit of weight – as he smiled back, his cheeks looked pudgier. And yes, there was a definite paunch round his belly. He must be living comfortably with his new partner, she mused. She felt the rawness of hurt still there, but weirdly no envy. All she noticed was that his hairline had receded a touch more at the temples.

'Tea or anything?'

'Ah, thanks, but no, can't stay long. I just wondered if you'd got the message?'

'Message? About . . . ?'

'The house.'

'No, but I was out food shopping earlier on.'

'I tried both your mobile and the house. Left a message on both.'

'Oh, I'm sorry. My mobile needed charging so I left it here. I haven't looked at either since I got back.'

'Right. Well, I've had a call from the estate agent. We've had an offer.'

'Oh . . . right.' She'd known this was coming, but it

still felt odd. She really would be leaving this place soon.

'The couple from the other week. It's an offer, but it's ten thousand less than our asking price. I was trying to contact you to see what you thought. Anyway, as I couldn't get in touch, I've gone back trying to negotiate an extra five grand. I hope that's okay. I didn't want to miss out on their interest.'

'That sounds fine, and if we can get a bit more for it, all the better.'

'I'm just waiting to hear back now. I thought I'd pop in and get some more of my stuff. If things are likely to be moving ahead soon.'

'Okay, well, go ahead. I've actually put some things in a couple of bags. Your music collection and your favourite DVDs.'

'Okay. Thanks.' He seemed relieved that she was being so reasonable.

'Go and pick up what you need. We'll have to talk about the bigger stuff like furniture later, I suppose. Have a think if there's anything in particular you'd like. I'll be somewhere smaller for sure . . . in my next place.'

She tried to be polite – staying bitter and angry with him wouldn't get either of them anywhere. She found the box of DVDs, handed them over and then went back to the kitchen to get out of the way while he went upstairs to find the other things he needed. Soon the house would become a part of someone else's lives. She stared out at the garden from the kitchen window and felt a quiet sense of loss.

Splitting up a house, a marriage, a life – no, two lives – was inevitably painful. Even when you knew in your heart it was over.

It was the nights that were the hardest. The days seemed to fill themselves. There wasn't so much time to think. But in the dark hours, in a double bed, on her own, her mind would roam not back to Paul, but to the two cottages by the sea, and Ed. She just couldn't help herself. She wondered what he was doing. Did he ever think of her? Was she just an annoying neighbour for a couple of weeks that he nearly made a fool of himself with? The sad truth was that he probably didn't think about her at all.

Just let it all go, Claire, push him out of your head, she urged herself. Get on with your life here, get the house sold, find a cosy place of your own, get a kitten – hell yes, she'd love a kitten, something to curl up with when she watched telly in the evenings. A girl kitten. She'd have nothing to do with the male species any more. Hah, she might end up a mad cat lady, but at least she'd be content.

And then no one would ever have to see her scarred left breast ever again. Only her, but that didn't count as she'd already seen it. Problem solved.

But night after night with it all tossing around in her head, and five weeks since leaving her cottage on the coast, the problem didn't feel very solved at all. It felt like there was a big, muddy puddle in her heart. It was time to jump into it.

16

The view of the Cheviot Hills, the valley below, and the feeling of coming home
                    Harry, Leeds & Northumberland

She came off the phone with a silly grin on her face. The weekend of the 20th of August was free. Surprisingly, the Bank Holiday the following weekend in August was booked up. The poor devils – some unsuspecting family trying to hire a cottage in Bamburgh, no doubt, with no accommodation left bar the neglected Farne View cottage. She'd booked herself in for a long weekend, Friday to Monday; she'd taken a lot of this year's holidays already so it was all the time she could get for now. And the cheque was ready to go in the post; old Mr Hedley didn't 'do' bank cards. He also didn't do regular hot water, central heating, clean mattresses and a lot of other home comforts. Maybe she ought to warn that poor family. She was heading back to that wreck of a cottage, and yet, crazily, her heart was doing a little leap.

There were a couple of weeks to go yet, time to get the sale of the house sorted and get down to work, give her 'Magic Moments' column plenty of attention besides all the other articles she needed to work on. Her 'Magic Moments' idea seemed to have struck a chord already. Her story was getting so many hits on the newspaper website. Her email inbox was bulging at the seams and Facebook had gone ballistic after she'd posted an online video about the background to the feature. It was hard to keep up with all the interactions – though she tried to read every single comment. Some stood out in her mind: *'Fishing on a secluded Scottish loch on beautiful serene water surrounded by tall scented pines and curious wildlife, my lovely husband retrieves from his fishing bag a cake and champagne to celebrate my birthday'* – how lovely. And one from a child via their parent: *'My mum's smile which warms me more than any radiator.' Lucy, aged 9.*

In the past few days she'd received over two hundred replies, a combination of lovely comments and new magic moments, some funny, some that brought a tear to her eye, which was just wonderful. Her professional Twitter feed had gone nuts, with so many likes, retweets and comments, and a fab new hashtag, *#MagicMoments,* created by her followers, which made her feel extremely proud.

She'd even been invited to speak on local radio. She hadn't figured quite how nerve-wracking that would be: when the red light went on for 'live' she'd had a brief moment of panic and thought her voice wasn't going to work. She was used to being the one doing the inter-viewing, not the one being interviewed. Luckily her professional instincts kicked in – this was an amazing publicity opportunity and the chance to reach even more people with her feature, and it was actually quite an honour to be asked. The radio presenter soon put her at ease, and they chatted about the inspiration for the idea, a little about her past, the cancer, the way forward. Claire wanted the audience to know that it wasn't about money or the big things people thought they might need to make them happy, but the everyday things we could all have and enjoy, and find that little bit of magic in.

The snowballing success also meant that big boss Dave was going to let her carry the feature on for a few more weeks at least, and it kept Dragon Julia off her case too. In fact, Julia had popped across to Claire's desk with a magic moment of her own, which was when they'd found out they'd won the North-East Newspaper of the Year award last November and she could put a new frock down to expenses for the ceremony – little did Dave know she was planning on Vivienne Westwood.

Though all the professional buzz was great, Claire was also aware that she'd soon have to find and fund a place of her own and all the bills too. She'd need to keep her eye out for some extra freelance work to boost her income. The North-East's lifestyle magazine had shown some interest in the past, so she'd write something up, maybe on places to stay or dine in the area – that would be a nice thing to research – and target them once more. There was plenty to keep her busy.

And in just over two weeks, she was going back to her cottage by the sea. She hoped it would still seem as special; that she hadn't gone home with rose-tinted spectacles. She didn't want to find there was no magic there after all.

She could see Bamburgh Castle rising up ahead of her, all pink stone and powerful. Little flutters of excitement skipped inside her, making her hands twitch on the steering wheel. Then she was passing cream-coloured stone cottages, the butcher's, Lynda's deli – she gave a mental wave – the village green with its tall trees, tourists strolling the pavements, no doubt deciding whether to have tea in the pub, the hotel or the Copper Kettle tea rooms. There was the cricket pitch in its stunning location right below the towering castle walls, and then she was on the coastal road, skirting the low dunes for a further mile or so.

Would he be there? She couldn't stop herself thinking about him now she was so close. It wouldn't really matter, she told herself. She'd come back for the place, the sea air, those wonderful views. But in a corner of her mind, she hoped. Glutton for punishment or what! False hope and false starts, she chided herself.

In fact, would he think her a bit stalkerish, turning up again? But one awkward moment shouldn't stop her coming back to a place she loved, surely. If he was here, she could just keep out of his way. Keep a low profile.

And there it was, the driveway entrance to the two cottages. It seemed odd arriving in her own car – not such an isolated feeling this time. She made the turn, instinctively scanning the parking area by the bigger cottage. No black 4x4. No Ed. Ah well, there was never any guarantee that he would be here. So she could just enjoy a proper man-free chill-out at her cranky seaside escape. That was just fine, and much less complicated, to be honest.

She emptied the car, carrying in her suitcase and a box of provisions; this was so much better than coming on the train. This time she had wine – rosé and white – coffee, tea and, as she'd kept her baking hobby going back home, there were freshly made rolls and a quiche Lorraine, as well as bacon, some cheddar, fruit, a large bag of Kettle crisps and some fizzy water. She was set up nicely, though she'd still have to make a trip to the deli for a few local treats and to catch up on all the news with Lynda.

She checked the cupboard in the kitchen to make sure

the water heater was on; hopefully it would behave itself this weekend. Then she made up her bed with fresh linen from home. It felt quite cosy. Right – she grabbed her latest read, a glass of rosé, and set herself up in a chair in the patch of garden. The sky was turquoise, with just a few puffy clouds, and the sun was playing fair today, warm on her face even though it was late afternoon. Bliss.

She had just closed her eyes with the book propped in her lap when a crunch of gravel from the driveway disturbed her.

Could it be? But he might not be the only one who stayed there; he might well have let the place out to friends. There was no point getting excited over nothing. In fact, she shouldn't be feeling excited anyway. It was all a bit of a disaster last time. She opened one eye, scanned next door, but there was no sign of anyone. Whoever it was had gone quietly inside.

Oh well. She was determined to stay relaxed and enjoy her chill-out time. She was going to keep a low profile, she reminded herself. But she could always get up early tomorrow and see if there was a small pile of clothes on the beach, or even better beat him to it and catch the whole strip-down. It would be worth setting her alarm for that! She grinned to herself. Hmm. She'd forgive him his running away and everything for just one more glimpse of his naked body. To see those firm, peachy buttocks jogging down to the sea. She closed her eyes and lay back in the chair, felt the warmth of the sun on her face and allowed herself to dwell on that image a little longer.

'Hey . . . hi.' A soft Scottish lilt. Her heart lurched. Dream a little dream, or what. She opened one eye. *It was!* She must have a guardian angel hanging around somewhere after all.

'Well . . . hi.' She drifted back to being sixteen and all of a flutter in an instant, especially with those thoughts still dancing in her head.

'You're back,' he continued.

Well, pretty obvious, that. But hey, at least he seemed pleased to see her and had actually come across to say hello.

'Yep, it's me.' What a stupid response, but her voice seemed to be working without her brain.

'Well, great, good . . . Nice to see you.'

'You too.' She managed a smile. Probably a goofy one, if the racing of her heart was anything to go by. *Come on, Claire, you're thirty, not thirteen*, she scolded herself.

'Okay, well, I'll see you about.' He turned to go back to his house.

'Yes, see you about.'

She couldn't help the silly grin that spread wide across her face.

* * *

She was in the kitchen an hour or so later, putting together a supper of quiche and salad, when there was a knock at the cottage door. She supposed it might be Mr Hedley checking on the place or something. Though he hadn't appeared the whole time on her last visit. She headed for the hall. The door was solid wood, no glass, so there was no clue as to who it might be. She opened it.

'Hey.' Tall, dark-blond, handsome Ed.

'Hi.' She sounded coy, she realized.

He was holding a book out to her.

'What's this?'

'Just a little something I picked up for you.'

She was curious, scanned the front cover. Ooh, the latest baking bible from Paul Hollywood.

'I remembered you were into making bread and such-like.' He sounded almost shy.

'Well, yes . . . That's really kind, thoughtful of you.' She looked right into his lovely green eyes. 'Thank you.' Then it dawned on her. 'How did you know you'd see me again?' It was only on a whim that she'd rebooked the cottage.

'Well, I didn't really. I just bought it on a hunch. Saw it in my local Waterstones. And you never know, I might have ended up using it myself if you hadn't turned up. Maybe I'd have turned into a baking genius and ended up on the *British Bake Off* . . . giving that Hollywood chap a run for his money.' He grinned. 'No, it's definitely for you.'

She took it. A peace offering? A friendship token? 'Thank you,' she said again, flicking through a few pages. Images of scrummy just-baked bread greeted her, of pain-au-chocolat oozing with melted chocolate. Divine.

'I may just have to try some of the results, of course.' Again he smiled. God, he had a melt-you-down smile. But what the heck had happened to Mr Grumpy?

'Naturally.' She grinned back. Was there a little bit of flirting going on?

It was as if he'd had a personality transplant whilst she'd been away. Oh well, she'd enjoy it while it lasted. Was it too much to hope that he'd missed her in some way, that he had been thinking about her too?

'Are you here for long this time?'

'No,' she replied. 'Just a long weekend. I've got to get back to work on Tuesday. I've used up most of my holiday. And you?'

'Just the weekend. The world of Scottish architecture waits for me. I'm working on some designs for a new library for the university, and some apartments on the seafront at Portobello. It's pretty full-on at the moment.'

They were still standing on the step. She ought to invite him in – that would be the polite thing to do – but something held her back. It might get way too confusing after the last time's turn of events. She should just head back in on her own for her supper and a glass of wine; that would be the sensible thing to do.

'Claire ... would you, maybe, like to come over to mine for some supper tomorrow evening?' He looked slightly awkward. 'I mean ... I'd understand if you didn't want to, after last time and everything ...'

'Ah ...' So it had reared its ugly head.

'It's okay. I shouldn't have asked. Look, just forget—'

'Yes.' *What was she saying? Mouth engage brain, per-lease. Remember the disaster last time.*

'Yes?' He looked surprised.

'Yes, supper would be lovely, Ed. Thank you for asking.' *What are you doing, woman?*

He let out a long, slow breath, 'Well, great. Okay, right, well is seven-thirtyish okay?'

'Yes. I look forward to it.' For once she seemed like the calm one. 'And thanks again for the book.'

She stepped back from the threshold and slowly closed the door. Only then did she let the huge grin that had been bursting to get out spread across her face. Ha-ha, now *that*, Claire Maxwell, sounds very much like a *date*! Was he sorry nothing had happened? Was he wanting to put things right – desperate to rediscover what they had started that day in the rain? Or was it just to be friends? A little frown of confusion crossed her brow. Well, friends would be fine too – wouldn't it?

17

Dancing barefoot on sand in the moonlight

Standing on his step with homemade olive ciabatta, inspired by his cookery book and another lovely visit to Lynda's deli, Claire felt a little churn of anticipation. Would Mr Grumpy still be AWOL? Would it just be a friendly night, or might there really be something more to all of this?

She'd been spying on his preparations from the cover of her balcony this afternoon. He'd set up a table and two chairs out the back on the grass overlooking the sea, and she'd spotted him bringing out a large storm lantern ready to light later on. She'd approved of the setting, smiling to herself over her cup of tea. Then he was in and out with cutlery, napkins, glasses. It looked like he was making a real effort. Hmm, interesting. After that, he'd disappeared for an hour or so in the car, possibly getting provisions in. She wondered if he'd be a good cook or more of an assembler.

And here he was, opening the door for her, dressed in a pale-blue cotton shirt, sleeves rolled up to the elbows, a pair of dark jeans which fitted tightly over his long well-muscled legs and a lovely smile. His dark-blond hair was ruffled, and there was a shadow of stubble on his chin. Sexy or what. Or shouldn't she be thinking that? Just friends?

She hoped she looked all right. She'd taken a bit more care with her make-up, using a light foundation, some blusher and a slick of red lip gloss as well as a hint of pale-gold eyeshadow; she hoped it wasn't over the top. And she'd been in and out of three different outfits in the past hour, settling on a strappy dress with a floral pattern that came to just below the knee; she hoped it might look pretty and summery, but not overdressed. On her arm was a cardigan for later; from the setting-up this afternoon it looked like they'd be outside, and she might well need it.

'Come on in. Welcome to my humble abode.'

'Not half so humble as mine next door,' she quipped.

'No, maybe not.' He gave her a small peck on the cheek.

He smelt gorgeous, all aqua and citrus notes, fresh, like you could just bury your head in the crook of his neck and sniff. Just a sneaky second then, hmmn.

She pulled herself away.

'You look lovely.' He sounded slightly nervous.

'Thanks,' she answered, giving a mental air-punch – phew, she'd got the outfit right. She then found herself at a loss for words, feeling shy and wondering what she was doing here. So much for keeping a low profile.

She followed Ed through to a spacious lounge. The room had French doors that opened out onto his garden, overlooking the beach and the sea. The furniture was off-white wood, and the soft furnishings various shades of blues, greys and cream, suggesting the sea and sky – perfect for leading you through to the beach. There were various knick-knacks of boats and shells – all very tasteful, but not quite what you'd expect a man on his own to choose. Mind you, she remembered it was his family's second home, so maybe a mum and sisters had been involved, or even an interior designer had come in and done the lot. He'd probably be able to afford it, probably had the right contacts through his trade – didn't architects earn a lot?

'Right, well, would you like a glass of wine? White, red?'

'White would be lovely, thanks.' She settled herself onto one of the stripy blue and cream sofas, sinking into its cosy cushions. His Labrador bounded through, wagging her tail exuberantly and settling down beside her for a rub.

'Hi, girl. You okay?'

The dog lay upside down for a tummy tickle.

'She likes you.' He smiled. 'She's called Bess. I hope she's okay out here. I can put her away if you'd rather.'

'No, she's fine. Aren't you, Bess? Just wants a bit of affection, don't you girl?' She knew the feeling.

'Well, I hope you like seafood.'

'Sounds good to me.' She'd try just about anything – she'd never been a fussy eater, except when the chemo stole her appetite. But her appetite had made it back good and strong recently.

'And thanks for the bread, it will go lovely with the langoustines I got today.'

'Mmm, I've never tried those before.'

Ed headed off down the hall to fetch the wine. Claire heard the pop of a cork. Soon, he was coming back through, his voice getting nearer. 'They're like a big prawn really.'

'They sound great.'

'Would you like to sit outside?'

She smiled, having seen all the preparations he'd made earlier. 'Yes, that would be nice.'

He swung open the French doors and Bess followed them out. The sun was low in the sky, making the sea glow gold and pewter. A few last tourists were packing up their wind-breaks, rolling up towels, and a dog-walker was striding by. But soon it would empty. Claire loved this time of day, when everyone went home and it felt like it was just their two little houses left in the whole wide world.

It was a touch chilly in the gentle sea breeze; she was glad she'd brought her cardie and slipped it on as she sat down.

'Sorry, is it a bit cold out here?'

'No, it's fine. It's lovely, in fact.' The view was beautiful – she didn't want to leave it.

He lit the chiminea that was near their table, and it wasn't long before the warmth of the coals reached her bare legs and sandalled feet. Bess settled down beside it happily.

'So.' He sat back in the other chair, resting his long legs out before him. 'How have you been? Back to work and everything?'

She couldn't remember how much she'd told him; about the cancer, but she knew he was aware that she'd been off work. 'Yes, I've been fine. I've enjoyed going back to work. Luckily, I was full of new ideas and energy, and my column with the newspaper's going pretty well.'

'So the break here did you good.'

'I think it did.'

'I took a look at your column in the *Herald* and some of the stuff you'd written before.'

Whoa. So he'd looked her up. Then it wasn't just she who'd been thinking of him. She'd drawn a blank though:

googling *Ed from Edinburgh + architect* hadn't given her any clues.

'Yes, I've been reading some of your cancer blogs. You've had a lot to cope with, haven't you?'

So he did know. 'Well, it's not been the best of times . . . But hey, I'm still here to tell the tale.' She paused, her mouth drying as she thought back to the unlucky ones, the ones who never got their second chance. How arbitrary it all was, how bloody cruel. She stared out across the sea. Sometimes it got to her – the emotions just crept up on her.

'Claire, I'm so sorry. Are you okay?'

'Oh . . . yes, I'm okay. It's just that some of my friends on the ward . . . they didn't make it.' She had to stop talking as she felt the clutch of emotions at her throat, in her gut.

He looked at her sympathetically, then looked away to sea, giving her a chance to compose herself. They were both quiet for a while.

'That's tough.' He spoke first. 'But I bet your column's helped a lot of people. Not just those going through it, but family and friends. It certainly helped me understand a lot more.'

'I hope so. That was the idea. And I suppose it was good for me too, in a way. Writing it down kind of helped me understand my own feelings better. Even writing down the weird and funny things. I remember my mother sitting with me at the first chemo session, reading all the pamphlets. 'Oh look, Claire,' she comes out with. 'At least you'll get free pedicures.' Trust my mum to find a silver lining. I had to smile. And the nice folk at Macmillan Cancer Support offer all sorts of things to prop you up, from headscarf-tying sessions to free massages. People still laugh in a cancer ward, you know.' Laugh and cry and live and love, she mused.

He nodded, looking at her intently.

'Anyway.' She wanted to lighten the mood. 'That's all done now, and here I am. A new chapter in my life. I'm one of the lucky ones.'

'Good.' He nodded, picked up his glass and clinked it with hers. 'Cheers, Claire . . . to your very good health.'

'You too – to health and happiness.' They smiled at each other.

He gave a small sigh. Now he was looking out across the sea, as though happiness was somehow a very long way off. Then he turned back, raised his glass and clinked it gently against hers. She wasn't sure why, but that gesture seemed significant, made her feel that this might be the beginning of something.

They sat chatting. He told her a little more about his work. He'd been developing designs for the new library building for the university, something quite cutting-edge by the sounds of it. How did you dream up a building? She admired the fact that he could. But when her questions got a little more personal about his home and his life, he brushed them aside.

'Ah, there's not much to tell about me. It's a pretty quiet life I lead. Home. Work. That's about it.'

She persevered. 'Do you live on your own, then?' She was being nosy, but she *really* needed to find out if there was someone else on the scene. If there was anyone else involved at all, then this was going nowhere. After everything with Paul, she could never do that to someone else. She needed to be clear. No point getting into him, if that was the case. It would just be a polite, neighbourly dinner and she'd be on her way.

'Yes.' A one-word answer, and the stony look on his face told her she really shouldn't ask any more. He got up to his feet. 'Right well, I'd better do something with the food or we'll never get supper at this rate.' He filled her glass. 'I won't be long – don't go anywhere.' He smiled and raised an eyebrow ironically as though very aware of his own rapid departure last time.

'I won't.' She sipped her wine, relaxing back into the chair.

'Right . . . good.'

She sat looking out across the evening seascape. The colours were now beautifully muted from the bold shades of a summer day – a gentle blue with a pale-gold horizon that reflected in a shimmer on the waves, a hint of peach just filtering through. Ten minutes later Ed was back. He added a small log to the chiminea, and then checked on the barbecue she'd watched him set up that afternoon.

'Starters won't be long,' he announced as headed back towards the French doors. 'It's nothing too complicated.'

Claire watched a pair of black-and-white oyster-catchers wander about at the seashore, dipping their bright-red bills into the sands. The waves hushed as they broke into gentle white froth: the sea was calm this evening. She warmed her toes by the chiminea, gave Bess a pat on the back as she lay there relishing the warmth. Felt the peace of the place. How wonderful it was just to be.

Soon Ed was on his way back bearing two plates. 'Goat's cheese – hope you like it. It's from the local deli.'

Claire had to smile. So he'd been in to see Lynda. She wondered briefly if her friend might be in on tonight's meal? Knowing how Ed guarded his privacy, probably not.

'Looks lovely. Thanks.'

He lay the plate in front of her, then sat down opposite. The cheese had been grilled golden and was on a bed of mixed salad leaves with a dressing. She lifted her fork – balsamic dressing by the taste of it. Gorgeous. The cheese was slightly melted, so oozed as she cut into it. Scrummy.

'This is really good.'

'Great.' He looked relieved. 'Fairly simple, I know, but my culinary skills are limited, I'm afraid.'

Okay, so he *was* more of an assembler than a chef, but she could settle for that. And with delicious ingredients like this, the end result was great anyhow.

'It's so beautiful here, isn't it?' she said. 'Especially when you get a day like this. That view . . .' Sea and sky and golden sand, so many shades of blues and greys and golds – she'd never tire of it.

'Yeah, there is something pretty special about this place. Don't get me wrong, I really like Edinburgh too, but here it's so different – that sense of space and nature. There's a little bit of magic about it. It keeps you coming back.'

'Yes, I know.'

'And every day it changes: the sea, the sand, the sun or the stormy skies. Even when it pelts with rain . . .' He stopped, realizing where his words had led them back to . . . To that day in the rain. They shared a poignant look, but said nothing.

'You're so lucky having a place of your own to come back to whenever you like,' she said, swiftly moving the conversation on. 'Somewhere with heating and hot water, no less!' she quipped.

He nodded. 'Yeah, this is a great place for a holiday home. My parents chose well. I remember playing in that stream as a kid, building dams. Fishing for crabs and shrimps in the rock pools.'

'Do your parents still come here?'

He didn't answer straight away. Oh bugger, she hoped

she hadn't put her foot in it. She could be quite good at that.

'Mum died a few years back. Ovarian cancer.' He stared out across the bay.

Well done, Claire – *shit*. 'Oh, I'm so sorry.'

'It's okay. Dad comes occasionally, sometimes with my brother and his family. But I don't think it feels the same for him without her.' He let out a long, slow breath and stared down at his shoes.

Claire was at a loss what to say next. He saved her by standing up.

'Right, well I'm off to sort the main course. Won't be a mo.'

So they'd both had hurt and pain in their lives. But she wanted to make the most of tonight. She had a feeling he did as well. Life could roll and punch you, but it could also lift you. Like the flotsam and jetsam at sea, you were tossed about chaotically, but then you somehow made it to shore. And there wasn't anywhere she'd rather be than this shore right now.

He came back out with a bucket of shellfish that looked a bit like mini lobsters and proceeded to barbecue them over the coals whilst she sat sipping her wine. Life at this moment was pretty good. The smell was delicious, especially when he warmed a frying pan of garlic butter on the barbecue and popped the shellfish into it right at the last. He dished them out into white bowls and served them with a wedge of lemon and some thin slices of the olive bread she had made.

'Langoustines, madam,' he announced.

Eating them was gorgeous – messy but finger-lickingly good. Lucky he'd thought of paper napkins.

'Wow, these are really delicious, thank you. Are they local?'

'Yes, I picked them up this afternoon just along at the fish merchant in Seahouses.'

She carried on peeling and plumping juicy, garlicky langoustines into her mouth, then mopped up the sauce with her bread. Bowl emptied, she sat back in her garden chair feeling warm, content and full. Ed relaxed too, stretching his legs out in front of him. His jeans clung nicely to his quads beneath. Her mind flitted back to her first ever glimpse of him . . . of those legs . . . and more . . . the early morning swim. She felt the heat of a blush rise up her neck.

They carried on talking and she learnt a little more about his brother and family, who lived just outside Edinburgh too. He didn't seem quite as closed-off as earlier. And she mentioned her sister Sally and her two boys, and her memories of holidaying here as a child. The sun shifted lower, the pale-blue sky fading to an orange glow, then diffusing to indigo as dusk crept in with the promise of a few early stars. He lit the storm lantern and a couple of tea lights that were on the little wooden table they were sharing. She sighed, feeling utterly content for the first time in ages.

'Dessert, madam?'

'Crikey, is there more?' There might just be a teeny space for something else. 'What have you got lined up?'

'Meringues from the local farm shop, with raspberries and cream.'

Lush. 'Okay, I'm sold.' She grinned. She hadn't eaten this much in ages. But her appetite was definitely back – and, looking at his tall, toned physique as he stood to go back into the house, in more ways than one. *Oh God, what was she thinking?* Especially after the disaster of last time. It was probably the wine sending her brain in weird directions, though she'd only had a couple of glasses. Still, she'd better ease off it a bit.

The meringues were amazing. He was definitely watching her lips as she licked off the crispy sugar crumbs. So she did it again, exaggeratedly, to test his reaction.

His gaze was intense, his pupils darkening within the green.

She started to feel a touch nervous. Or was it antici-pation? Perhaps she'd better not tease any more – she'd better be sure exactly what it was she wanted.

'That was gorgeous, thank you – the whole meal. Amazing.'

'My pleasure – and you're very welcome.' He gave her a wide, disarming smile.

Hah, there was still a tiny morsel of meringue stuck to *his* bottom lip. She could just lick it off. And then kiss those lips, which would taste of cream and sugar. Oh my, she remembered his kiss so well. It was making her feel all tingly.

'You okay?'

Oh God, she must have been staring? The wine had made her drop her guard, mind you she'd only had a couple of glasses.

'Yes. Fine.' Her voice came out high-pitched.

And now he was staring back at her . . . a little too intently. Were they going to go over old ground? Would it work out this time? And if things were going the way it looked like they very much were, she'd have to tell him this time. About her scars. So it would all be out in the open, so to speak, as her bra came off. Forewarned was forearmed and all that. But God Almighty, what would he think?

He leaned forward and softly, surprisingly, touched his nose against hers and then tilted his face so their lips brushed teasingly. Wow, that was sending shivers everywhere. Uh-oh, warning bells were clamouring, as well as the air-punch she was mentally making. Could this really be about to happen? Oh yes . . . The kiss deepened. Then she forgot to think and just let her lips take her to somewhere else. A longing swirled inside and her hand found its way to the soft curls of hair at the back of his neck.

Wow! As they pulled away, Claire recognized the music playing from the small speaker he'd brought out earlier. It was Coldplay, 'The Scientist'.

'Ah, I so love this song.'

And suddenly all she wanted to do in this world was dance. She stood up and swayed to and fro, as he watched her, softly smiling.

'Would you care to dance?' she enquired as if they were in a 50s dance hall. It would be so lovely to be in his arms, slowly moving to the rhythm of one of her favourite songs. It had been such a perfect night so far.

He looked a little taken aback. Then he smiled. 'Yes, why not? Though I'll warn you now, I'm not really much of a dancer.' He stood up to join her and held her rather formally, one palm against hers and an arm round her back. It felt somewhat stiff.

'Hang on . . . on the beach. I want to feel the sand under my feet.' She had already kicked off her sandals and discarded them under the table before dessert. Ed was in flip-flops, which he slid out of.

'Okay then,' and he led her the few metres out through his garden gate down to the sands. 'Better?'

It was darker out here, but she could see well enough to witness his wry grin that said he was going along with it just to please her.

'Better.'

She felt his arms close round her, and they danced

slowly to the remainder of the Coldplay song, then to the next, Keane's 'Somewhere Only We Know', with the feel of the sand under their feet, the stars above them and the hush of the waves on the shore, his arms wound around her waist and her head nestled against his shoulder. It was chillier out here with the breeze from the sea, and he pulled her in even closer. It felt like she had come home.

As the music paused between tracks, they stood staring at each other in the half-light. He dipped his head towards her and she leaned up for the most exquisite kiss. Tender, passionate, stirring every sense in her body. Oh, what a night. And she had the feeling that it wasn't going to end here.

As the kiss began to ease, reality moved in. Surely he wouldn't back out this time?

Okay, okay, so she was going to have to tell him.

'Ed . . .' She pulled away, felt a trembling in her hands as they fell away from his neck. Oh, sweet Jesus, she'd never had to say this to anyone before. 'Ed, umm . . . before this goes any further. That's if this is going the way I think it's going –' She managed a nervous laugh. 'Well, there's something I have to tell you.'

'Okay.' He looked watchful. 'Fire away.'

'Well . . .' God, this was *so* awkward. Nothing like killing the moment. But she knew she'd feel better if it was said. How he would react was another matter. 'Well, you know I've not been well.'

'Yes.'

'Breast cancer.'

'Yes . . . Oh God, you *are* okay, aren't you?' Fear rippled through his tone, his eyes still on her. 'It hasn't come back or anything, has it?'

'No, no. Thank God. But it's just . . . it's left scars. Bad scars.' There, it was said. She bumbled on. 'The left breast. I don't look *normal* there any more.' She gulped back a knot in her throat. It wasn't like this in romantic movies, where their bodies were perfect and they tumbled into bed and lived happily ever after. But there, she'd told him.

'Oh, I see.' Silence.

She didn't know how to gauge his reaction. It looked like he was thinking, processing the information. 'I didn't want it to be a shock. If you want to change your mind . . .'

'Hey, I'm not that shallow.'

'No, but . . . Well, it's not pretty, by any means.'

'Okay.'

'Sorry to kill the romance and all that.' Her voice dipped. 'It's been worrying me.'

And suddenly his arms were round her once more, strong, protective – dare she hope . . . loving? 'Hey,' he said quietly, holding her close. She felt his hand rubbing her back in a slow, soothing motion and relaxed into him. A few moments later he pulled back to speak. 'And

I thought maybe *you* were going to be the one to run this time.' He smiled with humour and understanding.

'No, not if you don't want me to.'

'I don't want you to.' And he took her back into his embrace, his lips moving towards hers. 'Let's carry on where we left off, shall we?' And his lips pressed hers before she could answer.

In her relief, she relaxed into his kiss. It was intense, a promise of so much more. They were still on the beach, with the sound of the waves rushing to shore, the dark of the night around them now, the storm candle flickering within its glass case from the garden. It was beautiful here, peaceful – but it was getting a bit chilly.

'Shall we take this inside?' he murmured between kisses.

'Yes,' she replied, though he could have taken her right there and then if he'd persisted. This was number 8 on her magic moments to-do list, after all. But yes, a bedroom might feel more protective, more private for her undressing. Oh jeez . . . she still had to get her bloody breasts out.

'Okay.' He led the way, back through the garden, the grass scratchy under foot, into the lounge, the hall, holding her hand all the way and on up the narrow staircase. At the top of the landing he paused, holding her gaze reassuringly. He led her into a cosy bedroom, lit by the glow of a bedside lamp, with wooden furniture painted in a cream shabby chic style. Crisp white bedding.

A king-size bed. It was a lovely room. But her nerves kicked in. This was the first time she'd had sex in ages. The first time since Paul's betrayal, since cancer, since the scars. Would she be any good? Would he be disappointed?

Ed seemed to sense her fears and held her to him once more, stroking her hair. Then he shifted his head back slightly to watch her as he lifted a fingertip to trace her cheekbone before kissing her on the lips again, very gently this time.

Okay, Claire, now or never. Let's do this thing. Her thoughts drifted anxiously for a moment, and then all she could think about was his lips on hers, responding with a longing she hadn't felt in a very long time. His body pressed so close, the scent of his aftershave, his skin, one arm tracing her back, the other holding her against him, the hardness of his erection firm and sexy against her hip.

She pulled back to take a slow breath, and he nuzzled her neck, sending little shivers down her spine. 'Oh, yes, that's good.' She wasn't sure if she'd said it out loud or thought it. Her lips close to his ear, she kissed the lobe. Then she took a step back, drew a deep breath, and pulled her summer dress off in one swoop. In her underwear, matching lacy stuff this time. Nothing like being prepared. *Would she ever be prepared?* Ed looked at her – she could see the desire in his eyes. She stepped forward to kiss his lips, then the tip of his nose and a little scar that rested on his forehead above his right eyebrow. He seemed to tense for a second, but then relaxed as she moved her hands down to his shirt, undoing the buttons one by one, appearing more in control than she felt inside. She traced her fingertips beneath the loose material, following the definition of his abs – my God, his chest was gorgeous, toned and solid. Her fingertips trailed down further, finding the line of dark hair that led down to his belt, his trousers. The skin of his stomach quivered under her touch, a sensual ripple.

She looked right at him. He smiled, but there was a trace of nervousness there in his eyes too. Maybe he hadn't done 'it' for a long time either. That thought made her feel better somehow.

She undid the buckle on his belt, unfastened the button on his jeans, and eased the zip down. She could feel the heat from him there, her hand brushing against his hardness. It made her feel wanted. It made her feel good. Not that she intended being good at all.

He peeled down his jeans.

Jesus, right then, we're really doing this. And, she had no intention of running away.

They stood staring at each other, both down to their underwear. She wanted to be the one to take off her bra. She took a long, slow breath. 'Oh God.' The words slipped out. Her hands found the clasp at her back.

'It's okay. It'll be fine,' he soothed, still holding her gaze.

Mists of tears were in her eyes. She hadn't meant to get emotional. Damn.

He took a step closer and brushed a thumb gently beneath her lower lashes, where the first tear had spilled. Then kissed her cheek, oh so gently.

He moved back a fraction, giving her space. He nodded. She nodded back. Then she slipped the bra from her breasts and stood before him. He was still smiling gently as he stood and looked at both breasts, at the scar laid bare. He lifted a hand towards her, tenderly touching her good right breast, trailing a fingertip over the nipple, which tensed under his touch. Moved his hand towards her damaged left breast. 'Is this okay? Will it hurt at all?'

'No, it doesn't hurt.' If anything, she had lost sensation there – the lack of a nipple, the long horizontal scar which had deadened some of the nerve endings.

He tenderly traced his finger along the scar and kissed the skin of her breast above it. 'It's fine, Claire. It's who you are. You're a survivor.'

And yes, she was. It *was* who she was now: a woman who had survived cancer and had the scars to show for it.

'And –' he lifted her chin with a gentle hand and looked her in the eye – 'you are beautiful.' He kissed her on the lips, then his tongue found hers.

Then he brought her so close she could feel him hard against her, sending warm pulses right through her, and she felt a huge sense of relief. He had seen her and he still thought she was beautiful and he still wanted her. His body was telling her as much.

She slipped her pants down, a giggle escaping her now. He stood staring at her with a grin. 'Okay then, if that's the way we're playing it –' and pulled his boxers down, launching them with humour across the room. He lifted her to place her on the bed, and her soft laughter was silenced as his hands got to work. Light, teasing touches, firm long strokes and massages all along her body. Then down, exquisitely, to tease her inner thighs until they quivered, his fingers tracing her secret curves, parting and stroking, gently at first, then rhythmically, until she was pushing back with him, against him. Taking her oh-so-close.

But she wanted to pleasure him too. She leant up on her side, pushing him flat down on the bed, delighting in the defined contours of his chest. She traced her hand down through the dark hair around his navel and below, reached his hard shaft, wrapping her fingers around its firmness and starting a slow, sexy glide. He lay back on the pillows, arms angled each side of his head, eyes closed, losing himself to her touch. She liked watching him there, the slow smile that lay on his lips, a quiver of tension beneath her fingertips as she moved faster, firmer, slowing as he began to moan.

'Whoa there.' He lifted a hand, opened his eyes with a grin. 'Steady, or it'll all be over before we get to base.'

She smiled back and knelt across him, her bare breasts brushing his chest, kissing his lips. Aware they were so close. One move and he'd be in.

But he sat up, rolled her down onto the bed on her back, slowly caressed her inner thighs, finding that perfect spot until a soft moan escaped her lips. He stared at her with longing in his eyes. 'Are you ready?'

Oh boy, was she ready. She nodded, thinking any words might end in a whimper. He leant to take a condom from the bedside drawer. God, how she wanted to feel him inside her. Even if she only got this one night. She wanted to feel whole again, loved again. He'd done everything right so far.

She watched him place the condom on; she didn't even know if she could get pregnant any more. There was a chance the chemo could have damaged her ovaries. She hoped not . . . there was still that dream of a family. But not to worry about that now. Better safe than sorry.

She felt the pressure of him hard against her, she took a slow breath, and then he was gloriously filling her, tight as he became part of her. He cupped her breasts, both scarred and good, as he glided in and out, the feeling exquisite – sensual, long and slow, and then faster, harder. She gripped his buttocks, pushing him deeper. Wanting him so much. Heard herself moan.

'Claire, oh, Claire.' His words came in a hot breath by her ear.

She was so . . . damned . . . close. Bucked her thighs up against him. Oh god, yes-yes-yes-and-YES. Golden waves of pleasure throbbed within her and around him. His deep groan above her was a joy.

They slumped down on the bed together, her brain a fuzzy, happy mess. Blissful fade-out.

Bloody hell, that was amazing. She'd not had sex like that for a long, long time. In fact, had she ever had sex like that? 'Aaaahh,' she sighed.

And he curled around her, from behind, his face against her hair, his chest lining her back, knees locked gently behind hers.

'Thank you,' she whispered.

'My pleasure,' he answered. There was a pause. 'It *really* was.' And she could hear the smile in his voice.

No one else could have made her feel that way – so relaxed, so wanted.

Ed, you are one special guy.

And she dozed off, nestling back against him, his arm wrapped protectively around her.

18

'There is no surprise more magical than the surprise of being loved.'

Charles Morgan

She woke to find his arm still round her. So this was real, not some wonderful fantasy dream. A slow, lazy morning smile spread across Claire's face. She lay there feeling the warm skin of the gorgeous man beside her, noting the dark-blond hairs on his forearm. Turned slowly to look at his face, all mussed-up blond hair, his eyes still closed, little crags of laughter lines and dark-brown lashes.

His eyes opened.

'Morning,' she squeaked, caught out staring at him.

He smiled slowly, as if he was remembering last night too. 'Hey.' His voice was honey-warm.

She couldn't think what to say, wanting to stay close

and not break the spell. Could it possibly last? It had just been so magical – a whole night of magic moments. There would be plenty to add to her newspaper column, though it might have to be X-rated, she smirked. And maybe, just maybe – she hardly dared let herself hope there might be lots more magic moments for them.

She moved a hand to his face, touched his cheek, which felt prickly with morning stubble. Brushed the waves of hair off his forehead. She wanted to kiss him, but wondered if her breath would be all fusty and garlicky after last night's langoustines. She could just nip to the bathroom and freshen up. She smiled at him, and began to wriggle sideways, realizing she was totally starkers. Could she brazenly just step out of bed? She knew he'd seen it all last night, but this was the cold light of day . . . She sat awkwardly with the duvet up around her breasts.

'Do you want me to shut my eyes?' he grinned, as if he knew she was being daft but was going along with it.

She nodded self-consciously.

'Shame. You could pop my shirt on. It's there on the chair next to you.'

'Thanks.' She leapt out of bed, betting anything he'd open his eyes anyhow and get an eyeful of her rear end. She whipped the shirt on and poked her head out. As she'd guessed, he was lying back watching her with a cheeky smile on his face, arms angled under his head on the pillows. She strolled out of the bedroom, trying to play it cool, found the bathroom opposite and brushed some paste around her teeth with her index finger. Had a quick pee too. That felt better. She had a cat-who's-got-the-cream look on her face as she caught her eye in the mirror – and why not.

The day was theirs, she mused. She could just slip back between the sheets, and if he wanted to spend the whole day shagging her senseless, then so be it. Who was she to argue? She didn't want to argue. *Where were these brazen thoughts coming from?* She'd definitely been out of action for far too long.

She slipped back under the duvet, still wearing his shirt, and snuggled up. His arm slid round her once more and she moved up tentatively for a morning kiss. It seemed a shy kiss compared with last night's passion, but it was warm and tender. And she lay her head on his chest, feeling the rise and fall of his breathing, taking in the warm-toast smell of his skin along with the lingering scent of last night's aftershave.

'Have you got much on today?' A leading question and she knew it.

'I do have some work I need to do, sorry.'

Ah, so maybe that was it, the get-out clauses creeping in already. For all her talk of one-night stands being fine, she felt gutted.

'Maybe later?' he continued. 'I just need a few hours to finish some designs I've been working on for a client.

Then I'll have some free time. We could go out and sample the delights of the village pub or something?'

A date. He was asking her on a date. It wasn't a one-night stand after all. Her heart soared.

'Yeah, I'd like that. That would be great.'

'I'll fix us some breakfast first. Croissants and coffee okay?'

'Ah, yeah, please.'

And he was up out of the bed, standing tall with his back to her, all naked buttocks, long legs and muscly thighs – gorgeous. A close-up of that first sexy vision of him on the beach. But damn, why wasn't he staying in bed for more hot sex? Had her shirt-and-shyness act put him off? Bugger. Oh well, she'd be seeing him again later on. She watched as he put on a dark-grey dressing gown that had been hung on the back of the bedroom door and slipped out of the room.

After a breakfast together of orange juice, strong coffee and hot, crumbly croissants served with butter and jam, sitting in his lounge overlooking his beachside garden, she decided she ought to go back to her own cottage. He seemed a little distracted this morning, was probably keen to get on with his work, she supposed. She could go and have a nice leisurely shower and wash her hair – she'd better be looking good for tonight. Hopefully they could recapture some of that closeness of last night.

In her shower – the old-fashioned type hung from a pole over the shitty-green coloured bath in her chilly cottage bathroom – she started rubbing shampoo through her hair. She was suddenly blasted with a rush of ice-cold water. Damn and bugger! Ah, ah, ah, get out quick! Typical that the only time the shower produced decent pressure was when it was freezing cold.

She dashed from the peril of the icy blast and huddled in a towel she'd grabbed, the suds streaming down her face from the unrinsed shampoo. She rubbed it from her eyes, managing to rub more suds in than out, and then could hardly see as they began to sting. She shoved on a dressing gown and wrapped her hair, turban-like, in a towel. There was only one thing for it. Surely he wouldn't mind saving her from hypothermia and hair like a nest.

She rapped at his door and rang the bell for good measure. Getting colder by the second, she realized coming out with bare feet was not a good idea. The gravel had spiked her soft soles. And although it was August, there was a chilly sea breeze – it was draughty right up and under her dressing gown, in places she'd much rather keep warm.

He seemed to take an age getting to the door, then looked through the glass panel quizzically at her. 'What on earth –?'

'Bloody hot water's done a bunk.' She launched herself

into the warmth of his hallway. 'Mid-shower, no-bloody-less. Can I use yours? Pleeease?' She felt herself shiver and her teeth beginning to rattle.

'Of course. Go on up before you catch your death. So the house from hell's at it again.'

She'd rather have liked his arms around her at this point to warm her through, but it didn't happen.

'Yes, I'm sure the old bugger's set it up as a death trap to torture unsuspecting guests so they never want to come back again, and he doesn't have to bother any more. I have persevered, but . . .'

'I bet you're his only ever repeat booking.' Ed grinned. He spotted her shivering. 'Oh, go. Go on up and thaw out in the shower. Top of stairs to the left.'

'I know.' Having been to the bathroom only this morning. She gave him what she hoped was a sultry look through soap-squinted eyes.

'Of course . . .'

She began to thaw under a stream of hot, power-jetted water and helped herself to a squeezy blob of his bodywash and shampoo, which smelt all fresh and manly. She half hoped he might pop his head round the door for a sneaky, sexy peek at her, or indeed whip off his clothes and leap in to join her. She'd enjoy soaping up that lovely chest . . . and more. But he didn't materialize. Oh well, it felt kind of naughty and nice just thinking about it. And a proper power shower was a delight – hot, bubbly bliss.

Ed obviously had a lot of work on and stayed downstairs. Hopefully trying to finish whatever project he had, to free up some time tonight. She began to soap herself slowly, sensually, remembering the feel of his touch. She couldn't wait for round two. Just a few hours away.

Finally, stepping out, she couldn't resist using one of his huge fluffy towels, hot off the chrome radiator rail, folding her old damp cottage one on the floor. Aaah, she felt so much better. She towel-dried her hair and found a comb on the side to neaten it up a little, having left her own brush at the cottage in her rush. She wandered out to the landing. All was quiet. Glimpsed his bedroom, where they'd lain and loved only last night. Could this be the start of something beautiful? It surely felt like it. She was drawn to the open doorway and looked at the bed, which was still a little crumpled. She could smell his aftershave and was almost tempted to pull a pillow up to her face and sniff. God, she'd got it bad. She smiled.

Then her gaze locked onto a photo frame that was set on the far bedside table. It hadn't been there last night. She'd slept on that side – she would have remembered it, for sure, especially when she'd got up this morning. She moved in closer, froze. It was an image of a woman, a very attractive dark-haired woman with a toddler, and behind them, with arms wrapped around them both, was Ed. The child's eyes were the exact same green as his.

Oh my God, what was she seeing? They looked so

happy, so close. It *had* to be his son. And the way his arms were held tight around the woman – she looked so much more than a sister, a friend. *A wife, partner, lover?*

So was everything last night a lie, a betrayal? What kind of a man was he? Oh no, she should have trusted her first instincts – the grumpiness, the offhandedness. The coolness again this morning. Had he got a family at home all the while? Had he just lured her with food and wine into his bed because he fancied a bit of playing away? She'd fallen for it hook, line and sinker. He must have been using her all along. She felt sick.

She'd always steered clear of married men, of anyone taken. This was not her thing at all.

She wrapped the towel tightly around her, left the bedroom and its memories, now tainted with betrayal, grabbed her dressing gown and the damp towel up off the bathroom floor and ran.

What an idiot she'd been. And she'd given herself so freely – believed him when he said she was beautiful. He'd probably put up with a scar for a quick shag. How could she ever be beautiful with a body like that? She'd so wanted to believe it. Believe him. Another liar, another man. She'd just been an easy lay.

She got to the front door and dashed out, not bothering to close it. Shit, the gravel was nipping under her bare feet. Bugger it. No more. No more men, no more so-called bloody romance. No more being duped and made a fool of.

She ran into her own cottage, slamming the door behind her. Heard his shout across the yard – 'Claire . . . Wait . . . what the . . . ?' She turned the key in the lock and ran up to her room, grabbing her case and shoving clothes and shoes in haphazardly. She pulled on some knickers, jeans and a T-shirt, and slipped into plimsolls. There was no point staying now, stuck next door to that prick of a man. She never wanted to set eyes on him again.

Let him work it out. That she wasn't playing his game any more. She wouldn't be someone's bit on the side.

She stormed into the kitchen, grabbed the food she'd brought and shoved it all into plastic bags. Time to get out of here. Time to go home.

She scoured the driveway – no sign of him for now. Bolting out of the door, she piled her bags into the boot, locked the cottage door and put the key back under the flowerpot outside. Security wasn't tight, but who the hell would want to break into that hovel anyhow.

'Claire.' His voice was taut. Shit, he was out of his house, striding across. 'What the hell's going on?'

As if he didn't know. She tried to make it to the car.

'You tell me, Ed. You tell me.' The bitterness spilled over into her voice.

'What the –?'

How dare he play the innocent.

'Oh, come on, I've had enough of being lied to, Ed. The woman, the photo by your bed.'

His face dropped. He paled. At least he didn't try to deny it. He just didn't say anything.

So he'd been caught. No defence. No, *'You've got it all wrong.'*

She opened her car door, got in, slammed it closed. Pulled the gearstick into reverse and turned the car with a satisfying spin of the gravel. A few more inches back and she might have hit him. The bastard would have deserved it. She pulled out into the main road, throwing a glance at the rear-view mirror. He was just standing there staring after her.

19

The first time I heard my daughter giggle

Sean, LA

Back to work. Back to reality.

Sitting at her desk on Tuesday morning, Claire stared out of the window, past a section of the brick-built office block opposite them at a corner of the Tyne Bridge and a fragment of blue sky and puffy white clouds.

'Earth calling . . . Claire? Do you read me?'

'Uh . . . Oh, hi, Andrea. Sorry, not quite with it there for a mo.' This was no good, drifting off into some lost zone in her head. She was meant to be writing her latest article. Focus woman.

'I can tell. I was asking if you wanted a cup of coffee? I'm just about to make myself one.'

'Yeah, okay.' Maybe caffeine would do the trick, perk her up a bit.

She'd been finding it really hard to settle since getting back from Bamburgh and the seaside cottage. Not that she should even be letting that tosser of a man into her thoughts. And it was a bloody shame he'd spoilt her seaside retreat now too. She really couldn't face going back there now, not with that asshole next door.

Okay, enough of that – she shouldn't even give him the credit of head space. Andrea was heading off in the direction of the kitchen. 'Thanks,' Claire called after her. She flicked to her emails on the laptop screen – thirty-nine new messages. Twelve appeared to be junk, and – ooh, great – she was getting some more in with the subject line 'My Magic Moments'.

She clicked on the first one: '*Hi, Claire. Loved the last blog! My magic moment is the five minutes' peace I get sitting alone in the kitchen with my first cup of tea of the day, before my hubbie and the kids get up. It's so quiet and still, sometimes I might just hear a bird tweeting outside and that's it. I can sit and sip my Tetleys and then the lovely but crazy family bedlam takes over.*'

She clicked on the second: '*Claire. Magic moment. Bubble bath and a book!*'

And there were more when she looked at the *Herald*'s Facebook page: '*When Newcastle United beat Sunderland 5–0! Now that would be a magic moment!*'

'*A winter-wonderland Icelandic evening with a good friend, a cosy bar, a guitar player, hot mulled wine and the snow falling softly outside.*'

'*Hi Claire. The first time I heard my daughter giggle. Thanks for a great feel-good column, Sean x*'

Then she spotted a hand-written envelope, addressed to her, that must have been put on her desk by one of the secretaries a little earlier. The paper was crisp white vellum, the handwriting neat and gently looped but with a slight wobble, suggesting the writer might be someone elderly. She leant back in her chair as she read:

Dear Claire,

Hope you are feeling much better now, my dear. My magic moment is the kiss my husband gives me at night before we go to sleep. It's the last thing he does every day, and he has done this since the day we got married. We've been married for fifty-five years this July. We are also very lucky to have a lovely family, including six grandchildren and four great-grandchildren.

Very best wishes,

Jean and Duncan Brown.

Ah, how sweet. Her heart felt a little tug. So there was some romance left in the world after all. She leaned her elbow on the desk, rested her hand on her chin, and gave a small sigh.

'Coffee time.' Andrea delivered a large steaming mug of Nescafé, just a dash of milk, no sugar – just as she liked.

'Thanks, you're a star.'

'You okay, hun? You seem a bit quiet since you got back from your weekend.' Andrea looked at her quizzically. 'Is everything all right? You *are* feeling okay?'

Her closest friend hovered beside her desk, waiting for her reply. Since she'd had cancer, there was always this extra layer of concern from her friends, colleagues and family. It was only natural, but so many conversations seemed to have this backdrop of worry. *What if 'it' came back?* Like an elephant in the room, cancer loitered. Waiting to gate-crash her life with heavy, stomping feet and a desire to crush her all over again. But she couldn't allow herself to dwell on it, couldn't let it stomp all over her when she'd been told it wasn't even there any more.

'I'm fine, honest. Thanks for asking. All good on the health front. Not due for any more checks for another two months.' She pasted on a bright smile. She really did have so much to be thankful for.

'Well, that's good. So you'll be fancying another night out soon, then? What about a few drinks and some dancing down on the quayside? I could get Gary from the sports team out, and a few of us from the office?'

Not Gary again. It seemed Andrea was still dedicated

to hooking them up. It's true he was pretty fit – obviously practising sport in his downtime as well as writing about it – but he really wasn't her sort. A little too full of himself for her liking, and she'd heard he'd been a bit of a player in his time.

'Are you *still* harping on about Gary? Give me a break, Andz.'

'Recently spilt with his girlfriend,' she added.

Another heart-crushed casualty, no doubt. Even more reason to steer clear. 'I'm off men, anyhow.'

'Pray tell. Anything I should know about?'

'No.' There was no way she was taking the lid off the recent can of worms. 'Just the whole ex-husband saga. That's enough for anyone. The house sale is going ahead and I'm packing up, trying to get ready for a new place on my own, so as far as Gary is concerned, thanks, but no thanks. Though I might be up for a couple of drinks one evening and a boogie with the girls.'

'Fine. I'll see what I can get fixed up. Check out when the others are free. It'll do you good to let your hair down a bit.' Andrea looked at her friend's crop; the still-recovering head of hair. 'Ah, shite, I've done it again, haven't I?'

See – there was that elephant again!

'It's fine. No worries!' Claire laughed. Hair was the least of her issues; at least she had some now.

David, the newspaper's main editor, came out of his

office, and strolled down the aisle towards the pair of them, pausing pointedly to say, 'How's that article going, Andrea? Deadline for two p.m. I need that copy filed asap.' There was obviously far too much chatting going on.

As he turned his back, they pulled a told-off-at-school face at each other, and Andrea sidestepped her way back to her desk. Claire looked fondly across at her friend's computer, which was draped in a fuchsia-pink feather boa. Photos of her and Danny together were Blu-Tacked onto the partition board between hers and the next desk, and an assortment of Malteser and Twirl packets, both empty and full, were strewn alongside the keyboard. Andrea's main role was compiling the 'What's On' listings, and she did a lot of reviews. She often took Claire with her to see first nights at the Theatre Royal and the Comedy Club, and to various cinemas for new releases. It had its perks.

Head down for her next article. Alongside 'Magic Moments', which was a weekly fixture now, Claire was working on a couple of human interest stories for the newspaper's website. She was hoping to get a piece in the main paper too – an item on a local lad who was undergoing treatment for Hodgkin's lymphoma, and who'd been doing a lot of fundraising locally. David thought Claire the ideal person to interview him. It was going to be quite an emotional visit – she was scheduled to meet him and his family in two days' time at the hospital. She'd heard about him on the radio and she wanted to write up the best article she could, to highlight his charity. At times like this, Claire really loved her job. She felt she could make a difference, do some real good, hopefully brighten someone's day.

'Something happened, didn't it?' Sally eyed her across the kitchen that evening. 'Come on, spill the beans. It wasn't that hunk next door, was it?'

It was the first time she'd seen Sal face to face since last weekend. She felt herself flushing up, the telltale heat rising at her neck. Trust Sal to hit the nail on the head.

'Hah – it did, didn't it! I knew it. You lucky thing. Was he as delicious as he looks?' Claire didn't answer. 'Okay, so why the long face? And why did you get back a day early? You never did say. And come to think of it, you look like shit.'

'Well, thanks.' You could always rely on a sister for an honest opinion. Too bloody honest sometimes. Claire let out a slow sigh and hugged the mug of coffee that Sal passed to her. 'Oh Sal, why does it always turn into a bloody mess?'

Sal came to sit down across from her at the wooden kitchen table. 'What happened?' Her tone had softened.

The boys were out playing football with Mark, so there was no one to interrupt them.

'Okay. We did get it together.'

Sal couldn't help an envious quirk of her eyebrow, she noticed.

'I spent the night. It was great . . . or seemed to be. And then it all went bloody wrong, as per usual. I should have known better . . . Why would a guy like that be on his own?'

Sal sat quietly listening, love and concern etched on her pretty features.

'Well, I had to go back later that next day. The shower had packed up in my cottage.'

'No surprise that, hey.'

'No, well anyway, I went to use his, and when I came out of the bathroom, I shouldn't have been so bloody nosy, but I took another look in his room. Well I'm glad I did in a way, or I'd never have found out.'

'What exactly?'

'He's married, or got a girlfriend at least. And a kid, by the looks of it.'

'Did he tell you that?'

'No, I saw a photo by the bed. It had to be.'

'But did he *say* that? That he was married, in a relationship?'

'No, not exactly. But it was bloody obvious. Just the look on his face. He didn't deny it or anything.'

'Oh, Claire, what a bummer. You'll just have to put it down to experience.'

'Maybe . . . but I just feel awful. You know, it's just not me. I'd *never* have been there if I'd known there was anyone else involved. Oh Sal, I feel so shit that I might have just buggered up someone else's life.'

'Claire, you can't blame yourself for something you knew nothing about.'

'I know, I know. But getting involved with someone who's already in a relationship . . . Aagh.' She knew first-hand how much that could hurt. The damage of deceit and lies. Why would she do that to someone else?

'It's not your fault, Claire. You're not a mind-reader – give yourself a break.'

'S'pose . . . I think I'm just feeling a bit vulnerable at the moment.'

'Yeah I can see it's got you. Just when you were getting back on your feet, too. But are you absolutely sure? If he never *said*.'

'Well, I can't think of any other explanation, can you?'

'A sister, a friend with a kid?'

'Right by his bedside? And it's funny how it wasn't there when he had me in that bed. Anyway, if it was a sister, wouldn't you put that kind of pic on a sideboard or in the lounge or something? I wouldn't have you stuck next to me every night. Much as I love your pretty face.' She managed a wry grin.

'Cheers. But, yes, maybe you're right. So you didn't give him the chance to explain?'

'He didn't deserve a chance. He had guilt written all over his bloody face.'

'Okay. Well, best left well alone, then. I imagine he had a fit-looking body – it can't have been a totally bad experience.' She gave a wicked smile, trying to lighten the mood.

'*Sal . . .*'

'Okay, enough said. I was only trying to cheer you up. Staying for some supper? It's just cold chicken and some salad for when the boys come back, if you fancy it.'

'Sounds lovely, if you're sure. I feel I'm gate-crashing a lot at the moment.'

'How can it be gate-crashing, you wally – you're my sister. You are *more* than welcome.'

'That's a yes, then. Thanks.'

At home in her half-empty house the next evening, everything felt very real, very final suddenly. The solicitor had advised that the sale of the marital home was going ahead and would all happen in a week's time – cash buyers, no chain involved. The time had come to leave the house that had been home for six years.

She'd been looking around in the area and found a lovely quirky flat for herself at the far end of Gosforth where it merged with Jesmond. It was nearer to the city centre and on the bus route – ideal. It had a small court-yard garden out the back, two bedrooms, a compact but newly painted living room – three walls cream, one teal, which she actually didn't mind – and a decent-sized kitchen with a good oven, ideal for her baking hobby, which she'd kept up. She'd hung on to the 'Hollywood' bible – no point wasting a good cookery book, even if the purchaser was a tosser.

She'd been packing in earnest every evening this week so she'd be ready to move when the day came. Most of Paul's belongings had gone now; he'd arranged to come in with his set of keys whilst she was at work. It would have been an uncomfortable experience having to watch that. But then he'd wanted to chat about the main furniture items and turned up again once she'd got home to discuss practicalities. The sofa – hers (it was really comfy), the marital king-size bed – his (he was welcome to it, the cheating bastard). She'd opted for the kitchen table and chairs, whilst he'd have the dining-room furniture. It had all come down to that – the splitting of goods, furniture, CDs, DVDs, lives. It left her with a heap of mixed emotions.

So here she was in the kitchen, starting to box up her cookery books, and there in her hand was the Paul Hollywood bread bible that Ed had given her. She paused, flicked through its pages, a weird nagging ache in her gut.

Her sister's comments niggled in her mind. It had felt so lovely with Ed, so genuine at the time. Could she have got it so very wrong? She hadn't given him a chance to explain, Sal was right. Did he deserve one? Was she so afraid of getting hurt again that she'd jumped to conclusions? Or was she just clutching at straws again even now?

Ah, sod it. Her intuition was probably right. She wouldn't be going back to that seaside cottage again, ever. And, she certainly wouldn't be giving Ed a second chance to hurt either her or his own family again either. Just let it be, her conscience told her. She didn't need any more upsets in her life.

The doorbell rang. She put the book into the box with the others and went to answer it.

'Need a hand with your packing?' It was her mother. 'I thought you'd have a lot to do, and it might be a bit grim doing it all on your own.'

'It's not so bad – I'm getting there. But I'll not say no to some help.'

How did mums have the knack of knowing when you needed them, even when you hadn't thought about it yourself?

Late the next morning, she got a phone call on her mobile from her sister. 'Hi, Claire. I'm just in town. I've managed to escape for a couple of hours. Mum's got the boys. It's nearly lunchtime and I wondered if you might be able to nip out and join me?'

'Actually, I'm not quite back at the office yet.' She'd

been out that morning interviewing Reece, the lad with cancer, and his family. It had been quite emotional. 'Where are you?' It would be her lunch hour in twenty minutes. She may as well carry on and take it now and head back to work afterwards – no-one was expecting her just yet. And chatting with her sister might be just what she needed.

'Centre of town, near Grey's Monument. I've just been in Waterstones.'

'Right, I'll head that way now. Meet you at Carlo's in, let's say, ten minutes?' Claire suggested.

'Perfect.'

'Well this is nice,' Sally greeted her in the foyer of the bistro.

'Yes, it's worked out well for me too. Another ten minutes and I'd have been back at the office and probably have been collared by Dave off-loading some urgent task on me.'

They were ushered through to a cosy table by the window, where they took their seats. Sal ordered a glass of Pinot Grigio, Claire a cup of tea.

Claire sat quietly, thoughtfully.

'Everything okay, Claire?'

Her gaze was fixed on a brightly coloured painting of the Tyne Bridge on the opposite wall. 'It's not bloody fair. I've been to the hospital today, interviewing that lad Reece and his family. The one with lymphoma. Sal, he was so brave, all wired up to that chemo line and chatting away talking about his charity. The lads in his football team are doing all sorts of things in support – car-washing, grass-cutting, cake-baking. And his school's putting on a big summer fete.'

'Well that sounds good. That there's so much going on for him.'

'But he shouldn't even be there. He was so pale, no hair, all wired up and putting on a brave face. He should be out playing football with the other lads, running around like your Ollie and Jack.'

'I know . . . God knows how I'd feel if it was one of my boys in there. It seems so cruel, doesn't it? But Claire, life's like that sometimes. Shit happens, and often to the best of people, people who don't deserve it. You know that well enough.'

'But a little kid.' Claire drummed the tabletop with her fingertips. 'He's never smoked or had a drink or done anything. He might not even get the chance to, bless him. Might never drive a car, have a girlfriend, have kids, even bloody grow up . . .' Claire's eyes were misting now.

'I know, it's crap. Cancer's so fucking arbitrary.'

Claire looked up. Her sister hardly ever swore.

'It doesn't discriminate – young, old, class, colour, creed,' Sal continued. 'But it is what it is. An illness. An awful, horrible illness.'

'It's a bloody bastard.'

'It is that. There were many times I cursed it when you were going through all those treatments.'

'But at least there *were* treatments, and I got through, didn't I.' Claire was trying to see the bright side. 'God, I hope that little boy gets better.'

'Yeah . . . Fingers crossed for him and his family. But he's fighting it, Claire, and doing so much more. All this charity stuff. He's got support from his family, friends, strangers, and you. You can make a difference by telling everyone about it, putting it in the newspaper. Your article can make so many more people aware of his charity. And that's all you can do, sis. Make something positive happen from it.'

'Yes, I can do that much for him. You're right – life isn't always so bad, is it? It's just been a hard few days.' And she let her mind drift to a better place, to Bamburgh and the sea, the views and the quiet, special moments she'd had there, at least before the latest incident. Life could be harsh, but it could also be beautiful and awe-inspiring, scenic, peaceful, playful. All the good stuff really did outweigh the bad stuff. It had to.

The waitress appeared with their drinks. 'The tea?'

'Thank you.' Claire raised a smile.

'And the wine.' The girl placed the glass down in front of Sally. 'I'll be back in a moment to take your order, unless you already know what you'd like?'

'Well, I'm ready. I'd like the brie and bacon panini, please,' said Sal.

'And I'll have a smoked salmon and cream cheese baguette,' Claire added, suddenly realising how hungry she was.

When the waitress had gone, Sal placed a comforting hand over Claire's. 'You go back to work this afternoon and write the best article you can. Let everyone know about that brave little boy.'

'I will.'

'And why don't you pop round to our house later and we can carry on with a large glass of wine out in the garden.'

'That sounds lovely.'

20

A smile across a dance floor
                    Norman, Newcastle-upon-Tyne

'Hey, you okay?' It was the next day. Friday, back at the office.

She raised her head. Refocused. 'Yeah, fine. Sorry, I was off in a world of my own there for a mo.' Claire smiled at Andrea; she'd been feeling really tired of late.

'Well, hun, 'spect you've been busy and you've got a lot on your mind. When's the move? Do you know yet?'

'We've got the actual date now. A week to go. And yes, it has been busy, but I'm pretty organized now.'

'Ooh, house-warming time soon then!'

'Hah, I haven't really thought about that yet, to be honest.' She was still trying to get packed up in time. Hadn't imagined having a party or anything, was just hoping to move in quietly and collapse for a day or two! The way she was feeling at the moment, a onesie and a mug of hot chocolate in the evenings might be in order for the next few weeks. What she *was* thinking about, however, was getting herself a kitten to celebrate. A cute cat friend to cosy up with at nights.

'So . . . ?'

'Ah, I'll think on it. Maybe. But I'll definitely need a week at least to find my feet, get the main stuff unpacked and all that. It'll be something small, if I *do* do a party.'

'Fine by me. And let me come round and help you with the unpacking. Lighten the load. I could call in after next week's training session. We need to keep them up, Claire. We missed last week's. I know you've been busy and all that.'

'Yes, you're right – we must,' she agreed. 'We can catch up a bit tonight, at least.' The Bella's Babes team had been trying to keep up a regular run, but for the past two weeks life had got so hectic, it had drifted.

'How does the following weekend sound for a celebratory girls' night at yours? Or we could tie something in after race day? Our little gang from the office and a few bottles of Prosecco? A joint celebration.' Emma and Jo were looking across, smiling hopefully. So they'd been scheming.

'Actually, that does sound quite nice. I might still be in chaos, mind, but yes, I could do something at my new flat. I'll do a few nibbles if you lot bring the booze. After all, it *is* a time to celebrate.'

Andrea was grinning from ear to ear. Her plan had obviously worked.

Claire was warming to the idea. Once she'd settled in. She could invite Lou and a couple of her other friends too.

'Has no one got any news articles to write up round here? Is there nothing happening in the North-East at the moment?' Julia's boom of a voice came from the end of the aisle. Oops.

'Just on it.' Andrea marched back to her desk, raising her eyebrows as she left Claire's and pretending to crack a whip behind her back. Claire stifled a giggle, then quickly got on with checking her emails. There were always tons of emails in her work inbox. Approaches for articles, often from the same batty people. Complaints about parking charges in the city centre, or requests to post an image of a lost dog – even if it had been missing for about a year.

Then she spotted one entitled 'My Magic Moment'. She opened that first:

Dear Claire,

My granddaughter, Sarah, is kindly helping me to write this email. My magic moment was when my Valerie smiled across the dance floor at me at the Oxford Galleries Hall in Newcastle fifty-nine years ago. It gave me the courage to go and ask such a pretty lady to dance. I remember it was a waltz, and boy was I beaming when I held her in my arms. We never looked back. We were married for fifty-eight years, very happily, may I add. I lost my lovely Valerie last year. But never a day goes by when I don't think of her, or her beautiful smile at me across that dance floor that day.

Yours sincerely,
Norman Jones

Claire's eyes filled up, and her fingertips trembled at the keyboard. How lovely, how very sad. Life and love and loss. And the world carries on spinning. Each of us on our own journey, sometimes a very bumpy ride, journeys of happiness and sorrow, of love and of pain. Magic moments along with the sad.

Where was her journey taking her?

Another message pinged into her mailbox. Another with a Magic Moment header.

She pressed 'Open'.

Hi Claire,

Great column by the way. My magic moment was meeting a wonderful, beautiful woman on a rainy, windswept beach. I got to know her a little, danced with her on the sands, and she made me smile again.

E.

Her heart went into freefall. *Could it be?* Or had she just got all sentimental and wrapped up in Mr Jones's romantic story and let her imagination run riot? But E . . . No, come on, there were loads of names beginning with E. Edwin, Elvis . . . and it might be a lady – who knew? Eleanor, Evie, Emma, Edwina. And even if it was an Ed, there were thousands of Eds around, and thousands of beaches. And England was not a place where rain and wind were unusual. *Button the excitement, girl.* It was just a flukey coincidence, that was all.

Though . . . should she reply? Try and suss out the sender a bit more? Nah, she'd look damned stupid and lose her journalistic credibility if it was a total stranger. 'Oh, by the way, were you the guy that kissed me by the open fire, that slept with me after a candlelit barbecue by the beach? Were you the bastard with a family at home while you were playing away with the next-door neighbour by the sea?' *'Sorry, love, no, not me. I was thinking of my girl Suzanne and I've never played away in my life.'*

No, she'd made enough daft mistakes. There was no point risking her journalistic reputation, embarrassing herself and getting a bollocking from the boss. She'd just send a polite thank-you and add the message to her list of maybes for this week's post. Mr Jones's was a definite.

After work that day, and with Andrea's reminder, she'd arranged for another training session with Bella's Babes. Yes, she was busy, but the Race for Life was only four

241

weeks away, and they needed to up their game. They had a pre-run warm-up routine organized by Lou, you could tell she was a teacher keeping them all in check, and they had now got up to a mile and a half in one go. And, they could actually manage to breathe and even stay upright thereafter. Onwards and upwards!

The muscles still groaned the next day, which didn't help with the post-work packing, but it was going to be all for a good cause.

She was round at Sally's again that evening after her run. Claire watched her nephews out of the kitchen window, as they kicked a ball round the grassy patch out back, Ollie in goal, Jack shooting. They were making the most of the last days of the summer holidays. It would be September next week, summer drifting into autumn. The first of the leaves would soon be starting to drop, the apples were plump and beginning to ripen on the old tree at the end of the garden. They'd be ready soon. In a couple of weeks she might take some apples if Sal didn't mind, get the boys to fill a carrier bag for her, make a couple of apple pies or something – one for Sal and one for their mother.

Sounds of laughter, the thwacking boot of a ball, filtered through the kitchen window. She'd have loved a family of her own. But that dream seemed so far away. And who knew if cancer had stolen her chances at that too? Oh well . . . she had so much to be grateful for, she reminded herself. She had her health back, her new home to move into in a week's time. And she was going to view a kitten soon too – she'd spotted an advertisement for a litter at the local sanctuary and given them a call. They'd be ready to collect from two weeks – perfect timing. She might have to peek in and view them; choose her little girl cat before anyone else got in there.

Her nephews were dashing about, boisterous, happy. She loved being Auntie and spoiling them. She would always have them in her life, whether or not she was destined to have children of her own. (Hah – she mused, that would be pretty difficult anyhow, with no man in her life.) Anyway, it was lovely that she and Sal were close again. Her sister had made her feel so welcome lately; she was making her supper again tonight, as most of her own kitchenware was all packed up and ready to go. One week to go. Sal and Mark were going to help her with that too. Family was just magic.

Sal passed her a cup of tea. 'How's the training going? Are you all geared up for your charity run?'

'Well, the training's going okay. Still on the build-up to two miles this week.'

'Do you know what, I quite fancy doing it with you. It's about time I got back into some regular exercise. I used to be at the gym every week. It's kind of slipped. Would you mind if I joined in?'

'Of course not – the more the merrier.'

'Great. And I'm sure all the mums at the school gate will be really supportive with making donations. I can ask Mark's work colleagues too, to drum up some more sponsorship.'

'Sounds fab. You can be one of Bella's Babes.'

Sal's brow furrowed.

'It's our group name.'

'Okay, I sort of get it. But . . . Bella?'

'It's the bar we were in at the time.'

'Well, why not. It has a good ring to it.'

'It'll be lovely having you there, sis.'

'You know, after everything you went through, I'd really like to do it. I'd like to think I can help other people in that situation too. So how do I get signed up?'

'It's all online. Just look up the Race for Life, Newcastle.'

'Okay, I'll do that a bit later. Once dinner's all sorted. And I'll dig out my trainers and get myself motivated again.'

Back at her house later, surrounded by bare walls and cardboard boxes, the phone buzzed into life.

'Hi, Claire. You know the Race for Life – well, I'm on the website now. There are three dates. Which one are you booked on?'

'The 24th of September. The Saturday.'

'Ah . . . right. Are you sure it's the 24th?'

'Yes, I'm pretty certain that's the date I put in my diary.' It was the day after Andrea's birthday, that's how she remembered. They'd decided to postpone her birthday drinks until after Race Day. A hangover might seriously affect performance.

'Okay, the muddy one. Did you know you were doing that one, or were you meant to be doing the normal run on the Town Moor?'

'The normal one, as far as I know. What's the muddy one all about?'

'Three miles of mud and obstacles at Newcastle Racecourse, apparently. Thick, gloopy mud by the looks of last year's photos.'

'I'll check with Andrea – she's the one who booked it. She might have jotted down the wrong date. We're on the normal run, I'm sure. Andrea wouldn't want to mess up her hair – a bit of sweat will be bad enough. Leave it with me and I'll give her a quick call. Get her to check her email confirmation.'

'Okay.'

Ten minutes later, after explaining the situation and sending Andrea off to check, the call came back.

'Do you want the good news or the bad news?'

'Go on . . .'

'We're definitely booked in for Saturday the 24th . . . and it definitely is the muddy one. Soz. I'm not sure how

I managed that. It's still three miles, though. We're not on a half marathon or anything.'

'Oh my God. Three miles of mud and grime and assault-course battering. What have you got us into, girl?'

'We could just rebook on the other one and not turn up for the muddy one.'

'Mmm.' Claire's mind was buzzing. It might actually work better for publicity and sponsorship. The mud-wrestling-style images would work really well in the paper, if Dave let them have a slot. If she could get through cancer, she could get through a bit of mud. It might even be fun in a weird, horrendous kind of way. 'No, let's do this thing!'

'You sure?' Andrea sounded horrified.

'I'm sure. Just think of the publicity we could get. We're bound to raise more money.'

'Okaaay. I think. What am I agreeing to?'

'It'll be fun!' The slogan of the 'Pretty Muddy' campaign had stuck in her mind: '*Cancer plays dirty, but so can we!*' she chanted down the phone. And she thought about little Reece and his family.

'Okay, your call, Claire. We're on.'

'I'll just ring Sal back – tell her the good news.'

They both laughed.

21

After a long day working in the garden, sitting down on the patio with Mum, enjoying a glass of wine and listening to the birds

D., Cornwall

It was just three days to go until the big move. She had a day off booked for Friday when the removals van was coming, thanks to Mark, who'd elected himself as driver, at eight-thirty a.m. Half the furniture had already gone off with Paul, who'd turned up last night looking rather sheepish in a self-drive with his mate. At least he'd had the decency not to bring the new girlfriend, but actually it hadn't hurt as much as she'd feared. She'd booked a smaller van than Paul's, and Mark was going to give her a hand with moving the sofa and larger furniture items, and then all the boxes. It was a bit daunting, but she felt very ready to face the next chapter. A fresh start.

Her mum, one of her moving out support team, let herself in that evening, calling 'I'm here, love, where can I help?'

'I'm in the kitchen. You can help in here, that would be great. That's where most of what's left to pack is.'

'I'll do your china and glass then. I'm a dab hand with scrunched-up newspaper. I take it you've kept some back?'

'Oh yes, I've kept all my old articles. I thought they'd come in handy to wrap round my mugs,' Claire quipped. Her mother raised a grey-pencilled eyebrow. 'Actually, you can use the sport pages. Gary's soccer specials are enough to bore the socks off anyone.' She smiled.

Her mother shook her head. She was used to Claire's ironic humour about her work. Her daughter was always modest about her writing.

'I'm liking your "Magic Moments" articles, by the way. What a lovely idea. Makes you think about all those special moments and slow down a bit. Brings us all back down to earth.'

'Thanks.' Claire started on a box for her oven trays and casserole dishes.

'Oh, and Mrs Evans, next door but one, said to tell you that her magic moment is an hour with *The Times* crossword and a coffee when her husband's out at golf.'

'Cheers. I'll jot that one down when I get a mo.'

'Do you want to know what mine is?'

'Ah, okay yes, of course.' Ooh, she hadn't got round to asking her mum. She should have done by now, really.

'It was after your dad died . . .' Her mum held a half-wrapped mug aloft as she remembered. 'I'd been racing around trying to block it out. Keeping myself busy. I thought that was best for a while, and then I realized that what I actually needed was to slow down. It was the garden that did it. Gave me these magic moments. At first it hurt like hell, even there. I'd be cutting the grass and it felt all wrong. Your dad always did that, not me. I did the borders and weeding. I just stopped mowing one day and smelt the grass, freshly cut, and I felt the sun on my face. And although it hurt and I ached inside, I felt like it might just be okay again, one day soon.'

Claire listened quietly as her mother reminisced, giving her space to talk.

'Yes, the smell of freshly mown grass. The warmth of the sun on your face. Watching a butterfly on a buddleia. My magic moments . . . Oh, and when you were so poorly, Claire. It was the garden that kept me sane. Doing the weeding, watering the pots, keeping myself active. Thank God you're all right now.' Her mum's eyes had misted. 'Sorry, I'm going on a bit, aren't I?'

'No, it's fine. It's lovely to hear that. And I'm fine. So we're all okay, aren't we?'

'Well, except for that bloody husband of yours.'

'Ex-husband.'

249

'The bloody bastard. I still can't believe he's making you move out.'

Claire was taken aback to hear her mum swear like that, but she gave a smile. 'Mum, I'm okay with it. I can see the sense in it now. We were both clinging to a lost cause.'

'But waiting to tell you until you got better, indeed. He shouldn't have been messing about elsewhere in the first bloody place.'

'The ship had already sunk, Mum, way before I even got cancer. I suppose it just made it harder for him to leave.'

'Well, I'd not be so forgiving.'

'Hey, I've tried the bitter, angry and twisted route already – it just left me exhausted. So I decided to go with it and see things for how they were.'

'Hmm . . .' She obviously wasn't convinced. 'Do you want me to leave the kettle out?'

'Yes, last thing to pack away. Actually, let's have a cuppa now, shall we? I'm parched.'

They had a ten-minute breather, munching on crumbly shortbreads and sipping strong Yorkshire tea.

'Thanks Mum, for your help. For everything.'

'My pleasure, darling. I'd only have been watching the *Bake Off* or repeats of *Strictly*. Talking of *Strictly*, what do you make of the new Romanian male dancer? Rather gorgeous, don't you think? Makes it much more exciting viewing this year, I must say.'

My Summer of Magic Moments

Claire smiled. His eastern European charms hadn't been lost on her either. Nothing like a taut torso, even when it was all spangly lycra and orange spray-tan.

They packed a couple more boxes, then her mother said she'd better be heading off. She'd promised to pop into Mrs Clark's down the road on her way back and drop off half a dozen eggs and a madeira cake from Sainsbury's before it got too late.

'Are you all organized for Friday, darling? Do you need a hand on the day? Maybe I can come and help unpack all this stuff at the new place over the weekend.'

'Friday's going to be pretty manic. Sal and Mark are going to help. Mark's driving the hire van for me, and he'll help with all the heavy stuff. It'll be enough hands on deck, I think. So thanks. But, Saturday would be good. By then we could unpack some of the smaller stuff together.'

'I'd like to help both days if I can. I'll keep them free and we'll chat about what I can do. Ooh, shall I make you some supper over at mine on Sunday evening? I'm sure you'll be in need of some good food and rest by then.'

'Oh yes, that sounds great.'

'Lovely. But ring me if you need anything before then, won't you. No point struggling away on your own.'

'Thanks, for everything, Mum.' And she gave her a big hug. Family was precious.

251

22

Family

Back at the *Herald* the next day, Claire had her head down typing up her 'Magic Moments' blog for Monday's edition.

All night her mind had been buzzing with that email from 'E'. She thought she'd put the whole thing to rest, but what if it really was him? But no, a cheating git wouldn't try and contact the woman he'd had a fling with once she'd sussed him out. On the other hand, dammit, what if she had, after all, got the wrong end of the stick?

She typed up Mr Jones's message of enduring love. Focused on that. She'd get herself a coffee soon; she was feeling bloody tired – hadn't got a good night's sleep at all. Why the hell was she allowing thoughts of Ed and Bamburgh to affect her? The race training was taking it out of her a bit too.

She vaguely heard the sound of the swing doors opening at the far end of the office – it happened all the time, so it hardly registered. A male voice, possibly Gary in Sport, said, 'You'll find her just down the far end on the right, mate.' Then there was a weird hush over the office. The usual sounds of typing, chatting, had ceased.

Claire glanced up to see Emma's head and ponytail swish in a turn. There was a mass swizzle of chairs. Then Andrea's face popped up over the dividing screen just across from Claire, her eyes wide. Why the hell was everyone in the office looking her way?

A deep mellow voice with a hint of Scottish lilt. 'I'm looking for Claire?'

As she turned, he stopped.

'Hi, Claire.' He stood, looking rather awkward, in front of her. As tall and handsome as ever. Dark-blond tousled hair. He gave her a nervous smile.

Oh My God!

'Hi.' She just about squeaked the word, stunned. 'Ed.' She seemed to be incapable of normal speech.

'Hi,' he replied. He didn't seem to know what to say next either. It didn't help that the whole office was staring at the pair of them.

They stayed a polite metre or so apart, Claire still sitting in her office chair, Ed standing before her. Ed who she'd kissed, had sex with, whose body she'd seen every inch of. Her colleagues were gawping. Andrea's eyes were still peeping over the top of the partition, entranced, as if she was thinking '*Who the hell is that!*'

'I'm sorry to just turn up like this. How are you?' His voice melted her like chocolate.

'Fine,' she managed to say, her tone all high-pitched. 'And, it's okay.'

'It took me ages to find you.'

'It did?' *So he'd been looking for her.*

'Well, after you'd stormed off that day . . . You never gave me the chance to explain.' A furrow crossed his brow.

Andrea's face slid down behind the screen to give them the pretence of privacy, though she'd be earwigging on the far side of the partition, for sure.

To explain. So had *she* been the one to make the mistake? She suddenly felt very unsure of herself.

Ed scanned the office, looking uncomfortable. Most people's eyes had shifted back down to their computers, their phones. Most people's ears were probably still tuning in, though – this kind of thing didn't happen every day. 'Look, do you get a break or something? Can we maybe go for a coffee?'

'Ah, yes – yes, of course.'

'And . . . how are you, Ed?' Claire returned the question.

'Fine.' He nodded slowly as if reassuring himself.

'Okay then, I'll just need to finish off here. But I could take my lunch hour a bit early, say in ten minutes. There's a little coffee shop just over the road opposite the main entrance, Brooklyn's. We could meet there.'

'That sounds good. I'll go and set myself up in there with a cappuccino or something. I'll see you in a minute.'

He turned to walk away, the eyes of the office lifting again. Curiosity fizzed through the air like static. In her work environment he looked gorgeously out of place. Just as the swing doors closed on him, Andrea's head popped up like a meerkat's. 'And *who* the fantastic fuck is *that*?' She wiped her brow exaggeratedly 'Hot or what!'

Claire stifled a giggle as Dave loomed out of his office doorway. 'Okay, gang, enough of the side show. Back to work. Claire, my office.'

Oh shit, was she in trouble? It wasn't as if she'd asked Ed to call in at work.

She saved the editorial she was working on, took a slow breath, and walked up the aisle to David's door. Andrea gave her a small thumbs-up signal of encouragement from her desk.

She braced herself as she took a step inside.

'Have you done the article on the old people's home being threatened with closure yet?'

'Yes, I finished that this morning. I was just going to give it a quick glance over, then forward it to you.'

'Good, that's fine then. Get it checked and into my inbox for three thirty. In the meantime, scarper. You can go. Believe it or not, I'm a bit of a romantic at heart. Go meet your man.'

Claire grinned. 'Thanks.'

Though she wasn't at all sure he was her man.

Her stomach was in knots as she put her computer into sleep mode and quickly neatened the paperwork on her desk. She grabbed her jacket and headed out of the office.

Why had he come? What was this really about? She was torn between elation and the fear of getting hurt yet again, the fear of learning something that she'd really rather not.

She walked down the two flights of stairs and out through the glass double doors at the front of the newspaper building.

He was there, sitting in the window of the coffee shop over the road. He hadn't seen her yet. He lifted his head instinctively as she crossed.

Okay Claire, here goes. She tried out a smile, pushed open the coffee shop door. He was sat on a stool at a high table in the corner. He looked gorgeous, if somewhat apprehensive. *And breathe.*

'Hey,' was all he said, with a gentle smile.

'Hi.' A whole host of butterflies were jittering away in her stomach.

'Come and sit down.'

'So . . .' She picked up the conversation they'd started in the office. 'You found me.'

'Yep. I did. Can I get you a coffee or anything?'

'A latte would be great.'

He had a half-empty cup in front of him. 'I'll just be one sec.' He headed over to the counter, spoke with the waitress and was soon back. 'Right, well . . .' He sat down on his stool across from her. They were close enough to touch, yet she felt a world apart. He took a slow breath as Claire held hers. 'Claire, I didn't want to leave things like that. With you thinking . . .' he paused, looked out of the window for a second, then began rearranging the sugar sachets that were in a small white dish. 'Ah, this is so hard to put into words. Sorry.'

'Shall we make these a takeaway? There's a nice park just along the road. We could walk a bit.' Walk and talk, hopefully. She could do with some fresh air herself.

'Yeah, that sounds good.'

The waitress was still making up her latte, so she asked for a takeaway cup and, after checking with him, another Americano for Ed.

She rejoined him, offering him his paper cup. 'Have you been back to Bamburgh lately?'

It was two weeks since they'd both been there. Since she had dashed off, full of anger, accusing him of all sorts. She felt herself flush a little as she remembered.

'Yes, last weekend.'

Of course. The bank holiday. 'It's such a beautiful place,' she added.

'It is.' He smiled softly.

Beautiful, she mused, and full of memories. Shaken up right now like a kaleidoscope – the meal in his garden, the tea lights glowing, the taste of raspberries and cream, the smell of the sea, dancing barefoot on the beach . . . the gut-wrenching twist of betrayal, or so she thought . . . Despite the horrible ending to it all, the truth of which it seemed she was about to find out, she had missed it so much. And him.

'Right, I'll show you where this park is. I escape there sometimes on my lunch hour.' Yes, she'd watch the children play, feel the sun on her face or the wind in her hair. It had been a really important place to her when she'd first gone back to work after her chemotherapy sessions. The park kind of grounded you. Reminded you that life was still carrying on, and that was a good thing.

They walked fairly close together, but not touching in any way. The unspoken was keeping a polite space between them. He might still be a shitty adulterer, for all she knew. But would you seek someone out to tell them that? Track someone down to say another goodbye? Too many questions were flitting in her mind. She took a sip of her latte as they entered the stone gates of the park and wandered along a leafy grove, dappled sunlight beaming across their path.

'I've been reading more of your column. The magic moments.'

Curiosity burned. 'Was it you?'

He quirked an eyebrow at her.

'The "E" last week? Was that you? All those things about the beach. Our evening.' Her voice faded, realizing she'd look a right idiot if it hadn't been him. If she'd been clutching at similarities.

But he smiled broadly, showing white, even teeth. And his lips. Boy, she remembered those lips. 'Might have been.'

She smiled back tentatively, the sensible part of her brain still keeping her in check.

'Okay, I need to be honest with you. Yes, it was me.'

Her heart did a little skip.

'Look, I didn't want you to think – I *don't* want you to think – that I didn't care about you, Claire. Or that I used you in any way. It wasn't like that.'

So here it was, the truth.

They stopped walking. There was no one in earshot. In the distance, there were some children on the swings, a toddler standing next to his dad feeding the ducks. She could hear them quacking animatedly.

'So tell me.'

He took a long breath and looked at her. 'That photo. It's of my wife and child.'

Ah shit, the cheating dirt-bag. So she'd been right all-a-bloody-long. And there she'd been, getting all soppy again. She should have known better. She hardened her stare.

'Sarah and James.'

She watched his Adam's apple bob uncomfortably in his throat. Well, she didn't want to hear how they were 'taking a break', how his wife 'didn't understand him' or any of that bullshit.

Ed was biting his lip. She saw his hand tremble as he ruffled it through his hair.

'They're dead.'

Claire froze, registering his ashen face. 'Oh my God. I'm so sorry, Ed. Both of them?' Oh no, no, no. How could they both be dead? That cute little boy in the photo and his mum. Her eyes filled with tears. Fuck, poor Ed.

He nodded blankly. Yet she realized it wasn't blank at all; it was as if pain riddled his whole body, making it useless.

Claire didn't know whether to reach out for him, to hold him. But his body language was so stiff, so raw with grief, that it was as if he needed that space between them.

'Oh, Ed. That's so terrible.' She was curious to know how his world had fallen apart so horrendously, but sensed not to ask just at that moment.

He started walking again slowly along the path. She kept time in silent support.

What the hell should she say now, after that?

As they reached a bench, he slowed and sat. She sat

beside him, her leg gently propped beside his, and he looked down at her thigh, and then up, as though he'd only just realized she was still there with him.

'How?' her voice was soft.

A second or two passed. His voice came out broken. 'A car accident last November.' Then he looked right into her eyes. His pain so acute, it was almost hard to look back. 'It was my fault. I was driving.'

Oh, fuck.

'I was driving. It was an icy morning. I was meant to be dropping them off at her parents . . .' He paused, staring across at the toddler and the man by the pond. 'Spun off the road. Hit a tree. They never made it out of the car. Yet I walked away.' His voice hardened. 'Why the fuck did I get to walk away? It should have been me, not them. It should have been fucking me.' His fist screwed into a punch, but there was only air to hit. 'It should have been me,' he repeated, softer now, his anger, his regret, tensing every limb, the muscles in his jaw tight.

'Ed, I'm so sorry.' She reached an arm around his taut shoulders, but it felt like he was a world away from her. She had no idea what to say next. What words could possibly help that pain? *Are you okay?* was so obviously not right. How could you ever be okay after that? She knew pain and fear and hurt, but she didn't know *this*. This grief so raw. She just left her hand there on his shoulder, leaning in slightly against the warmth of his taut body, stayed silent.

It seemed like he was hardly registering her presence, lost in his nightmare world.

There were birds tweeting from the trees around them. Children laughing and playing. And a beautiful man with a heart full of hurt beside her. She felt her eyes misting, but that would be no good. If she could support him at all, she would, but she really didn't know how.

She lay her hand over his where it rested on his thigh, gave it a small squeeze of support, of humanity. He didn't withdraw his hand, let it be sheltered by hers. Yet it stayed perfectly still below hers. Time seemed to freeze around them. He finally lifted his head, looked out across the park and gave a low sigh of a breath.

'So there you are. You know now.'

They walked back to the newspaper building, her hand having slipped away from his as they stood up from the bench. At least she could begin to understand now, had a grasp of the awfulness of the situation. But she really didn't know where they could go from here. He seemed so very far away, trapped in his past. Too many hurts within him. And she was still healing herself. Yes, she was all clear from the cancer. The scars on her breast a reminder of the deeper scars within. But Christ, she was lucky, she had life, a future ahead. Ah sweet Jesus, Ed's poor wife, his baby – never to grow up, never to have those chances. She felt sick for them, for him.

'Thank you . . . for coming to explain.' They were standing on the threshold to her office, a strange calm between them. 'I really appreciate that. It couldn't have been easy.'

'It was just something I had to do. I didn't want anyone else hurt, not by a misunderstanding.' He tried a weak smile. Then took her into his arms and gave her a stiff brotherly hug. 'No hard feelings.'

'Of course not.' She hugged him back, holding him close to her for an extra second. If only things had been different for them both. Then she stood back, giving him the space he needed. 'Bye, Ed. Take care.' She turned to climb the steps.

Life could change on the spin of a coin, a cluster of rogue cells, a bend in the road, a patch of black ice.

She knew he wasn't going to ask to see her again. They had gone as far as they could go. She would only get hurt. She had hoped for more than he could ever give, she understood that now. It was best this way. She stopped and waved from the top step, then watched him walk away. There was a weird ache in her heart. And she knew he had come here to explain, not to love.

23

PJs, popcorn, sofa, movie

A new start in a new flat. She had two evenings left to pack, so much still to do. Another box to fill with remnants of her old life. She had the music on loud, and was stuffing DVDs and her favourite CDs into another square of cardboard – Adele, Coldplay, Keane. The soundtrack to her marriage, her illness, treatment, her separation. She had put *The Best of The Stereophonics* on as a backing-track to her packing, and 'Dakota' was blasting out. The words about summertime and June striking her – and it wasn't her ex-husband on her mind. All she could think of was Ed and their up-and-down summer of magic moments. What a bloody shame he wasn't carefree and single. Well, he was technically single, but the past was still burying him. No one had the right to tell him to let go or how to grieve. At least he'd had the guts to come and explain. If Ed wasn't to be a part of her life, then so be it, however sad that made her feel.

Three more boxes sealed with brown tape. It was only eight p.m. She had the feeling it was going to be a long night, felt the need for some company, so she rang her sister.

'Hi, Claire. How's the packing going?'

'It's going. Stage by stage.'

'So you're getting there.'

'Yep.' She tried to sound bright and breezy. But felt awfully tired.

'Have you got time to break off? We're just going to watch a movie here, if you fancy joining us. The boys are staying up a bit later as a treat. If you fancy a bit of *Transformers*, you're more than welcome. May I add it has Mark Wahlberg in, so that's a bonus. I'm about to open a bottle of red wine too.'

That did sound good. Cosying up on a sofa with the family. She could pack a couple more boxes when she got back.

'Okay, I'll bring the popcorn.'

'Fab. That'll please the boys no end.' It was only a fifteen-minute drive to Sally's townhouse in Jesmond. She'd stop by the Co-op on the way.

* * *

The credits rolled.

'Right, you pair, time to pop your pyjamas on. Then you can come down and see Auntie Claire for another ten minutes before you go to bed, okay?'

'Okay,' they chorused reluctantly.

'Cup of tea? Or another glass of wine, Claire?'

'I'd love the wine, but I'd better not. My car's outside.'

'You could always get a taxi. Or Mark hasn't had much – he could take you. He's upstairs finishing off a bit of paperwork so he gets a clear weekend.'

'No, tea will be fine. Thanks, though. I'd better keep a clear head for the last of the packing up.'

Sal flicked the switch of the kettle on and found a mug. 'Everything all right?' She must have picked up on Claire's mood. She bustled about with teabags. 'Earl Grey?' she asked mixing the mundane with the leading question.

'Bit of a strange day yesterday,' Claire started.

'Oh? Well, I suppose this weekend's move must be a bit difficult.'

'It's not that. In a way, that'll be a relief now.'

There was a pause. Sal passed her a steaming mug of tea with just a dash of milk, as she liked it.

'I saw Ed yesterday.'

'Ed the guy from the cottage at Bamburgh? The hottie?'

'Yeah.'

'Wow. Well that's a bit of a turn-up. I thought he was a cheating scumbag at the last count. And?'

She didn't reply.

Sal was staring at her. 'So is he separated or something? Was he asking you out on a date?'

Claire wished it had been that simple.

'Spill, then. What was all the palaver about – his ex? Or is he still married?'

'He came back to tell me that he was married, yes. With a child.' She could feel a lump forming in her throat, knowing what was to come. 'Oh Sal, the horrendous truth is that they both died in a car accident.' Claire left out the horror that it was actually Ed driving at the time, wanting to protect him somehow.

'Oh, Jesus . . . how bloody awful. No wonder he was a right grump with me that time.'

'He wanted to explain to me. Just turned up at the office out of the blue, which caused a bit of a stir.'

'Yes, I can imagine.'

'You should have seen Andrea's face when he walked up to my desk. And the whole office just went quiet.'

'Well, he is a bit of a hunk.'

'And then the whole office never stopped quizzing me when I got back, after we'd had a walk in the park on my lunch break. It was hard to even talk about it, though.'

'Sounds romantic.'

'It might have been. But he's just so gutted by it all, Sal. I think it was more of a goodbye.'

'Oh, what a shame. The poor guy. That must be so

tough on him. But he must have thought something of you to come all this way to explain. Didn't you say he was based up in Scotland?'

'Yeah. But I've just felt really odd since. Hearing how cruel life can be at times. It kind of knocks you, you know. How do you ever get over something like that?'

'I don't suppose you do. Not really.'

'No, I don't suppose you do.'

24

A new start in a new home

Friday. Moving Day. All hands on deck.

Mum, who insisted she came and helped, was ordering everyone about whilst Claire finished packing up the last few things in the kitchen. Sal and Mark were there, helping to ferry the light stuff out to the van that Mark had hired for the day.

Claire didn't have an awful lot of stuff, she realized. Split two ways, there was not that much furniture left, but it was plenty for her needs and for the size of the new flat. Paul had taken away the king-size marital bed – she was happy to keep the spare-room double, less memories and significance – as well as his office furniture, the dining set, an armchair and some other smaller items. And so, the house and its contents were split; a marriage brought down to a division of possessions and a heap of ragged memories. But it hadn't all been bad, she reminded herself, there had been good times too. It had just been brought to its knees these latter years. Time to get up and move on. She had seen him, Paul, just a few days ago, coming for the last of his things. It was all fairly amicable. She had felt a little empty if anything. She'd been through too much these past eighteen months to worry any more about this lost relationship. She'd done all her crying and hurting many months ago. Their marriage was spent. There was no going back. Trust had gone, and all their dreams from the early days were damaged beyond repair. At least there weren't any children to split down the middle. Not that she hadn't wanted children, she had always imagined they might be part of her world at some point.

'Claire, can you give me a hand with this box of books? It's a bit heavy for me.' Her mother's voice brought her back from her reverie.

Three trips in a stacked-up, white hire van, and her house was empty. Being the last there, she checked every room, making sure nothing had inadvertently been left behind. She traced a hand down the wooden bannisters, wandered into the kitchen, checked the cupboards were all emptied, went through to the lounge. It looked smaller without all the furnishings. She noticed the darker patches on the walls where her pictures had been.

She thought back to the day they'd moved in, full of

excitement at their new home together – so much more spacious than the flat they'd rented together previously – a place of hope and dreams. She thought of the years drifting along. Then how it became a place of illness and recovery. Of lying in a stupor after the chemo cocktail, wiped of every ounce of energy, lips like parchment. It didn't just kill the bad-guy cells, it killed the good stuff off too. But you had to deal with it, it was just something you had to do. He'd looked after her then, her husband, as best he could, tucking her in with a blanket on the sofa, carrying her up to bed when her legs couldn't cope any more. He'd tried to do right by her through her illness, despite all his other failings. Relationships shifted like sand, and they had let theirs slip through their fingers. But, there was no going back.

Okay, stop dwelling on the past, Claire. Say goodbye to this house, lock the door. It's time to move on.

She stepped out over the threshold and quietly closed the door on that part of her life.

Another set of keys. A new door.

Mark had got a mate at this end to help heave the heavier boxes and furniture in. No stairs this time – it was on the ground floor. She thanked God that she had her lovely family there with her, ferrying packets and bags and boxes like a mini-colony of worker ants. Even her nephews had cheery smiles as they passed with an 'Auntie

Claire, where do you want this one to go?' Luckily Mum had been busy with her black marker pen back at the old house before most of the boxes had had a chance to escape, making the task so much easier. She spotted the large 'K' in Mum's twirly writing. 'Kitchen for that one, thanks Jack. You're doing a great job.'

An hour or so down the line, Ollie had started to loiter, taking quick peeks at his Nintendo DS out in the back courtyard, and Jack commented that his arms felt like they were two metres long. She'd also noticed that her mother's steps were slowing. They were nearly done – it was past five o'clock – and as long as everything was in the flat and the van was emptied ready to return by six p.m., they could all stop and she could unpack later in her own time.

'A cup of tea is in order. I've found the kettle!' Her mum shouted.

'I have shortbread,' came an echoey call from the bedroom. Sal, organized as ever.

She had rented the bottom half of a semi-detached Victorian red-brick house just at the Gosforth end of Jesmond. It overlooked the Town Moor and was near a little run of shops with a convenience store and a little teashop. It was also a couple of stops further along on the bus route for her morning commute – perfect. It was small, but cosy inside. She was pleased with it and was looking forward to settling in.

The daylight was dimming as Mark brought in the last box just before six p.m. Sal was going to follow him back to the hire place in Gosforth to drop the van off, and then they'd return. Claire felt shattered; a day of packing up and shifting it all out again taking its toll. Her energy levels were still not quite back to the good old days. But all the boxes were in the right rooms, and the main kitchen items were out. Her bed was all set up – Mark and his mate had done their best with a set of screwdrivers and an Allen key – and Sal and Mum had put all the pillowcases, a clean sheet and the duvet cover on for her.

'Right, boys, there's a fish and chip shop just along the next road and round the corner. The least I can do is get you all some supper. Who's up for that?'

'Yay!' the boys said in unison, as everyone else said, 'Sounds good to me', 'And me.'

'Right, boys – we'll give it five minutes to let your mum and dad get sorted. Then I'll pop along in my car. Want to come and give me a hand?'

'Yep!'

'Yay.'

'Mum, can I leave you in charge of finding plates and some cutlery?'

'Of course.'

On the way back from the fish and chip shop, Claire nipped into the Co-op in her little run of shops and picked up a bottle of champagne. It wasn't chilled but she'd pop it in the freezer, which she'd thought to plug in as soon as it was in place. It was definitely a time to celebrate.

So they sat on the floor of her new lounge, Mum, Sal and the boys squeezed on the sofa, she and Mark on the floor, eating deliciously salt-and-vinegared crispy battered fish and chips, straight from the wrapper with little wooden chip forks, the cutlery not having been traced yet. Luckily the champagne flutes had.

Sal raised a glass. 'To your new home, Claire.'

'Cheers, everyone! And thanks so much for all your help today. I really couldn't have done it without you all.'

'You're welcome,' Mark smiled.

'The sore arms are worth the fish and chips,' grinned Jack cheekily.

'Cheers,' they all chanted, and there was a clinking of glasses all round. Even the boys had a small taste of champagne to toast with. Though Ollie pulled a face, gulping down his can of cola straight afterwards.

Mum added, 'To your new home, darling – be happy and healthy.'

They were all too well aware of the shadow of ill health. She could tell it still hung around in the corners of their minds.

'Cheers! And thank you all so much. For everything.' Claire smiled. Boy, was she ready for her new start.

25

Precious Prosecco moments with friends

'Surprise!' Andrea and Lou were on the doorstep beaming at her, dressed in training shoes, shorts and tees, each bearing a bottle of Prosecco.

'First, we run as planned. Then we party. Happy new home!' Andrea announced.

It was the following Friday evening, the end of the first week in her new flat. The last thing Claire felt like at that moment was going jogging – she'd not long been home from work and she was absolutely jiggered – but once she got going, she was usually fine. They had got to two and a half fairly comfortable miles now, with two weeks to go to the Big Race.

Andrea looked down at Claire's work clothes. 'Had you forgotten the Friday training session, lovely?'

'Might have done – sorry, guys. It's been a topsy-turvy week, with moving in.' She had in fact envisaged a night in with feet up, TV on and a box set at the ready, possibly with a trip to the Co-op for a tub of ice cream. It had just been such a busy week, with work as normal and unpacking every evening. But she rallied. 'It's fine – I'll get changed in a flash. And thank you. Come on in. Welcome to my humble abode.'

'Ah, it looks lovely,' said Andrea as she entered the hallway, which was painted a pastel green – not Claire's favourite colour, but she could live with it for now. She'd hung up an ivory shabby-chic-style mirror to give it a sense of space.

'The living room is really sweet.' Lou had popped her head in through the open doorway. Claire had more or less sorted that room out. Her comfy beige sofa was installed with a couple of new cushions, taking up much of the space. And she'd kept the small wooden coffee table and matching TV stand from the old house.

Andrea was already through into the kitchen. 'Hmm, now this is nice.'

The kitchen had been recently done out with light oak-style units and a dark-grey marble-effect work surface. It did look good, and was Claire's favourite room. It was fairly compact, especially with the kitchen table and chairs in it, but it was proving easy to work in. She'd give the oven a go soon and try out some baking; see how it handled cooking a loaf or two. It had only had to deal with warming up a pizza so far.

'Okay, I'll nip upstairs and quickly change. Let's get this run over with, then we can chill out with that bubbly. Go ahead and pop them in the fridge, if you like. Thanks so much, guys.'

A quick trip round the corner to the shops once they got back would soon sort out some nibbles, she mused on her way to her bedroom. She'd get some spring rolls and starter-style treats to heat up, and she'd do some cheese and biscuits too. That would serve as supper for them all. Other than the ice cream scenario, she hadn't even planned what she was going to have for tea up to that point, anyhow.

Sal turned up five minutes later in running gear with yet another bottle of Prosecco and some gorgeous-looking Belgian chocolate truffles, obviously having been kept in the loop too.

Five minutes later, Bella's Babes were grouped on the pavement outside Claire's new home.

'Right, ladies – quads, squats and pods!' Andrea was making up her own exercise terms for good measure, which made them grin. Lou started off the warm-up routine she insisted they do to ensure there were no pulled muscles before the big day.

The stretch they were currently performing involved balancing on one leg with the other leg pulled up behind as you held onto your ankle. As they were wobbling like a gaggle of half-drunk flamingos, two lads pulled up beside them on chopper bikes, smirking. They looked about twelve. 'All right, ladies?' One of them gave a cheeky grin. The other winked, then burst out laughing, before they scooted off.

'Great, thanks,' Andrea shouted after them. 'Cheeky little gits.' She turned back to the group.

'All for a good cause,' reminded Claire. 'Let's set to it.'

And they were off.

Twenty-seven minutes and forty-three seconds later by Lou's Garmin measurements, they were staggering back up to Claire's front gate.

'Hah, we did it. *And* in under twenty-eight minutes. Well done, ladies!' Lou congratulated them.

'Blimey – that last bit nearly finished me off. I'm sure you were speeding up, Lou.' Andrea was still out of breath.

'Might have been just a teensy bit – I saw that we might do our best run yet. And we did!'

'Yay!' cheered Claire. 'Right, time for showers, then Prosecco. Actually, did you lot think to bring a change of clothes?'

'Ha-hah, yes indeed, we're not daft, you know. All organized. There's a bag of stuff we left in the hall,' said Andrea.

'Perfect. Don't want you lot all smelly in my new lounge,' Claire teased.

'Well, you know who your friends are,' quipped Andrea. 'We're doing all this for you, and what do we get for it?'

'A shower, Prosecco and chocolates, and when I get back from the shop in a mo, you can have some supper too. I'll nip for some nibbles while you lot get cleaned up.'

'And what about you? God, I feel sorry for the checkout person. Are you going like that? You'll be all stinky,' her sister added.

'Well, we can't all shower at once.'

'Might be fun.' Andrea was on full form.

Sal looked horrified.

'Don't mind her, she's only joking.' Claire was accustomed to Andrea's quirky sense of humour.

'Might not be.' Andrea kept it up with a cheeky grin.

'Behave, you nutter. There's no way I'm getting in a shower with you.'

The popping of corks sounded fabulous. Precious Prosecco moments with friends. They had a lovely evening chatting, griping about their aches and pains from their training, and discussing the impending run and the implications of the Pretty Muddy event.

'God only knows what you've got us into, Andrea,' Claire laughed.

'Ah, it'll be fun. We'll just throw ourselves into whatever. And boss Dave from the office is fully backing us. He's even sending a photographer from the paper on the day to get some action shots.'

'Jeez,' groaned Lou. 'I can't wait to see those plastered all over the newspaper. Us lot looking like a load of mud wrestlers!'

'It'll raise a load of cash.' Sal was looking on the bright side.

'And plenty of laughs,' added Claire.

'Oh well. In for a penny, in for a pound,' Andrea said, trying to look excited.

'And let's hope we make *loads* of pounds for Cancer Research,' said Lou.

'Absolutely.'

'Well, if all those poor people can get though their surgery and their scars and the chemo and everything else, then I'm sure we can all put up with a bit of mud,' Claire said bracingly.

'Exactly,' Sal agreed.

'Well said, that girl.'

'Cheers guys.'

'To Bella's Babes,' they said together, raising their glasses.

'To Bella's Babes and the mud wrestling!' added Andrea.

26

A hug

Boom! Just when you thought your world was settled.

Claire was showering before bed, rubbing her hands over her abdomen, frothing up her favourite mint and ginger scented bubbles. It was tiny, a bump in her groin area. She felt again, probed slightly deeper into the skin. It was hard under her fingertips, the size of a pea. She went cold. It was always there, that fear, once you'd already had a cancer. Any lump or bump sent an icy dread through you. You tried to put the thought away, close it down, but it was there just below the surface, the feeling that you were on borrowed time.

It was probably nothing, she rationalized. But she'd better get it checked out to be on the safe side. She'd ring the doctor first thing in the morning, get an appointment.

The doctor had been great with her through the whole thing the last time. The last time . . . She hoped to God this wouldn't be the *next* time.

In bed, she wished it wasn't too late to phone the surgery. She wanted to act on it, now. She couldn't tell anyone about this scare, not yet. Not till she knew what she might be facing. It was just a lump, a tiny little lump. There was no point worrying her mum or Sally with it, no point three of them worrying. That would be unfair on them.

Whoa, how sodding typical. A new start, new home. Things were really on the up. Or they had been.

Okay. Stop it! Banish all negative thoughts. Carry on tomorrow as normal. Get your work done at the newspaper. Then go and get checked out. Do not worry about it until you know it's something to worry about.

Claire pulled the covers up tighter across her. Shame she hadn't got her new kitten yet. She could really do with a cuddle. She'd phoned the animal rescue centre and asked if they had any kittens ready to go, but had decided to get herself settled in properly in her new flat first. She was thinking of going along in a couple of weeks' time, knowing for sure that she'd fall in love with a cute bundle of fluff and take it home on that first visit. But hey, this could change everything. She'd better make sure she wouldn't be to-ing and fro-ing to hospital before she committed herself to getting a pet.

Oh no, this could have all sorts of implications. She tried to rein in her fears. She so hoped she could still do the charity run with Bella's Babes. She couldn't let them down, let alone all those people who had now sponsored them. She was all trained up and ready. It should be okay to do, surely, whatever might be wrong with her; she only had to get to Saturday and get round.

Lying in bed on her own, her thoughts and fears buzzed in her mind. Boy, she could do with a big hug right now. She found herself picturing Ed's warm, strong arms around her on the beach. Remembered that night dancing on the sand. She closed her eyes and began to play the movie in her mind. She could pretend they had just met, that there was no history. The memory was still so clear – trying to feel it again wasn't as good as the real thing, but it helped – just her and Ed and the music. So very close. Safe in his arms on a beautiful Northumberland beach with the sand under her feet and the stars up above. She'd hold tight to that memory, that magic moment, keep it with her to cheer her up, hold on to Ed in her mind until she knew what she had to face.

The next morning she booked an appointment with her surgery for straight after work. They knew her history, and said they'd fit her in that same day.

Somehow she got through the working day, but it was hard to settle, though she tried her best to get her head down and focus on the task in hand. Five o'clock couldn't come soon enough. She got the bus back as far as Jesmond and then popped into the flat for her car keys and drove the five minutes to the surgery at Gosforth.

'Okay, Claire. So you say you've found another lump?'

Claire was sitting opposite Dr Reynolds, her lady doctor at the surgery. She had been great with her eighteen months before when Claire had first found the lump in her breast. Dr Reynolds had made sure she was seen quickly, and since then had always made it clear she was available to chat with about any concerns, even when Claire had been under the hospital's treatment programme. Dr Reynolds was in her fifties, and her black hair and olive complexion suggested a Mediterranean background. Today she was smartly dressed in a black suit and green blouse.

'Yes, I spotted it just last night. In my groin area. Here.' Claire pressed her fingertips against it.

'Right, let's run through a few questions. So you first spotted it just last night?'

'Yes.'

'And, how big is it, and has it grown at all overnight?'

'Pea-sized I'd say, not big, but quite hard. And it's the same size this morning.'

'Okay.'

'And how have you been feeling?'

286

'Oh . . .'

'Tired at all?'

'Well, yes, I have been tired, more so than normal in the past couple of weeks. But I've had a recent house move and been really busy.' She didn't add about the running regime she'd been on as well. 'I just put it down to that.'

'Okay, well that links in. There's a chance you might have an underlying infection. Now then, I'll need to give you an examination so I can check out the lump. I'd also like to feel your other main gland points. It could well be lymphatic, being in that area.'

Claire must have paled. Lymphomas – lymph nodes. They were near your breast as well. She'd had a couple of nodes taken out from her armpit area as a precaution at the time of the mastectomy.

Dr Reynolds continued, 'Look, we both know your history, but try not to worry too much at this stage – there are lots of reasons why there could be a lump.'

'Okay.'

'So if you could just undress for me, down to your underwear, and pop yourself onto the examination bed behind the curtain there.'

'Right.' She stepped behind the curtain. Trousers down, blouse off. A little prayer sent to heaven for a good result. 'Okay, I'm ready.'

The doctor appeared and began to probe her right

groin area. 'Okay, I've got it. Sorry if that's a little uncomfortable.'

The fingers digging into the tender skin of her groin did make her squirm a bit. Claire tried her best to relax. The doctor went on to check her left groin area, then stomach, armpits and the glands each side of her neck. 'And you've been doing all your breast checks regularly. Nothing of concern there?'

'Religiously, morning and night. Not found anything at all, and I did a *really* thorough check in the shower this morning.'

'Okay. Good.'

The doctor finished her examination and Claire got dressed as the doctor went back to her desk. She came out from behind the curtain and sat down.

'Right, I'd like to send you for a CT scan. Just to be on the safe side, especially with your history. And they may then want to do a biopsy. I'll also inform your oncologist.'

'I see.' So this was how it all began. Oh God. *Shush, you'll be okay,* another voice in her mind soothed.

'I have a strong feeling this is more likely to be an infection. Something's set off your lymph nodes. But we'll err on the side of caution. Though it may well just settle down by itself. I'd like to take some bloods while you're here so we can test for infection, and I'll also ensure we do a complete blood count.'

'Okay.'

She readied herself for the needle in her inner elbow; she was used to it – needles became the norm after a while in hospital. Putting the line in for chemo. All those blood tests.

'I'm going to prescribe some antibiotics so that if it is bacterial, we're already countering it. And in the meanwhile, I'll refer you immediately for a CT scan and put it on fast-track. You should hear directly from the Freeman Hospital in the next day or so. Can I just check your contact details are up to date?'

So, Claire confirmed her mobile and email address. And then she would have to wait.

'Thank you.' She stood to go.

'You're welcome. And if there are any changes or concerns in the next few days, pop straight back in to see me.'

The worry of waiting. And then it was all a whirl. Two days later and she was in hospital for a scan. Drinking her cup of contrast dye. Being laid out on the flat bed, then moved slowly through the scanner, trying her best to stay totally still. It felt like she was in a sci-fi movie. Then another wait for results and a chat with the consultant – inconclusive on the nature of the lump. Her emotions were in roller-coaster mode. And, she had to keep feigning tooth problems and trips to the dentist to cover her time off from work.

A biopsy was booked for the following Monday, after race day. Another wait. Another few days of hiding her fear from her family, her friends. She nearly caved in and revealed all to Andrea at work on the Thursday, but she really didn't want to worry them all unnecessarily. And it was nearly the day of the Pretty Muddy race. At least that would keep her busy over the weekend. Training was all done. They'd had a gentle jog midweek as a wind-down, and now Bella's Babes were as ready as they'd ever be for their big charity event. She was a bit tired, but there was no way she was missing out on this, and if it was bad news from the biopsy, then it would mean more than ever to have done this. She wanted to kick cancer up its horrid arse.

27

Doing something to help someone else

Saturday – the Pretty Muddy Race for Life day. Bella's Babes are coming at ya!

'Oh my God, look at that!'

Claire was driving them into the car-parking field for the event. Women were staggering back to their cars clarted up with mud – it was in their hair, all over their faces, caked on to clothes that were hardly distinguishable, drying on their bare legs. It looked like something from an apocalyptic movie. The last of the walking dead or something.

'Whoa! Okaaay.'

'Looks like we're in for some fun . . .'

It was head-to-toe with the brown stuff.

'Right,' Andrea announced, 'so we're on at ten-thirty, and it's now a quarter to.'

'Time for some pre-run limbering up,' Lou said chirpily.

'How the hell do you limber up for this?' Sal asked wryly.

They all got out of the car. They had numbers to safety-pin onto their bright-pink T-shirts. Claire had had the tees taken to a printer's and got 'Bella's Babes' stamped across the back. Though if the other runners were anything to go by, no one would be able to read anything printed on them after a few minutes.

They did a few hopeful stretches, including their flamingo move, propped against the side of the car.

'Ready?'

'Not really,' Andrea responded.

They spotted two more women heading back to the car opposite. They smiled across at them, and the women gave a grin back – at least they were still smiling from beneath the mud.

'Ready as we ever will be,' Lou added.

'Bella's Babes are about to hit the mud!' Andrea sounded like a Viking warrior.

They all laughed.

They walked through to the starting area. There were pink banners and pink information tents, and coffee stands and food stalls had been set up nearby. There was a DJ commentating and setting the participants off. The runners went off in fifteen-minute slots, and there were the 'ten-fifteeners' off and on their way. Along the racetrack, no less, then up a hilly bank. The girls joined in the cheering to support them, all feeling a little bit anxious. Bella's Babes just wanted to get going, get round and do themselves and everyone who had sponsored them proud.

'Oh look, there's Danny.' Andrea spotted her boyfriend in the crowd.

'Hi.' They all waved across.

'Good luck,' he shouted back. 'Go Andrea. Go girls. Good on ya.'

And then six little heads were shouting away by a barrier fronting the course. 'Go, Miss Jones.' Some of Lou's primary class had come along and were lined up with their parents in support. 'Good luck!' How lovely.

'Well done, ladies.' Strangers were cheering them on now too, as they funnelled into the waiting zone ready for the next wave.

There was a buzz of anticipation within them, and from the crowd.

Mark and the boys then appeared. 'Sorry, took a while parking,' he explained to Sal.

'Good luck, Mummy. Good luck, Auntie Claire.'

'Thanks, boys.'

'You're going to get *very* dirty, Auntie Claire,' Ollie added.

'Yes, I think so, Ol. Oh well, it'll be fun . . . I think.'

'Yay. Get down and dirty, Sal,' Mark beamed cheekily.

293

Sal cringed while the other girls laughed.

A few minutes later, 'The Final Countdown' started playing from the DJ station, and a few thanks and mentions were made. Many of the ladies who were taking part today were running in memory of someone special. That brought it home. Reminded them all why they were there. Claire felt a horrid knot in her throat as she thought about her biopsy due on Monday. She gave her sister's hand a squeeze. Sal smiled, unaware of her sister's fears, and squeezed it back.

'Okay, ladies, are we ready? In five, four, three, two, one!'

A hooter blared out and they were off. They'd positioned themselves mid-pack, but people were soon spreading out, some in teams like themselves, some as singles. Some were struggling straight away, and they overtook them with an encouraging smile as they passed them on the hill. This was not your usual race – some of these women might still be undergoing treatment, determined to battle this out.

The first obstacles seemed fairly straightforward – jumping over big bouncy balls and through tyres that had mud at the bottom, only ankle deep. They were obviously leading them in gently. The running seemed okay; their training was standing them in good stead. They'd agreed beforehand that they were running as a team, and as a team they'd stay.

Suddenly they were faced with heavy nets on the ground, like some army assault course.

'On your knees, girls,' a marshal advised.

And down they went on knees and bellies, scrambling under the nets. Their knees and chests were plastered now. On the next running straight they passed a couple of ladies who seemed to be battling with the running part.

'Well done, keep going,' Claire encouraged them. There were probably still two miles to go.

A short burst of a run and then they were at the next obstacle. There were climbing frames, a balancing pole, tunnels of mud, a cat's-cradle-type zone strung with rope barriers to try and work your way through.

'Come on, girls, we're doing great.' Lou was in full teacher mode.

Andrea was lagging a little, and Claire was finding it hard to get her breath with the running. This was so much tougher than a normal three-mile run. Crawling, climbing, scrambling. But hey, this was also *nothing* compared to chemo, or surgery, a mastectomy.

'Come on, we're doing really well!' Claire rallied her team.

After the next jog, they were faced with a massive ten-foot-high wooden wall with netting up the sides – to climb up and over, obviously. There was a male marshal at the top helping some that were struggling.

'Let's go, Bella's Babes,' Claire shouted. A battle cry. They tore up the sides of the wall, balancing precariously at the top. Thank Christ for the rubber crash mats each side, but you could still break an ankle in a fall, mused Claire as she wobbled at the top. Sal was up and over in a flash – Claire hadn't realized what a little power pack she had for a sister. It was probably all those years keeping up with three males in the house – but Lou was clinging on warily near the top.

'Hate heights,' she shouted nervously.

'Ah, here, take my hand. I'll help.' Claire reached out, reminding herself not to look down. She was feeling a little wobbly too. 'Don't look down, Lou. Just concentrate on this bit – hang on and swing a leg over the top.'

'Okay, ladies.' The very nice marshal man gripped Lou's other hand as she mounted the top beam and guided her over. 'Best to turn at this point,' he suggested, 'then go back down facing the wall step by step. You'll be fine.'

Just like life – step by step, with a guiding hand along the way and a friend or two in tow.

Andrea had already made it over the top and was perched just below Lou, who was still on the net the other side. 'Come on, let's beat the fucker,' Andrea shouted up at both Claire and Lou.

Three other ladies and the marshal stared down from the top looking slightly shocked.

'Sorry, I'm talking about cancer! Not you lot.'

'Ah. Right.' Understanding softened their furrowed brows.

'Yeah!' Sal shouted up from the base. 'Absolutely,' joined in Claire from the top, and a little cheer rose up from around them.

'Yay, we did it!' A couple of minutes later, and they had all reached solid ground on the far side.

There was a click and flash of a camera as they assembled at the bottom. Steve, photographer from the *Herald*, had caught up with them. 'Go Claire, go Andrea,' he cheered. 'Got a great shot then. Just remember to smile next time,' he added cheekily.

Andrea grimaced at him.

The team began running once more, though every joint was aching now. They had to have done over two of the three miles now, for sure. They passed another group of four ladies who had decided on walking.

This was becoming hard work as there was yet another hill to run up. Claire was certain there'd been more ups than downs. How did that work?

'My legs are killing me,' groaned Andrea.

'Well, don't mess about now. Do you realize we're the first ones in the group? Come on, we might just come in first.' Lou was getting competitive.

'Yeah, come on. We can do this this,' Sal urged.

They pushed on, with plenty of moaning and groaning.

'Don't stop now, there's another group gaining on us,' Lou shouted, eager to keep the pace.

Not that there were really winners or losers in this. It wasn't a race where people or teams were placed. It was a challenge against yourself only, and to help others. It was just a matter of Team Bella's pride, and coming in first out of their section would be the icing on the cake.

They could see the racecourse buildings as they reached the brow of the hill, so they couldn't be far away from the finish now. Claire looked at her team, already clarted in mud from chest to toes, feeling very proud of them. They turned a corner into a courtyard area, and here it was, the grand finale of obstacles. The mud-wrestling pit.

Wow – a huge tub of mud, probably knee-deep, and you had to lie down in it and crawl, and oh my God, there were Ollie, Mark and Jack sporting plastic shovels, as well as a couple of the marshals. Yes, people were ready to scoop mud all over them. So that was how the other charity runners had it in their hair, their eyes, their mouths. This was the apocalypse scene. And the cameras were flashing away.

'All in a good cause!' she shouted to the others as they plunged in. Oh Jeez, it was filling every nook and cranny. Oh good lord, it'd take weeks to clear it out of all the cracks. Her shower was going to have a hard time; she hoped the drains were good in her new flat.

'Go Mum. Go Auntie Claire.' Slop. She got a scoop right in the face.

'I'll remember this, Ollie,' she managed to laugh, though the mud was now in her mouth, on her teeth, gritty and earthy to taste. This was so bloody crazy.

'Thanks, Andrea,' she shouted ironically across the tub as they were crawling to a stand. Mud glooped off them as they straddled the far end trying to get out.

'Yes, *thanks*, Andrea,' the others joined in.

Danny and a couple of his football mates were standing laughing on the sidelines, and then there was the line-up of schoolchildren seeing them back in. 'Go, Miss Jones!!'

'Is that really you Miss Jones?' a little girl piped up.

'Yep, sure is.'

'Wow, you look like the Gruffalo,' the same girl shouted out.

'Or a poo monster,' the lad next to her joined in, which caused a fit of giggles through the children and other spectators.

'Come on, they're gaining on us!' Sal shouted, glancing over her shoulder.

They rounded the racecourse stands, were nearing the finish line, and put on a final flourish.

'Well done, Claire. Go, Bella's Babes.' There was a shout from the crowd. Claire scanned the spectators, and – how lovely – there were Jo and Emma in support.

They gave her a big thumbs-up as she made a blast through the big pink finishing posts, hand in hand with her team-mates. It was *such* an amazing feeling – she forgot about the mud and the aches and the pains. She forgot about her imminent biopsy. All four of Bella's Babes jumped up in the air like muddy warriors. *We did it!* Air-punch time.

Claire stood bent over for a few seconds, catching her breath. Her vison went a little fuzzy and she had a little wobble. Her sister steadied her. 'You okay?'

'Yes, think so. Just need . . . to breathe.' She leant against Sal for a second or two. 'Must have just pushed myself a bit hard there at the end. I'm fine.'

There were a couple of last shots taken of the team for the paper – once they'd caught their breath and could manage to stand up straight again. Steve lined them up professionally. 'Well done, you lot. This'll make great coverage. Bit different from your fashion shoots, Andrea.' He gave a wink.

Then Ollie and Jack piled in to congratulate their mum with big hugs, not worried in the least about dirtying their clothes as Mark watched in amusement. It was probably the first time *ever* she hadn't berated them for getting muddy. Claire walked across and caught up with Emma and Jo in the spectator section.

'Aw, thanks for coming, guys.'

'Had to cheer you on, of course,' said Emma.

'And see for ourselves you lot covered in mud,' Jo added. 'Great effort!'

Claire moved in to give them a kiss on the cheek. They jumped back out of the way. She looked down, realizing the state she was in. 'Ah, yes of course – sorry. Totally forgot.'

The others from the team caught up with them.

'Hi, thanks for coming,' Andrea smiled beneath her mud pack.

'This was definitely worth coming to watch, just for the entertainment value,' said Jo. 'But yeah, well done. You did amazingly.' She and Emma chuckled.

'Cheers.' Andrea pretended to be disgruntled, but then grinned.

'Right, I think it might be time get back to the car and peel off these muddy clothes, then we can get ourselves home to some hot showers and warm up – asap.' Claire was definitely beginning to feel a chill now. Even with the silver-foil blankets around them they'd been given as they got through the finish line.

They were all in agreement.

'Well done, everyone. And thank you.' Claire was so proud of her team. 'We did it. And we'll have raised loads for charity. Our Just Giving page was at £720 yesterday. And it seems to be going up all the time. Brilliant. Thank you.'

'Aw, that's really great, Claire. We did good, ladies,' Andrea added.

'I actually enjoyed it, in a weird way,' said Lou.

'It's the school-teacher thing,' Andrea bantered back.

Sal went off home with her family, after muddy hugs all round. Then it was time to strip down to underwear in the field, aka the car park. There were plenty of other women doing exactly the same thing, so no one was bothered, and otherwise Claire knew she'd be cleaning mud off her car seats for evermore. She'd had the forethought to provide two bin bags per person, one for dirty clothes and one to sit on, and once they'd stuffed their tumble of filthy clothes into carrier bags, and the carrier bags into the car, they all got in themselves, now sporting tracksuits, comfy trousers and tees. Claire noted her mascara-streaked eyes and the mud splashes all over her face in the rear-view mirror, then turned to look at her mates. They all looked as bad as each other.

'Can't wait for the photos,' Andrea said drily.

28

The magic of being alive

Monday. Biopsy day. Another 'dentist's appointment'. She had the afternoon off work. She got herself to the Freeman Hospital on the bus, and after waiting ten minutes or so was greeted by a friendly nurse. A few questions, a quick change into a hospital gown, then an examination, and after a local anaesthetic they took a small sample with a needle from the lump. Thankfully, it was a fairly straight-forward procedure. She was advised to sit quietly for a few minutes, then got dressed, her groin area a little tender with just a small dressing on. The nurse told her to wait a further fifteen minutes just to check she wasn't dizzy or anything, and then she'd be allowed to go. She wished she'd brought a friend with her now, or Sal – someone to chat to at this moment would be nice – but she still didn't want to worry anyone. She smiled across at another patient who was waiting too, and then read a leaflet on organ donation. She was already signed up to the register, but it passed the time.

Given the nod to go, she travelled back home on the bus and then curled up on the sofa, feeling so very tired and still aching from the Pretty Muddy race. She felt a little odd and emotional and had a little cry. Then she blew her nose and pulled herself together. It might all be fine yet. She'd go and make a nice honey-and-sunflower seed loaf, try the oven out at last, and when it was baked and still warm and doughy, she'd spread it thickly with fresh butter. She'd walk to the Co-op right now and get the ingredients she needed.

Wednesday. Her mobile buzzed at work. She recognized the hospital number and headed out of the goldfish-bowl of the open-plan office to the landing area of the stairwell to get some privacy.

'Hello.'

'Miss Maxwell?'

'Yes?' The tension was palpable in her body. *So this was it.*

'It's Mr Bartholomew's secretary here. I'll just put you through.'

'Hello?' She waited a second. A couple of reporters from the newspaper wandered past, chatting away between themselves. Life was going on all around, yet she felt frozen.

'Miss Maxwell.' The familiar voice of her oncologist came on the line. 'I'm pleased to confirm that the biopsy was negative. There was no sign of any cancerous cells within the lump. And your CT scan and blood tests were all clear too.'

'Oh, wow . . . thank you.' She felt a little light-headed. 'That's so good to hear.'

'It's most likely you've had an infection and that your lymph gland in the groin area has swollen in response to that. It should naturally go down by itself in the next couple of weeks. But just keep an eye on it and how you're feeling in general, and if you have any future concerns please refer back to your GP or myself directly.'

So she wouldn't be back into hospital, back into chemo and that grinding routine of illness and treatment she knew so well. She could let go of the fear that had hummed along in her mind for the last week, a fear you never dared voice aloud because this time it might actually get you. 'Yes, I will, and thank you. Thank you.'

'It's nice to be giving out good news.' She could hear the smile in his voice.

She pressed 'End call' and gave a mental air-punch. 'Yes!' And then the relief overwhelmed her and she suddenly found herself sobbing.

Just at that point the glass doors to the main office

swung open. Dragon Julia appeared beside her, no doubt checking what she was up to, wasting time out here.

'Are you okay, Claire?' Her face turned from its usual scowl to concerned within a second. 'Can I help?' She placed a hand on her arm.

'I'm more than okay,' Claire smiled through the tears. 'I'm all clear.'

'Gr-eat . . .' Julia was obviously still confused.

'It was just a scare. I've had a scan, a biopsy . . . The cancer hasn't come back.'

Her colleague's arm moved to wrap her in a short and sweet hug, much to Claire's surprise. The ice queen had thawed.

'Well, that's good news.' Julia pulled back stiffly. 'Now, let's get back to work.' Sympathy really wasn't her thing.

But Claire didn't mind at all. Getting back to work would be absolutely bloody wonderful!

Back at her flat that night, the relief still pulsed through her body, and for some reason she kept thinking about Bamburgh, imagining herself walking on that gorgeous beach. Enjoying the ever-changing view of the sea, the sound of the gulls, the soft hush of the waves on the shore. Tasting the salt of the sea air. She had this driving urge to get back to the coast. To her happy place. She still couldn't afford the luxury hotels or cottages that were on offer in Bamburgh village, especially after all the expenses of the house move. Her half of the money after paying off the mortgage was safe in the bank till she bought again. There was only one thing for it. She had two days left of her annual leave. Life was too short to wait.

29

Catching up with an old friend

Louise, North Yorkshire

She felt a surge of joy as she saw the castle rising up from its dark rock base. She wound down the window of her car and got an exhilarating whiff of salty sea air.

It was a beautiful crisp, early October day. It was Friday, and she'd taken the whole day off work. Julia had been very understanding in the light of their recent encounter on the office stairwell – and she'd booked for the weekend with old Mr Hedley, who had seemed rather irked that he'd have to open the place up again and get the hot water tank back on, but when she offered an extra £20 towards electricity, he caved. She'd packed extra jumpers and a spare blanket just in case, not trusting the ancient fire and portable gas heater to do the job.

She drove easily along the last stretch of lane winding its way from the A1, past farms and cottages behind a tractor that slowed her journey, but no matter – and then there it was in all its glory, the majestic Bamburgh Castle and the little village below it. Driving past the butchers, Lynda's deli (she looked forward to saying hello later), the tea rooms, the hotel, the high castle walls and the cricket pitch below, the tourists and the seagulls, her spirits soared.

The tension of her recent cancer scare was well behind her now. Okay, so she would never be totally free from the fear of its return, but she couldn't be ruled by it either. She was going to grab life by the balls and enjoy it.

As she neared the driveway to the cottages, she was a little nervous that Ed might be there, and how he might feel about her turning up. Naturally she hadn't told him she'd be coming; there'd been no contact since their walk in the park – though she had spotted a charity donation on the Bella's Babes Just Giving page for a generous £50 from someone called Ed; she had a feeling she knew who that was. She had felt he needed his space. To find his own life again, however that might be. She had no wish to upset him or possibly make him angry by appearing next door, but the compulsion to come had been so great. To watch the rush of the waves, hear the sea's roar or its hush, feel the sand under her feet. Watch a pinky-pearl sunrise over the North Sea. The place had drawn her back, like the tides themselves.

Well, if he was here, she'd leave him alone. She'd say 'hello' if he was out and about, no more. There was no way she was going to intrude on his privacy. She had to respect it. Many times she'd thought about his devastating loss, felt gutted for him, but she realized there was no real way for her to help. All he ever wanted was to have them back, for it never to have happened. How could anyone put that right?

She indicated, feeling a little shiver of excitement as she pulled in off the road. No black 4x4 parked outside his cottage. She felt a sense of relief, and yet a weird pang too. How she wished the situation wasn't so damned complicated. But it was what it was, and it would probably be better if they didn't have to face each other again. She hoped he wasn't going to turn up later.

Here was her stone cottage by the sea – the ramshackle, quirky yet lovely old place. She smiled as she got out of the car and found the rusty front-door key under the flower pot. She couldn't wait to get a cup of tea in her hands and sit up on the balcony overlooking the golden sands and the rolling waves. She'd keep her coat on this time though. The air was cool, the sky a subtle grey. Getting the fire going was definitely going to be her first job. She knew how to light it now, thanks to Ed. Dumping her bags in the hall, she went straight back out to the lean-to at the side of the house and stocked up the logs and kindling next to the hearth in the lounge. She'd brought some old copies of the *Herald* that had been lying about at the office, a box of firelighters, matches (the long ones) – the works. She was armed and ready, tackling the house on its own terms.

Fire lit and warming the house through, she was soon sitting on the old deckchair, with her mug of tea in hand, overlooking the stubbly-grass garden where Ed had lit storm candles and tea-lights, made her langoustines and luscious meringues. Neither of them had known quite what a storm they were heading into. Knowing the truth of his situation, she didn't regret their one romantic night – even if that was the only one she would ever know with him. She could only wish him well. She wondered if he would ever find happiness again, or at least some calm in his ocean of grief. She dearly hoped so.

She sat watching the dog walkers, the terns. There were no children playing in the stream today, too chilly for that, and of course they'd all be at school anyhow. The summer holidays were long gone.

She'd go and put all the groceries she'd brought with her away in a minute, and then go for a walk. The light would soon fade this time of year. The days were so much shorter – it would be dark of an evening. She'd get cosy with a book and a mug of hot chocolate later. Hah, she grinned at herself – she was sounding like a ninety-year-old! Outside on the balcony the chair was comfy, and though the air was cool, the sun was directly in her face; she closed her eyes for a second or two.

Awaking with a start, fuzzy-headed at first, she took in where she was – the sea view, the cool air. Gosh, she must have been tired – over half an hour had passed. The activity of the move, her charity run, the worry of the scare must be catching up on her.

The light would soon be beginning to fade; four o'clock. If she got going, she'd still have time to reach the village and get back before dark. A walk would be nice; she'd pop in and see Lynda at the deli for a quick hello, buy some fresh bread if there was any left, and a nice wedge of local cheese. She popped her trainers on and set off. The rhythm of her stroll took over and she relaxed into the walk. The sand slowed her down, but it was also soothing. A couple were walking towards her in the opposite direction with a black Labrador that reminded her of Bess. Ed. She hoped he was okay, that he was finding some way through his devastated life. How could fate be that cruel? Life was beautiful, yes, but it could be harsh sometimes too. She would have loved to be able to wrap her arms around him, tell him that somehow everything would be all right. But it wouldn't, would it?

'Hey, honey, lovely to see you. How are you?'

'Hi, Lynda, I'm really well – thank you. It's so good to be back. I've missed my rickety cottage by the sea.'

'Hah, you'll be the only one misses that place! You look great, by the way. The hair . . .' She studied her with a smile.

'It's grown a bit.' It was now in a long wavy bob of chestnut brown. She felt a little more like her old self, though her hair had been far straighter pre-chemo.

'Yeah, that's it. Suits you. How long are you up for?'

'Just the weekend, unfortunately. I've just about used up all my annual leave.'

'Ah well, a quick recharge of the batteries, hey. What can I do for you, petal? Or are you just in for a quick chat?'

'Both a chat *and* some of your gorgeous food. I'd love some of that scrummy local cheese. Do you have any of the blue one from Doddington Dairy? That was great.'

'I do indeed.'

'And any bread?' She looked hopefully along the shelves.

'Sorry, petal, too late in the day. It all went by lunch-time, except for these two wholemeal rolls. But I'll put a loaf by for you tomorrow, if you like. Any preference? Plain, wholemeal, rosemary and sea-salt bloomer? Or I'm doing a nice Red Leicester and caramelized onion at the moment?'

'I'll go for the caramelized onion one – sounds great.'

'And for now, I do have some lovely black olive crostini – they'll go nicely with the cheese.'

'Okay, I'll take a pack of those too, with a wedge of the blue.'

'And how's life been back down in Newcastle?'

'Pretty good. I'm getting back into it all at work. Oh, and I've moved house, so it's been all go.'

'You have been busy.'

'I had a bit of a health scare, too, but it's all fine now, thank goodness.' Claire found she didn't mind talking about it now that it was good news.

'Well, that's good to hear.'

'And how's life in Bamburgh?'

'Much the same as ever here. I've had a busy spell here in the shop in the past couple of weeks. September's been a good month. The weather held, so we saw a lot of re-tired couples – ramblers and so on. I like all the different people coming in, and I've got to know the regulars over the years. Nice to have a chat, catch up with everyone. Some people have been coming back year on year for about fifteen years, since I first started this place. It certainly makes the day pass quicker.'

'Yeah, that must be good.'

'I haven't seen much of your neighbour lately.'

Claire's ears pricked up as her heart did a skip. 'Oh.'

'You know, that fella in the cottages, the good-looking one.'

Claire knew all too well who she meant. Despite everything, Ed was never far from her thoughts. She nodded.

'Yes, that Scottish guy. He used to pop in most week-ends. Not been about for ages.'

Claire felt her throat tighten. How could she even begin to explain what had happened between them? She could barely get her head round it herself. And she knew that she wanted to preserve his privacy; she didn't want his dreadful, sad story to become part of the village gossip. He needed to come here to escape. This was his bolt-hole, she was sure.

'Oh well, I'm sure he'll be back at some point.' Claire tried to keep the conversation light, noncommittal. Like she didn't really know him very well. Like she'd not been in his bed, or held him when he cried.

'Ah, well I thought he might have had a bit of a soft spot for you. Came in asking after you, that last time you stayed. Which seemed unusual as he never stops long enough to chat normally. He was asking if I knew where you lived, or if I had a contact number.'

'Oh, right.' That must have been when he was trying to find her. She didn't want to start going into the story of his visit to her office and why. Her provisions were ready and an elderly lady came in, so Claire took the chance and said a breezy goodbye. 'See you tomorrow when I come to pick up my bread. Take care, Lynda.'

'Lovely to see you again, petal. See you tomorrow.'

* * *

Back at the cottage, Claire popped the kettle on, made a mug of strong tea and sat back out on the bedroom balcony to watch the sun fade in the sky. The peace of the beach, the sea and the sky, diffused through her. She was so glad she'd come. It pulled her to it, this place; it felt like home. Her Jesmond flat hadn't quite reached that status yet. She wrapped a fleece top round her shoulders to keep off the early evening chill, and let the hot mug warm her hands.

Another Labrador was chasing a ball with its owners away down the beach, and reminded her of Bess, of Ed, all over again. She couldn't shake him from her mind. What a hard hand he'd been dealt. How *did* you ever get over something like that? Was it even possible? Or did you just endure a shell of an existence and live through hollow days? She so wished she could go and put her arms around him, hold him close to her, tell him that she'd help him, love him . . . Oh shit, where had that thought come from? Did she *love* him? A little voice in her head acknowledged her heart. Oh bugger. Bad, bad timing. Far too many complications.

She went inside and fetched her latest read from the bedside table. She'd take her mind off it all by drifting into someone else's world, a nice easy romance. She settled into the velour sofa in the living room and started reading. Yes, that was better. Enjoy the magic of the melting colours of dusk, she told herself as she looked out at the now cloudless azure sky fading into gold, orange and purple. Enjoy the magic of a storybook world, where dreams come true and love is easy.

Supper was a medley of cheese, pâté and crostini with some salad she had brought with her, and a small glass of red wine. It was a tad chilly, so she added a couple more logs to the fire in the lounge. She was glad she was armed and ready with a portable electric heater to warm her bedroom before going to sleep. She had the measure of this house now. Old Mr H would probably have a fit at the next electric bill, but as utilities were included and she'd paid a decent amount this time, having frozen her butt off in the summer months, she decided to make the most of it. He'd earnt enough from her already.

After supper, she treated herself to some dark-chocolate brownies from her local baker on Gosforth high street and enjoyed the cocoa-meltiness with a cup of tea whilst she sat in her cosy onesie listening to some chill-out music on her iPod, curling up on the lumpy sofa, which she'd evened out by bringing her duvet downstairs to lay over it. The fire crackled and popped, mesmerizing her with its dancing glow.

All in all, life was pretty good. She was so relieved about that bastard lump. She was safe for now, at least, though she felt for those poor souls who were having to face it right now. But that was all we have – the now.

This moment, whether it was magic or ghastly. Whether you were apparently healthy or not, you never knew what the next day might bring. Every single moment was precious.

She could hear the soft lull of the sea outside, saw the crescent of the moon over the bay. And here she was, all cosy, tucked up in her cottage by the sea. She'd made the right decision to come back here. Some places suited your soul.

30

The waggy-tailed welcome of a dog
                    Amie, Newcastle-upon-Tyne

Cradling her cup of tea at seven-fifteen the next morning, Claire was struck by what looked like a little pile of clothes and a pair of trainers on the beach. She'd had an early night, had vaguely heard a car late on, but thought it must have been out on the main road. *Could it be?* She dashed to the spare bedroom that overlooked the driveway, and yes, there was the black 4x4. Her heart did a little somersault, but then she wondered how he would have felt seeing her vehicle in the driveway? Would her being here spoil his weekend?

She zoomed back to her viewpoint on the balcony, and yes, there out to sea, was a black shape arcing through the water, looking a bit like a seal if she hadn't known better. Should she stay out here? Watch from a distance?

A warm glow filled her with the memory of that very first time. When she'd first watched his beautiful body. But everything had changed since then. She knew that body now. Oh boy, did she know that body. She also knew his past, his hurts . . .

She decided to keep a low profile, but couldn't quite tear herself away from the balcony. It would only be a fleeting glance, a lovely silhouette of his physique, and then she'd go in and make herself scarce, keep out of his way. Her reasons for coming had not included Ed, she told herself. To be honest, it would have been easier if he hadn't come. She didn't want him to think she was chasing him or trying to push herself back into his life. Whatever she felt for him deep down, she understood his distance, his grief, and respected it.

The dark shape was swimming for shore now. She held her breath. And then he was coming out of the shallow waves, tall, broad shoulders, slim hips and waist . . . eek. She caught a sexy glimpse of peachy buttock as he turned to pull on his shorts. His top, then his trainers went on, and he started to jog back up the beach, staring right at her cottage. Time to make a hasty retreat. She backed through the open door into her bedroom wistfully.

Well, that was some start to the morning. *So*, Ed was here . . .

* * *

She'd packed a little rucksack with the two rolls from the deli filled with cheese, a cereal bar and a couple of apples.

She decided to walk up the coast as far as Budle Bay, probably about three miles away. The forecast didn't look too great for tomorrow, so today, with just a few puffy clouds in an autumn-blue sky and a mild breeze, seemed the better day to take a long walk. Her energy levels had increased again in the past couple of weeks, thank goodness. She must have just been at a low with that infection that had affected her glands. The bump in her groin had disappeared now, thankfully. She'd head off, get out of Ed's space and do her own thing. Perfect.

There was no rush, no timescale, no deadline, no one to please but herself. It came with a great sense of freedom. On days like this, it was a joy to breathe in fresh salty air, to hear a gull's cry, the laughter of children, watch lovers holding hands as they wandered the sands. A couple of turns of the bay and there was Bamburgh Castle, as grand and stunning as ever. Ochre sands stretched before her beside a gunmetal sea, the sandstone-pink castle rising majestically against a cool azure sky.

She walked on past the castle today, to the far end of the beach where the rocks started. You could climb them and follow a track around the headland at the base of the golf course, she'd found out, where there was an old whitewashed coastguards' building. She skirted the base of the grassy dunes and found herself on a wide open bay with a stunning view across the estuary to Holy Island. She sat a while, eating an apple and a bread roll, thoughts of Ed still drifting through her mind. Being so near him was hard, harder than she'd imagined. How she wished things could have been different for them.

She'd called in to the village on her way back and collected her bread order from Lynda, stopping for a quick catch up. Being a Saturday, the village was busy with cars and people. There was a buzz of activity that had pulled her back to real life after her quiet stroll along the shore, where most of the time it had been just her.

Now she was walking back down the beach towards the cottages. She took her time – there was nothing to rush for. She stopped to eat another apple, perched on a rock, then set off again, turning the corner to her bay. A hundred metres or so from the cottages, a black Labrador came bounding up to her. She recognized this one.

'Bess. Hey, girl. How are you?'

She was bouncing around Claire, tail wagging. She must remember her. As Claire continued walking, she spotted the dog's owner, looking decidedly less pleased to see her. He was standing at the end of his cottage garden, arms folded. Oops. Awkward moment ahoy.

'Hi,' she said to break the ice.

'Hi.' His voice was tense. He had a stern look across his brow.

So maybe he wasn't too pleased to see her here, but it was a free country. She could rent the cottage next door if she wanted. And she didn't have to be a bother to him. But she felt she ought to explain. 'I missed it here, the sea . . .' She nearly said 'everything', but that might include him, so she left it unspoken.

'Yeah.' He unfolded his arms. Bess was back around his legs. 'It kind of gets you that way.' His voice had softened.

'I'm sorry. I would have stayed somewhere else if I could have afforded it.' She didn't know why she felt she had to justify staying here.

'It's okay. It's fine. Bess is pleased to see you, anyhow.' He didn't add that he was.

Agh, this was so awkward. She'd invaded his private space, his place to get away. She wished she hadn't come now. Her being here obviously affected him more than she'd thought it might. It was so hard to stand here and be polite and keep a distance. Next time she'd save up and get a caravan down the coast, or stay at a little B&B. But somehow that seemed too sad – not to be here in her cottage by the sea.

Ed watched her. He was trying to smile, but she couldn't work out what he was thinking. He just stood there, looking so uncomfortable in the garden where he'd set out candles for her, where he'd made his gorgeous barbeque, talked and laughed with her. She wondered what had been on his mind back then? Was he thinking of his wife all evening, feeling guilty? Was it the first time he'd been with anyone since her death? Did it feel like a betrayal? Or something he had to get through? Tick the box – he'd done it, had sex with someone else. Got it over with.

'Right, well,' she said, trying to lift her voice with a breeziness she really wasn't feeling. 'I'd better be getting on in. I've walked six miles – I'm feeling a bit tired now.' Actually a hot bath was calling.

'Okay.' You could see he felt let off the hook. 'See you, then.'

'Bye, Bess.' The dog had nipped back to her side again, sharing allegiance. She ruffled the soft, silky black fur of her head. Claire lifted her gaze to Ed's. 'See you.' Not tomorrow, not later. She gave a gentle smile. Felt a weight inside. Wanted to lift all their hurts like a huge bunch of balloons and throw them up into the sky, watch them drift away so they could start afresh. Simple. Just Ed and Claire, two people who had no past, no hurts. Just two people.

She turned to walk away, then paused, looking over her shoulder. 'Thanks . . .'

His brow furrowed. 'What for?'

'For coming to explain that day. For finding me.' She knew in her heart she had to at least say that much. Understanding what had happened that night had meant a lot.

'No worries.' He gave a nod and a hint of a smile. 'Enjoy your break.'

'Thank you.'

And she was determined to.

After her bath, she decided to head to Seahouses for a supper of fish and chips. She sat in a little café with a plate of salt-and-vinegared delights. Crispy-battered, soft, flaky white fish, freshly made chips. She'd taken her book in case she felt awkward on her own, but was quite content watching a family tuck in opposite and listening to their friendly banter, and then an old couple came in and sat on the table beside her. They were evidently enjoying themselves too, chatting away. When they got up to leave, the elderly gentleman brought the lady's coat from the stand, held the door for her, and then took her hand as they walked away along the pavement. They must have been husband and wife, Claire mused – married for many years. They must have held hands so many times. It made her smile.

Later on, back at the cottage, she sank into a second bath of scented bubbles. The hot water tank, by some miracle, hadn't failed her this time, providing her with a second full and hot tubful. She lay looking at her scar, which she realized didn't frighten her any more. The reconstruction had given her boob a nice shape that pretty much matched the other side. True, the lack of a nipple appeared somewhat odd, as did the long scar, but she'd grown used to it. She didn't want to be messed about with any more, didn't want any more unnecessary ops, though she'd heard of new nipples being made from skin elsewhere on your body, somehow twisted into shape, or tattooed on – the wonders of technology. But for now that wasn't for her.

After the bath, she sat reading her book, listening to music. She wandered up the drive to get some signal to text her mum and Sal to let them know she was fine and enjoying her break. She'd been lucky with the weather today. The wet stuff was coming in tomorrow by the sounds of it – she'd caught a forecast on the radio earlier. But that would give her the chance to write up her next article for the *Herald* and a quick 'Magic Moments' blog ready for next week. The column was still doing well on the website, though it was no longer in the main printed paper, and she was still getting regular feedback. She remembered the list she'd jotted down back in June. She'd been using it as a bookmark since – she slid it out from the pages of her latest novel and held it in her hand. All those moments she'd longed for, many of which she'd now achieved:

A sea view and sunshine on her face.

Time with her family – her sister and the boys, Mum. She felt even closer to them all now.

Tea and cake with friends – yes, with Andrea in Café 9, and several times since.

Hearing the sound of children's laughter – many times, and it always made her smile.

A hot, deep bubbly bath – oh, yes, lots of those.

What else had she written? Ah yes, losing yourself in a great book. (This afternoon and before!) That was easy.

A hug – several, including a surprise one from Dragon Julia at work. And the ones from Ed had been pretty damned special. She so hoped he'd be okay. Her heart gave a little tug.

A chilled glass of wine on a summer's day. Yes, she remembered sitting chatting with Lynda out the back there, overlooking the beach, white wine and friendship, a perfect combination.

The smell and taste of freshly baked bread – well, a whole new delicious hobby had grown from that one.

A small deed to help someone else – they'd done the crazily muddy Race for Life, which would hopefully help lots of people, and she'd helped that teenager, Reece, with his own charity publicity. She'd been very happy recently to hear that he was now in remission. And she would keep looking out for others, finding ways to help if she could.

And, she wouldn't forget to keep enjoying the simple things in life, to be grateful for every day, every moment she had, and to live them one magic moment at a time.

Her column had grown and all those other lovely magic moments sent in by her readers filled her thoughts too – special places, a favourite walk, meeting a new grandchild for the first time. She was proud of her column. And she *would* make every day count. Winter was on its way, autumn already here, but she could still find calm, feel the sun on her face, wrap herself up and go for a walk, enjoy the log fire, a mug of soup, a hot chocolate piled with cream and marshmallows. In fact, she could whizz up some soup for lunch tomorrow before heading back – leek and potato was calling. Served with the rest of Lynda's deli bread – scrummy. Then, after she got back to Newcastle, where her flat was starting to feel more like home, it would be the Christmas season soon enough – woolly jumpers, giftwrap and bows, cinnamon scents, gaudy lights in the city centre, crowded shops. Life rolled on.

She felt tired this evening; the walk really had taken it out of her a bit. But it was a nice tired, an exercise-type tired. She went up to bed with a cup of camomile tea beside her, and couldn't help but think about the man next door. And yes, although it had been a little awkward with Ed earlier, it was kind of nice knowing he was just there. She sent him a mental hug, whispered 'Night, Ed', then drifted into a restful sleep.

She thought she was dreaming at first. The sound of barking and barking, with a whiny pitch that raised the hairs on the back of her neck. She bolted up in bed, startled. It didn't seem that far away. She registered the grey early-morning light at the window, got up, shoved on her dressing gown and ran out on to the balcony with wobbly legs that were trying to acclimatize to the sudden start.

The sound was coming from next door. Bess, it had to be Bess. But where was Ed? The dog didn't normally bark, she'd only ever heard a pleasant 'ruff' in greeting. She shoved on her slippers and dashed down the stairs, running out across the drive. The barking was frantic, getting louder as she neared Ed's house. She was halfway across the drive when she noticed the weather – the winds had really picked up. One of Ed's plant pots had toppled, leaving a small shrub strewn on its side. It began to spit with rain.

Claire got to the door of the other cottage. Heard the scrabbling of claws against the inner wood. It wasn't locked. She poked her head in, shouting 'Ed? Ed?', to be blasted by a powerful black lurch of fur and legs bounding past her for the beach. The beach. Claire turned – the waves were pounding the shoreline. Her soul chilled. *Clothes.* Dammit, she hadn't thought to look out from her balcony. Were there clothes on the beach? Bess was running straight for a little mound of something further away on the sands. Oh fuck.

What time was it? How long had she slept? She glanced at her watch. Eight fifteen. He usually went out just after dawn, and yesterday that was around seven o'clock. Oh God, if he'd been in the water that long . . .

And the water – this wasn't the usual waves, the gentle surf. This sea was mean and dark and menacing. She felt sick.

She ran out of his house, up the dunes. She might see better from there. Nothing, nothing, bloody nothing, just the boil of surf – even the sea birds had disappeared. They knew better than to be out on a day like this. Why the hell had he even thought of going swimming? Was he really out there? Or was the mound just something washed in on the tides, an old coat or blanket or something? But Bess's reaction . . .

She'd been wasting precious seconds. She had to phone for help, right now. Get the coastguard or whoever out. Why the fuck hadn't she thought of bringing her phone with her?

Bess ran up to her, circling her. 'It's okay, Bess. I'll get some help.' Claire ran back to her cottage. Bess lurched off in the opposite direction back to the mound on the beach. It had to be his clothes. The dog kept looking to sea frantically, then jerking her glance to Claire, who was now distant. Still the constant barking. There was no one else around. No one mad enough to be out on a morning like this. No one to ask for help.

She ran inside, grabbed her mobile from where it was charging on the kitchen bench and ran back out. No signal as ever down by the cottages; she'd have to run back up the dunes. Her legs kept sinking in the soft sand, snagging on the roots of the spiky marram grass. *Hang in there, Ed.*

One bar of signal, shit. She stood still, keeping it pointed inland to the best spot. Dialled 999. The ring tone. Answer. Answer. Please.

'Hello, which service please?'

'Ah . . . coastguard, I think . . . and ambulance.'

'What's the nature of the problem?'

'A friend, he's in trouble, swimming . . . in the sea.'

'And where is your location, madam?'

'Bamburgh . . . umm . . . further down the beach . . . halfway to Seahouses?' *Why was she being so bloody vague? A landmark . . . something.* 'The cottages. There's two cottages. One's called Farne View.'

'Okay, thanks, that's great. And what's your name?'

'Claire. Claire Maxwell.'

'Okay, Claire, please stay on the line. Don't hang up.'

Claire prayed that her signal would hold out.

'I'm going to put you through to the coastguard.'

'So you say there's someone lost at sea? A swimmer?' A male voice took over. 'Let me just clarify your position and the last position this person was seen. You're at Bamburgh, yes?'

'Yes.'

'And when and where did you last see the person you believe is lost?'

'Yesterday . . . but he'd have gone swimming this morning. There's a pile of clothes on the beach. His dog's going crazy.'

She began to think she sounded a little crazy herself. Did the guy on the end of the line think so too? Was that all the evidence she had of Ed going missing? Jeez, what if Ed had just popped to the dunes for a call of nature or something? Was about to come sauntering out as she had the HM Coastguard scrambling. But she knew in her gut something was wrong, just like Bess did.

And worse, a horrible creeping thought seized her mind. What if he'd wanted to go missing? To just vanish at sea. Let it all end.

She pulled herself together. 'He would have gone swimming just after seven, I think. From the beach where I am now.'

'Okay, keep this line open. We may need it to help locate your position on the beach. I'll contact the lifeboat and rescue-helicopter service immediately.'

The line was open, but no one was talking. She stood fixed to the spot, not daring to move in case she lost signal. She scanned the tumult that was the sea. Still no sign. No arc of arm, dark length of body. It would be hard to tell in those waters anyhow. He was fit and healthy, she reminded herself. He knew that sea, swam every day he was here. He'd swum for county, he'd told her. In a swimming pool, you tit, she realized. *Stay strong, Ed.*

Bess appeared beside her, nuzzled her hand. She patted the dog's head absent-mindedly. 'Okay, girl.' Claire was soaked to the skin now, her towelling robe heavy with rain, weighing her down. Stood there dripping in a dressing gown in the dunes. Her ear pressed to her mobile, just in case. And all they could do was wait.

31

Make the most of every day, every moment

Seconds hung like hours. Please God, please let him be okay. Whatever shitty life he'd had so far, he deserved his second chance, his future. He deserved some happiness. Her face was wet with rain and tears. Bess was beating a steady track to and from the beach, via his clothes.

Suddenly, there was something there bobbing in the waves. A dark torso shape. It didn't look good, tossed about, directionless. Ah, shit, shit, no. Her world felt like it was falling apart. *No*. Should she run to it, forget about the mobile signal? But then she looked closer. Bess wasn't bothered by it, and Claire realized she was focusing on a log that must have been swept out, then brought back in on the rough seas.

The weather was dismal. Heavy drops of rain were

coming down on her now. He *must* have got into trouble, must still be out there. Maybe it had been fine early this morning, and it just came in all of a sudden. She'd seen herself how the rain clouds could gather on the horizon, then sheet forward in a solid mass. You could see it advancing over the sea, an inky-grey shimmering wall. What if he wasn't strong enough to keep afloat? What if, right now, the sea was pulling him down – too cold, too tired to fight any more.

'*Ed!*' his name bolted from her lips, shouted across the dunes, across the sea.

And still the rain, the wind, whipping up the waves.

A loud burr of an engine, the mechanical chopping of rotor blades, startled her. Right over her flew a yellow helicopter, stirring up the sands, shooting grit into her eyes, lifting her hair from its roots. Thank God. At least they were here, they were looking.

She waved frantically. She needed to let them know they were had the right place.

And then a voice, tinny on her phone, hardly audible for the whirr of the helicopter. It sounded like the man she had last spoken with. 'The air–sea helicopter has located you, Claire. There's also a lifeboat launched. They are searching thoroughly. Please stay on the line. Okay?'

'Yes. Yes, will do.' *Find him. Go find him.*

'And Claire, you're doing great, just try and stay calm. They're doing everything they can.'

'Thank you.' That line of communication warmed her for a second; the thread to humanity, compassion. Then it went quiet once more.

She watched the helicopter move out to sea, then turn to fly parallel with the coast, first north, then south, back towards her. She thought she could make out a boat coming into view from the right side of the bay. Bess was back near her side, fretful after the roar of the helicopter, the poor dog pacing in figures of eight.

Even if they did find him, what would they find?

She stopped herself thinking that way, just stood, watching, every nerve taut in her body.

There were two figures on the beach now below her, drawn no doubt by the drama of the search. Something newsworthy happening.

Time seemed to stand still as the helicopter circled, then went up and down again, parallel with the shoreline. Then it seemed to hover, and almost pause. Something had been thrown down, a line? Had they found something? Had they found him?

'Miss Maxwell . . . Claire?' The chap was shouting down the phone like he'd been trying before.

Something was happening out at sea. Someone coming out from the helicopter, on a winch or something.

'Yes . . . yes.'

'They've located him, madam.'

'Is he okay?'

'I'm sorry, I don't have that information as yet. But they have definitely located a man at sea.'

'Thank you.' She noticed that she was shaking all over.

He had said 'man' not 'body', surely that was good. *Wasn't it?*

'You may now close the line.'

'Uh, ah . . . wait . . . do you know where they'll be taking him?'

'The rescue helicopter usually goes to the RVI in Newcastle, madam. That's the Royal Victoria Infirmary.'

'Oh . . .'

'It's okay to hang up now, Claire.'

'Oh, okay, thank you.' She still felt stunned, dread paralysing her.

'You're welcome.' And the gentleman closed the line himself.

So she could leave the dunes. She went to the wet pile of clothes, *his* clothes. Bundled them up.

'Are you okay, pet? Can we help?' The couple who'd been watching approached her.

'Ah . . . it's okay. They've found him . . . There was a man at sea . . . they've found him.'

'You're drenched, lass, and cold, no doubt. We have a car just across the dunes at the roadside. Can we take you somewhere?'

'Thank you, but I'm from the cottages just here. I'll get back there now. Thank you.'

Bess followed her back to her house. The pile of Ed's clothes were soaking, so she placed them in the kitchen sink. Then realized how wet she was herself. She stripped off her own robe and pyjamas and shivered her way upstairs. She needed to get herself down to the RVI hospital. She needed to find out how he was. Would they let her in, answer her questions? She wasn't family. She wasn't even a girlfriend. But the devil was going to have to stop her. She showered and towel-dried quickly, pulled on some underwear, jeans and a jumper, ran downstairs and grabbed her coat, her phone, her keys. Bess looked at her dolefully.

'Come on then, girl – we're in this together, aren't we?' She opened the passenger door for the dog, and she settled in the foot-well.

She queued impatiently for the car park, hunted for a space, paid a fortune to park in the narrowest space ever. When did it get so expensive to be ill, or to visit someone who was ill? She remembered to leave the window of the car ajar for Bess, and made a mental note to buy a bottle of water to give to her later. She found the main reception. She hadn't a clue which ward he might have been taken to.

'Hi.' Claire tried her best smile. 'Has there been a man brought in by the coastguard helicopter, about an hour or so ago? Ed.'

'I'll have to check. We have a lot of patients.' She raised

an eyebrow. 'Are you a relative?' The receptionist's well-plucked eyebrow arched further up. Claire was never good at lying, the receptionist had probably got her measure. But Claire hadn't driven all the way down here with a damp, distressed dog for nothing.

'Yes,' she lied. 'Yes, I'm his sister.'

'Okay, take a seat for a minute. I'll see what I can find out for you.'

'Thank you.'

The receptionist managed a polite yet sceptical smile.

Ten minutes later, Claire was given directions to the men's general ward. Thank God! Surely they wouldn't send her up to a ward if he hadn't made it? He must be okay – at least alive – and anything else they would deal with. She nearly hugged the receptionist.

A kind-looking young nurse met her at the entrance doors. 'You're here for Edward Baxter?'

'Yes . . . that's it.' She stalled for a second, realizing that she hadn't even know his surname. She hoped there wasn't more than one chap named Ed on the ward whose sister she was meant to be. This could be interesting.

She followed the nurse through to a cubicle, and she pushed the privacy curtain aside, announcing, 'Edward, your sister's here.'

He sat up, a quizzical look crossing his face, until Claire appeared at the nurse's side with a hopeful smile.

'Ah, yes . . . yes, of course. Hi, Claire.' He maintained the pretence. His voice sounded slow, like it was hard to find words.

He looked shattered, his face grey.

'How are you?' She wanted to lean across, grasp him in her arms, never let go. To check that he really was all right. All that churning fear pent up inside her from waiting for him on the beach, for the search to get underway, suddenly surfaced in tears. She tried to swipe them away with the back of her hand, which was trembling.

She took a seat on the grey plastic chair beside the bed. 'Oh, I was so worried. Thank God you're okay. What happened, Ed?'

He looked so pale in that hospital bed – a washed-out version of himself.

She feared that he had wanted to do it. Went out in that rough sea on purpose. She reached for his hand, which lay limply above the white, crisp covers.

He took a slow breath. 'How did you know? The helicopter . . . was it you that raised the alarm?'

She nodded, afraid it might have been the wrong thing for him. No, it could *never* have been the wrong thing, she reassured herself.

'Yes, it was me. Well, I can't take all the credit, to be fair. There's a very damp, stressed-out dog in my car in the car park right now, bless her.'

'Bess . . .'

'Yep, she was going crazy, shut up in your house. Like a mad thing. Woke me up . . . I'm so glad she woke me up.' And the tears were there, unstoppable this time. Relief at seeing him here, so close. Her eyes fogged up and she was sure there was snot coming out of her nose. She scrabbled for a tissue from the bedside table. 'Thank God for Bess.'

'And I nearly didn't bring her this time.' He closed his eyes for a couple of seconds, muttering, 'Ah, Bess.'

He still hadn't said why on earth he was swimming in a rough sea in October.

'Sorry.' He was rattled with a cough, struggled to open his eyelids again. 'They said I swallowed a load of water.'

Her hand was still over his. 'So what happened?' Her voice was gentle.

'It seemed okay, the sea, at first. Went out just after dawn, like I usually do. I was just going to swim for fifteen minutes or so. The sea gets that bit colder at this time of year . . .' He paused. 'It changed, just like that. Wind blew up. Black clouds. It was so choppy out there. I wasn't that far out really, but there was a current bloody pulling me the wrong way. It got harder and harder to swim against . . . I got so tired. Swimming all the time but never getting nearer to shore.'

'Oh, Ed.' She gave his hand a squeeze.

'Then it was so cold, my legs froze up. Weren't working

properly. All I could do was tread water, and even that was hard enough.'

He lay back on his pillows for a while, as if it was tough remembering, putting himself back there.

'It's okay. Don't talk too much . . . Just get some rest, my love.' The term of endearment slipped out before she could stop herself, but it felt so natural. Their eyes locked for a second. She smiled softly. But then she felt awkward, wondered what she was really doing here.

'Look, I just needed to see you were all right. I'd better go now. You might have some real family here in a minute.' *Ah, shit, she remembered his wife, his son – his real family – were gone.* 'Parents and that,' she added hastily. *Didn't he mention a brother?* 'I ought to go check on Bess,' she added. 'Get her some water and food. Check she's warm enough.'

'Don't go just yet . . . Stay a while. *Please.*' He looked exhausted, fragile, lonely. Began to drift off to sleep.

So she stayed, sitting quietly whilst he slept. She listened to the sounds of the hospital around her – the squishy-squeak of nurses' shoes, low chatter, a telephone ringing. Ed's laboured breathing. She studied his face, his eyelashes, which were long and thick. His hair was curled, matted from the salt of the sea. She could smell the saltiness on him; a faint white crust had formed around his jawbone. To think he might have drowned out there. She wasn't sure how her world would have been after that.

Claire began to feel tired too. The emotions of the day were catching up with her. She sat with her head in her hands, thinking for a while, her mind too busy to sleep. There was a swish of the curtain. The nurse from earlier popped her head in.

'Is he okay?' Claire spoke softly, not wanting to disturb him. 'Is he going to be all right?'

'Yes. We're keeping him in for observation. He was hypothermic when he came in and had swallowed rather a lot of sea water. But yes, he should be fine.'

Maybe in body, after a good rest, but with everything else . . . Claire knew that he was still a broken man. She sighed to herself as she gave a friendly smile to the nurse, who had no idea of his past, of all he'd had to cope with. She reluctantly let go of Ed's hand and scraped her chair back from the bed to let the nurse get on with her work. Ed came to as the lady lifted his arm to check his pulse. 'You're doing well, Ed. We'll have you shipshape in no time.' As she turned to leave, she added for Claire's benefit, 'He's doing okay.'

'Can I get you some water or anything?' Claire asked him.

'Yes, that would be good. Seeing as I've drunk half an ocean, I'm surprisingly dry.' He gave a wry smile.

She poured him a flimsy plastic cupful from a jug of water set on the bedside table. He sipped through lips that looked dry, and were beginning to crack.

'Thanks.'

'You're welcome.'

'For coming down here . . . everything. And thanks for staying. Did I sleep?'

'Yep, snoring and everything.'

'Really?'

She shook her head, 'no', laughing.

He suddenly looked serious, 'Thank you . . . for raising the alarm.'

'Thank God I did. And thank God for Bess.'

'It had started off as a normal swim.' He was trying to explain once more. 'Then, when I got into trouble, started getting dragged out, at first I thought it was maybe for the best. You know . . . Maybe that would be the easiest thing, just to let myself go. I could slide into oblivion. Join them.'

Tears were in her eyes. There was a mistiness in his too. 'I couldn't, Claire. I just wanted to live . . . I *so* wanted to live . . . Battling every fucking wave. There have been nights, so many nights, when I would have settled for that. For that oblivion. And then when I was faced with it, I wasn't ready. What a fucker of a way to go. Sod's law that when you *really* don't want that any more, it should happen.' He seemed tired again. His voice softer. 'I needed to live.'

Claire moved towards him and put her arms around his shoulders. Her head resting lightly against his chest, she held him like she'd been wanting to hold him for weeks, relief and love flooding her core.

He took a long, slow sigh, which she felt through his chest, then brushed her head with the lightest of kisses.

'Survival. That's the instinct to survive, Ed,' she said. She knew that all too well.

'I don't want to just survive any more.' He shifted up a bit in the bed so she had to raise her head to look at him. 'I want to live, Claire. Really live.'

It was how she had felt, facing cancer, seeing it all about to be taken away from her. You wanted to make the most of every day, every moment.

'To live, yes.' She understood.

They held each other, arms wrapped tight, until his breathing began to soften and he dozed off once more. He seemed peaceful. Claire pulled gently away and placed a tender kiss on his brow.

He looked like he was going to sleep for a while, so she popped out to the car to check on Bess, who seemed a little shivery but okay. She quickly nipped to the town centre to find a pet shop, to get a lead, two bowls – one for water (she'd had trouble trying to get the dog to lick from the tiny plastic cup she'd sneaked from the ward), the other for food, which she bought, and a dog blanket. She tucked Bess in after giving her a bit of a walk, a snack and a drink, and left her with a bowl of water. 'He's okay, Bess. You'll see him soon, promise.' She received a wag of the tail, which flicked the blanket loose. She tucked it back round. 'Got to go. Hopefully I won't be too long.'

Back on the ward, Claire couldn't bring herself to leave Ed, to drive away, until she knew he was really all right. And then he'd need a lift, wouldn't he? No one seemed in a hurry to push her out, though she realized visiting time had officially finished, so she kept a low profile, chatting quietly when he woke and letting him sleep in between times. He needed to regain his strength.

She went out to the car to check Bess once more, and came back to find that the doctors had been round and given him the all clear. Ed was trying to dress himself in chino trousers that were too short, a huge T-shirt and a well-worn grey fleece. He looked like a practising tramp.

'Ed, what's going on?'

'Great news. I can go.'

'Well, great, but . . . the clothes. Really?'

'From lost property. I can't go out as I came in.'

She screwed up her face, trying to understand.

'Naked as the day I was born,' he explained.

Oh God, yes – the naked bloody swimming. 'I knew all that nude swimming couldn't be good for you.'

'You've seen me?'

'Ah-hum.' A cheeky grin fluttered across her lips.

'How often?' He furrowed his brows.

'Quite often. I used to quite look forward to it.'

'Jeez, you peeping Tom, you.'

'Good view from the upper balcony,' she quipped. After all the tension, it was good to joke.

'Well it won't happen again. I can assure you.'

'Spoilsport.'

'Oh Christ, I hope the news hasn't got hold of it. Can you imagine the headlines? "Naked Man Rescued at Sea".'

'Hmm, might just have to make a call to the *Herald* office.'

'You dare!'

It was wonderful seeing him smile again.

'Well, come on. If you really do have to go out dressed like that, we'd better get you into the car as quickly as possible. And I know someone who's going to be *very* pleased to see you.'

They thanked the nurses on the ward and set off. Ed walking slowly, as though finding his feet on solid ground.

Bess went mad in the car as he approached, so excited to be reunited with her beloved master and friend, and plastered him with big greedy licks as soon as the door was opened.

'Okay, time to settle down, girl.' He patted her to calm her. 'So let's hit the road, Claire. I'm ready for home.'

And by 'home' she knew he meant the little cottages by the sea.

32

*I love the feel of my partner's skin, knowing that with
him next to me I can get through anything*

                                    Heidi, Southampton

It was pitch-dark, nearly eight p.m., by the time they
turned into the gravel driveway. She led him into his
house, offering her arm as support. He was still a little
weak. Then she fed Bess and let her out into the back
garden whilst Ed sat in the lounge.

'Can I get you something to eat? A cup of tea? A cold
beer, if you have any?'

'I'm still feeling a little chilled. Maybe something warm.
I might have some Bovril, hot in a mug. Yeah, I could fancy
something like that. There's a jar in the kitchen. Thanks.'

She busied herself, feeling comfortable in his house,
glad that he was letting her take care of him, for now

at least. In the back of her mind she couldn't help wondering what next. When would it be polite to head back across the drive? She *did not* want to head back across the drive.

Later, by the warmth of an open fire, with the hope of tomorrow, he asked her to stay. She sensed this wasn't going to be a night of passion. He seemed too shattered, too fragile. But they both needed to be together.

She followed him up to the room where they'd stayed before. The covers were cold as she slipped in next to him, naked. No need to hide. She was no longer afraid of her scar. She nestled up beside him with a sigh. He was here and gorgeous, and oh so alive. She slipped her arm around him as he lay on his side, with his back to her for now.

Soon his breathing slowed to a peaceful rhythm, and he fell asleep with her close around him. As she lay there, she could hear the rush and pull of the waves outside, calmer now. A sea that demanded respect and fear, yet held beauty and awe in its changeability. The fundamental power of water. A patch of ice on the road. How scary and arbitrary the world could be. Whoa – the extreme events of the day were still buzzing through her mind. But she snuggled against this man beside her, felt so very happy to be here, safe, with him.

She awoke the next morning, taking in the bedroom

and the gorgeous man next to her. The photo of his wife and child was there on his bedside table. And that was fine. That was good. They would always be a part of his life. A part of him. And they deserved to be.

Then she was struck by the realization that it was Monday morning. She glanced at her watch. She was due at work in less than an hour, in Newcastle. Ah, shite! She flew out of bed.

'Ed, I have to go. I have to work.' But as she was saying it and pulling on her jeans, every bone in her body ached to stay with him.

'Do you have to? Stay with me, please. Just for today at least. We've got some catching-up to do.' The look in his eye made her melt, then ignite.

All she wanted to do was to take her jeans right back off and jump back into bed with him. She felt torn inside at the thought of leaving him.

He stood up from the bed, and, in his full naked gorgeousness, made his way to her. Her top half was still bare. He smiled at her, took her in his arms – he was all warm and bed-cosy. He kissed her tenderly on the lips, oh-so-deeply. She felt his tongue on hers. His hardness, oh-so-sexy, at her hip. Oh, Jeez. His hands in her hair, on her back, tracing her breasts.

Don't go to work. Do not go to work today. He's bloody amazing. He wants to live. He wants you, Claire Maxwell. You, with your scars and your wonky breast.

She wanted him too. Body, mind, soul; his past and his future.

She pulled off her jeans and they jumped right back into bed, bouncing and laughing, arms tight around each other, kissing each other. With the promise of so much more to come.

'Okay, I'm staying,' she said, then kissed his earlobe. 'I'll ring in sick – for one day only, though.' Oh yes, another night to share. A day to be together after the dramas of yesterday. It felt so right.

'Come back at the weekend, then. You can stay here with me. Promise you'll come back?'

'I promise.' Nothing was going to stop her.

They had so much to do. So much to say. So much life to live. One day at a time. One magic moment at a time.

Epilogue

Eighteen months later

Light streamed over her face. Claire turned over, shifting to snuggle up against Ed; the bed strangely empty. She reached out, checking the space beside her.

Hmm. She peered out through half-opened eyes . . . he was definitely gone. There was just a telltale dint in the mattress, the covers pulled back over on his side. Ah, it was probably the naked early-morning swim. Despite being nearly drowned, in a wild October sea, he still hadn't kicked the habit. Though she'd made him promise not to venture out during the unpredictable winter months *ever* again. But it was April now, and a glorious spring day by the looks of it. Still, she'd better just check all was well. And of course it would be very nice to get a sneaky look at his sea-dripping torso. That gorgeous body still hadn't ceased to amaze her. It was all hers to explore now, and that always made her heart sing.

She got up, slipped on a silky robe, and wandered across to the window. The house seemed awfully quiet. Even Bess seemed to have disappeared for the moment. The dog would often sneak upstairs from her kitchen bed for an affectionate pat if she realized Claire was there. She stood at the window of Ed's bedroom overlooking the beach and the sea. There was no need to hire the cottage next door now. Claire still had her Newcastle flat, and Ed his place in Edinburgh, a beautiful old terrace in the Leith district. But this was the place that felt so much like home to Claire now.

She scanned the beach, spotted a dark clump on the sands not too far from the house, possibly his pile of clothes. But no, something was swishing behind it. Ah, Bess was out there, her tail wagging, sitting patiently watching for something. Oh Jeez no. A flutter of panic hit Claire's stomach. She felt instantly queasy.

But then something else caught her eye. Ed was on the beach, to-ing and fro-ing. He wasn't out swimming at all. He had something in his hand. She focused more carefully . . . a child's plastic spade. What the heck was he doing making sandcastles out there? They didn't even have her nephews staying with them. Curious now, she slipped on her flip-flops from beside the bed. This was going to need some investigating.

It was a beautiful morning. The pale-gold sun shimmered over a pewter-blue sea. The sky was now clearing to azure, yet there were still lingering brushstrokes of dawn peaches and pinks. Outside now, she remembered the wonderful night all those months ago when he'd set the garden up with those magical tea lights and cooked for her. Despite the confusion and heartache, there had been many beautiful days and nights together since. She still felt like pinching herself. And she was just so happy that Ed seemed to have relaxed, made a kind of peace with himself, found a place where he could smile and be himself once more. It would never be easy for him, she understood that. But she would be there to support him.

She looked over to the spot where they'd shared their first ever dance, barefoot on the sands, and there he was working away. She stood and watched him. Since she had made her way downstairs and outside, he had swapped his spade for what seemed to be a stick; yes, he was holding a piece of driftwood. The sandcastle shape was becoming clearer to her – a love heart or so it seemed, with lots of pebbles or something round the edge. Ed finished writing inside the heart with the stick, spotted her coming down to the gate that led to the beach, and stood back from his workmanship, giving her a huge grin.

What *was* he up to?

Bess came bounding up to her as she walked down onto the sands.

'Hey, Bess. What's up girl? And what *is* he doing building sandcastles at this time of the morning, hey?'

And then she paused, seeing what he had made . . . and what he'd written in the sand.

He was beaming across at her from the opposite side of his creation.

She saw a huge love heart – it must have been about seven feet across – built with a raised-sand border, and every few inches it was marked with a pebble, beneath which was placed a deep-red rose petal. There must have been at least forty pebble-roses.

Inside the heart he had written, 'Will You Marry Me?'

And there he was, with a big goofy grin on his face. How lovely it was to see that smile.

She ran up to him, shouting, '*Yes, yes and yes!*' Whooping as he picked her up and twirled her gently round him. He placed her down, and they kissed tenderly, so very meaningfully, silently promising the future to each other. For tomorrow and for ever love.

He finally pulled back, waving an arm out in a grand gesture towards the dunes, where she spotted a picnic blanket, two crystal flutes and an ice bucket, with what looked very like a bottle of bubbly all ready to go.

He put his arm protectively around her as they walked towards the champagne picnic.

'Now, just one glass for you, okay? Then I've got you some pink lemonade.'

'Okay, of course.'

And as Claire turned to him once more, leaning in for a hug and one more delicious kiss, the sunlight caught her profile, the mound of her tummy clear to see, raised and protective of its new life.

The most magic moment of them all.

Acknowledgements

Thank you to the lovely and inspirational Heidi Rehman for being so honest and open about her cancer journey. This book would not have been as special or insightful without her input.

For my family, Richard, Harry, Amie – thanks and love, always. Work hard, go for your dreams, and have lots of magic moments on the way.

My sister, Debbie, keep going, very best of luck and I'm looking forward to reading your books very soon. Mum and Dad, for the happiest childhood full of sandy beaches and books, and to all the wider family – thanks.

For my friends. What can I say . . . 'cheers' just about sums it up!

Thank you to Zoe Chamberlain and Ben O'Connell for their help with my journalism queries, and to my local doctor for allowing me to quiz him on his precious time off. If I have got anything slightly wrong, please remember this is a work of fiction and the mistakes are all my own.

An ongoing thank you to my friends in the Romantic Novelists' Association, for all their support and advice, with special thanks to Lorna Windham and Janet MacLeod Trotter.

Hannah Ferguson, my agent, thank you for believing in *My Summer of Magic Moments* from the start when I'd only written seven chapters. Your support has been wonderful.

My editors, the lovely Charlotte Brabbin, Charlotte Ledger, and Kimberley Young at HarperCollins. My magic moment was holding my first paperback copy of my debut novel *The Torn Up Marriage* after so many years of writing and trying to get published. What an amazing and very special feeling that was! Thanks to you and the whole HC team.

For my readers. A story is no good without someone to share it with. I hope you have enjoyed this book. Thanks for all the positive comments and feedback I have had for my novels so far – it makes being shut away with my laptop for months all worthwhile!

Finally, make the most of every single magic moment. Life is precious and beautiful, not always easy, but never to be wasted.

Caroline x

If you enjoyed this book, don't miss Caroline's other heartwarming novels.

Turn the page to read an extract from

The Cosy Teashop in the Castle

1

Ellie

Talk about flying by the seat of her pants. She hadn't really expected an interview. The ad had caught her eye in the *Journal*, and well, she'd been fed up, felt messed about by her twat of an ex, her bore of a job and fancied a change – of life, scenery, postcode, you name it.

So here she was, driving her little silver Corsa up the estate driveway that was lined by an avenue of gnarled-trunked, centuries-old trees. Her stomach did a backward flip as the castle came into view: blonde and grey sandstone walls with four layers of windows looking down on her – Claverham Castle. Did people really live in places like this? Did people really *work* in places like this? She felt like she'd driven onto the set of *Downton Abbey* or arrived in some fairytale.

The woman at the huge arch of an entrance did *not* look like someone from a fairytale, however; huddled in a huge fleece, dark jeans and wellington boots, and having a sneaky fag. She popped the offending item behind her back when she spotted Ellie pulling up on the gravel, but the wispy trail of smoke in the cool March air gave her away.

Okay, breathe, Ellie, breathe.

A quick check in the rear-view mirror. She hoped she still looked half-decent. She found her lippie and interview notes in her handbag, and tried to convince herself exactly why she was the right person to take on these tearooms as she popped on a slash of pale-pink gloss. It had all seemed such a good idea two weeks ago when she'd spotted the ad in the local press: 'Leasehold available for Claverham Castle Tea Rooms for the Summer Season.' A place to escape, and the chance to achieve the dream she'd harboured for years, running her own café, baking to her heart's content, and watching people grin as they tucked into fat slices of her chocolate fudge cake or strawberry-packed scones. A chance for change. So this was it! She *sooo* did not want to mess this up.

Her heart was banging away in her chest as she opened the car door. She stepped out with a pretence of confidence, aware of the woman still standing at the top of the steps. Sploosh! She felt a gloopiness beneath her feet, looked down. Shite! Her black suede stilettos were an inch-deep in mud and an attractive poo-like blob had landed on the right toe area. So much for first impressions.

She tried a subtle shoe-scrape on the grass verge, plastered a smile on her face and made her way to the castle entrance. A biting wind whipped at her honey-blonde hair, which she'd carefully put up in a topknot back at home in Newcastle-upon-Tyne this morning. Her black trouser-suit teamed with silky lime-green blouse was no match for the freezing cold. She hugged her arms around herself and headed for the door: a vast wood and iron creation – no doubt designed to keep out hairy, aggressive Border Reivers centuries ago.

The lady raised a cheery smile as Ellie approached, 'Hello, you must be here for the interview with Lord Henry.'

'Yes.' She reached out a trembling hand in greeting. 'Yes, it's Ellie Hall.'

'Nice to meet you, Ellie. I'm Deana.' The woman shook her hand warmly. She had a kind face, looked in her early fifties, with grey hair that hung in a grown-out bob. 'I'm Lord Henry's PA, well dogsbody really. S'cuse the attire, casual at the moment till the open season starts again. It gets bloody freezing here. Come on through, pet.'

Ellie relaxed a little; she seemed friendly. She followed Deana through the massive door to a stone inner courtyard, the sky a square of azure above. Wow – it was like some Disney set. And then into a circular stairwell that wound its way upwards – Sleeping Beauty or Rapunzel could well be at the top of that.

'There's no guests here at the moment,' Deana spoke with a gentle Northumbrian lilt. 'We close until Easter. So it's quiet. Come the spring, it'll be buzzing again. Well, kind of crawling,' she added with a wry grin, as though visitors were a necessity to be put up with rather than welcomed.

Ellie was offered a seat on a chair with a frayed red-velvet pad, positioned outside a closed door, which she imagined must be for Lord Henry's office. She could hear muffled voices from inside, formal tones.

Deana asked if she'd like a cup of coffee while she waited, said she wouldn't be long, and then disappeared back down the stairs. Ellie gathered her jacket and her nerve; it was bloody draughty there in the corridor.

Various artefacts stared down at her from the stone walls: black-and-white photos of the castle, the stuffed head of a weasel, or so she thought – ginger, hairy, teeth-bared, it looked pretty mean – a pistol in a glass case like something Dick Turpin might whip out: 'Stand and deliver'. This was *so* unlike her white-walled, MDF-desked insurance office, she felt she'd been shuttled back through time.

A scraping of chairs brought her out of her reverie.

Footsteps, the door opening, and out came a plump middle-aged lady, dressed smartly in a Christmas party jewelled jumper kind of way, thanking the gentleman for his time, adding she hoped she would be back soon. She smiled confidently (almost smugly) as she spotted Ellie sitting there. Lord Henry, for that's who she thought the man must be, was smiling too. 'Yes, lovely to meet with you again, Cynthia. I've been impressed with your work for us in the past, and we'll be in touch *very* shortly.' His tones were posh and plummy, the vowels clearly enunciated. It all seemed very amicable, and very *settled*. Ellie felt her heart sink. Was she just being thrown in the applicant mix as a token gesture?

Deana appeared at her side with a tray and coffee set out for three – perhaps she was staying for the interview. She ushered Ellie into the wood-panelled office.

Well, this was it. Ellie took a deep breath to calm her nerves. Now that she sensed she hadn't a cat in hell's chance of getting the tearoom lease, she suddenly realized how very much she wanted it. It was what she'd been dreaming of for years whilst stuck answering call-centre queries for insurance claims in a vast, impersonal office. She absolutely loved baking cakes for friends and for family birthdays. Her football party cake for her Cousin Jack had gone down a treat, and a champagne-bottle-shaped chocolate cake that she did for Gemma, her close friend at work, had led to a flurry of special requests. Oh yes, she'd offer to fetch the doughnuts and pastries for the office at morning break, standing in the queue at the baker's savouring the smells of fresh bread and cakes, wishing she could be the one working in the bakery instead.

Deana set the coffee tray down on a huge mahogany desk, which had a green-leather top. It looked big enough to play a game of snooker on. She smiled encouragingly across at Ellie, then left the room.

Lord Henry had a slightly worn, aristocratic appearance. He looked in his sixties and was dressed in beige corduroy trousers, a checked shirt and tweed waistcoat. He stood to greet her from the other side of the desk, offering a slim hand, shaking hers surprisingly firmly, 'Lord Henry Hogarth. Please, have a seat, Miss . . .' he paused, the words drifting uncomfortably.

Great, he didn't even know her name. 'Hall, Ellie Hall.'

'Well, Ellen, do make yourself comfortable.'

She was too nervous to correct him.

He poured out two coffees and passed her one, pouring in milk for her from a small white porcelain jug. She took a sip; it was rich and dark, definitely not instant, then she sat back in the chair, trying to give the air of cool, calm and collected. She was bricking it inside. She hoped her voice would work normally. As Lord Henry took his seat on the other side of the immense desk, she tried out the word 'Thanks'. Phew, at least she could speak, though she noted that her pitch was a little higher than normal.

'*So*, how long have you worked in the catering industry, Miss Hall?' He leaned towards her, rubbing his chin, his brown eyes scrutinising.

She froze, 'Ah . . . Well . . .' *About never.* Seat of the pants didn't even cover it. What the hell was she doing here? 'Yes,' she coughed into her coffee, 'Well, I've had a few years' experience.' *Baking at home, for friends, birthday cakes, cupcakes, Victoria sponges and the like, not to mention her 'choffee cake special'. And, yes, she made the tea and coffee regularly at the insurance office.* 'I *have* worked in a restaurant.' *Saturday-night waitressing as a teenager at the Funky Chicken Express down the road for a bit of extra cash.* 'And I have managed several staff.' Where *was* this coming from? She had trained another waitress in the art of wiping down tables. Though, she had filled in that weekend for her friend Kirsty at her sandwich bar, when Kirsty's boyfriend went AWOL.

Ellie thought that had planted the seed. She'd loved those two days prepping the food, making up tasty panini combinations – her brie, grape and cranberry had been a hit. She'd warmed to the idea of running her own company after that, spent hours daydreaming about it, something that involved food, baking ideally, being her own boss. That, and her nanna's inspiration, of course, lovely Nanna. Ellie remembered perching on a stool in her galley kitchen beating sponge-mix with a wooden spoon. Nanna had left her over a thousand pounds in her will – it would give Ellie the chance to cover this lease for a couple of months. Give her the time to try and make a go of it. She was sure Nanna would have supported her in this venture. Ellie would have loved to have turned up at her flat for a good chat about the tearooms and her ideas to make the business work, over a cup of strong tea and a slice of homemade lemon drizzle. But someone else was living there now, the world had moved on, and Nanna too. She really missed her.

Ellie managed to smile across at Lord Henry, realising she ought to say more but not quite sure what. How did you capture those dreams in words?

'And if you did take on the lease for the tearooms, Miss Hall, how would you propose to take the business forward?'

'Well . . .' Think, *think*, you've been practising answers all night, woman. 'I've had a look at the current income and expenditure figures, and I'm certain there's room for improvements. I'd bake all my own cakes and scones. I'll look carefully at pricing, staffing levels, costs and the like, offering good-quality food at a fair price for the customer, and keeping an eye on making a profit too. But, most of all, I want to give people a really positive, friendly experience so they'd want to come back . . . And, I'd like to try and source local produce.'

Lord Henry raised a rather hairy grey eyebrow. It sounded stilted, even to her.

At that, there was a brusque knock on the door. It swung open. 'So sorry I'm late.' A man strolled in. Wow, he was rather gorgeous, in a tall, dark-haired and lean kind of way. He offered an outstretched hand to Ellie as he walked past her chair and acknowledged Lord Henry. He looked late twenties, possibly early thirties. 'There was a problem with the tractor,' he offered, by way of explanation, 'She needs a major service, but I've got her going again for now.'

He had a firm grip, long fingers and neat nails.

'Miss Hall, this is Joseph Ward, our estate manager.'

'Hello.' Ellie smiled nervously. Another interrogator.

The younger man looked back at her with dark-brown eyes, his gaze intent, as though he were trying to suss her out. Then his features seemed to soften, 'Joe, I prefer Joe.' A pointed glance was exchanged between the two men. Ellie sensed a certain tension, which had nothing to do with her. Joe sat down, angling his seat to the side of the desk. There was something about him that reminded her of the guy off *Silent Witness*, hmm, yes, that Harry chap, from the series before, with his dark-haired English-gentleman look. He must be over six foot, on the slim side, but not without a hint of muscle beneath his blue cotton shirt, which was rolled up to the elbow and open at the neck. He looked smart-scruffy all at once.

'Sorry if I interrupted you there. Please carry on where you left off.' His voice wasn't upper class despite his appearance, having the Geordie lilts of her home town. He smiled at her.

On closer inspection she noted that his eyes were a deep brown with flecks of green. Her mind had gone blank. What the hell *had* she been talking about?

'Local produce?' Lord Henry prompted.

'Oh, yes, I'd certainly look to use the local farmers' markets and shops to source good local food.'

'Hmn, sounds a good idea,' Joe nodded.

'Well, Mrs Charlton, the lady who's been running the tearooms announced her departure rather suddenly,' Lord Henry took up, 'She's had the lease here for the past twelve years and we were rather hoping she would be back to start the season again in a month's time. With Easter being at the end of March this year, we would need somebody quickly. Would that be a problem for you?'

'No, at least I don't think so. I'd hand my notice in at work straight away. I'm meant to give a month, but the company owes me some holiday, and I believe they are usually quite flexible.' Did that actually mean Lord Henry was interested in her? What about Supercook Cynthia from earlier?

'So, what *is* your current position, Ellie?' Joe looked right into her eyes as he spoke, unsettling her. *He* wasn't going to miss a trick, was he? Damn, and it all seemed to be going so well.

Deep breath, how to phrase this one? 'Ah-m, well, I have been working as an insurance administrator. But, as I was explaining to Lord Henry, I have been building up my experience in the catering industry over many years. My friend owns a bistro, where I regularly help out.' *Fill in sandwich bar here*. 'And I have worked at a local restaurant.' *Funky Chicken, as a waitress*, the heckler in her mind added. She was losing her nerve rapidly.

'I see.' Joe was mulling her words over, rubbing his fingertips across his chin, definitely unconvinced.

'Ah, right. Well then. I see.' Lord Henry was cooling too.

'And what formal qualifications do you have in catering, Ellie?' asked Joe.

She began to feel sick. *None, I have none*. Her voice came out small, 'I haven't anything formal other than the standard health and hygiene requirements.' *Liar, liar pants on fire*. Well, she'd be getting those as soon as possible. 'Much as I'd have loved to, I haven't trained professionally as a chef.' A lump stuck in her throat. She knew she shouldn't have come, what had she been thinking? The dream was slipping away . . .

'But,' she had to grasp at something, tell them how much this meant to her, 'I want this more than anything. The admin, the insurance role, that's just a job, a means of earning money. But I'm passionate about my baking. I cook fabulous cakes and pastries and scones. That's not just me saying it, either, my family, my friends are always asking me to bake for them. I can make soups and quiches. I've wanted to run my own tearooms since I was a little girl.' The words were gushing out now. 'Just give me a year. Give me this season and I'll show you. I can turn the business around, pay you a good lease, *and* attract more people to the castle to do the tours that I notice you do. We could plan themed open days. I could cook medieval-style food.' *She wasn't even sure what kind of food 'medieval' might be.* 'Try cream-tea afternoons. Link up with local charities, host a fundraiser, a summer fete. Halloween, why not? It looks spooky enough here.' She ran out of steam then.

Joe was giving her a wry smile. She wasn't sure if he liked what she heard or was thinking that she was totally bonkers. Where had all that come from? She hadn't actually thought of any of it till now; it certainly wasn't what she'd been rehearsing in her head all night. Some last-ditch chance at getting hired, probably. A final fling at her dream or else it was back home. Home wasn't so bad, to be fair. Her mum and dad were great, but it was a narrow life, living in a brick-built semi in Heaton, and working in an office block in the suburbs of Newcastle. She couldn't afford her own place. Well, not now anyway. *That* particular dream had been ransacked by

Gavin-bloody-tosser-Mason. She needed this *so* badly, this new start. And a castle, surely, wasn't a bad place to begin.

They were staring at her, an awkward silence forming around them. Then Lord Henry stood up, indicating that it was time for her departure. 'Well, thank you for taking the time and effort to come all this way, Miss Hall.'

There was no 'We'll be in touch very soon' like good old Cynthia had. Though Joe did add, 'We'll let you know something in the next week or so. We do have several candidates to see and there may be second interviews.' He stood up, his hand outstretched. His fingers clasped warmly around her own.

'Yes, we'll be in touch.' Lord Henry gave an inscrutable smile.

Out in the cool corridor, Deana caught up with her. 'Do you want to have a quick look around the kitchens, the tearooms? Get an idea of what you're in for?'

'Okay, yep, that'd be good.' Go on, just dangle that carrot, show her everything she was about to lose.

They wound down the stone stairwell. She could almost imagine an old witch up at the top with a spinning wheel; all ready to prick the girl's finger, send her to sleep for a hundred years, and then there'd be her knight in shining armour galloping in to kiss her awake again. It happened like that in fairytales, you see, oh yes, those heroic men would hack down a forest just to get to you. Where were all the heroes nowadays? She sighed – she'd obviously been fed too many Disney movies as a child. Back out to the courtyard again and in through a heavy wooden side door that opened with a creak into the kitchen. It was big, *very* big, with rather drab mushroom-grey-painted walls; you could cater for a function easily from here. Weddings and parties were flitting through her mind. It had obviously been de-signed for bigger things than a tearoom. She wondered if it had been the original castle kitchen, but there were no signs of anything pre-seventies, really, no old ranges or copper kettles, no Victorian bells lined up on the walls for the staff (*Downton* was still flitting around her head), just practical stainless-steel work surfaces, a two-sided sink, huge oven, modern microwave, fridge, chest freezer and dishwasher.

Deana waltzed through, pointing out the various equipment, apologising for the general state of the place, explaining that Mrs Charlton, the previous lease-owner, had left in a hurry at the end of last season, only recently announcing that she wasn't coming back – some family crisis, apparently.

On closer inspection the walls were a bit greasy-looking, and the convection fan had a layer of tar-like grime; it needed taking down, scrubbing and bleaching. But Ellie didn't mind a spot of cleaning.

There was a narrow passageway leading from the kitchen. Deana set off, Ellie following her through to the tearooms themselves. Now *this* was back in time, a real contrast to the kitchens. History smacked you in the face – high stone walls, leaded windows, a massive fireplace; they'd need whole tree trunks, not logs, on that grate. A huge pair of antlers was fixed high above the hearth; that would have been one hell of a scary deer, like something out of the ice age. Deana was chattering on about how different it was when the visitors were there.

'Are they real?' Ellie asked, looking up at the antlers.

'Replicas, I believe, but the originals were from a real animal, fossilised. Can't tell you when they were dated, but, yeah, that would have been a brute of a beast, wouldn't it?'

'You're telling me!' It was like Bambi on steroids.

The corridor had taken them from twentieth-century kitchen – it hadn't *quite* reached the twenty-first yet, back to some sixteenth-century vault. Well, the tearooms certainly had character: reams of it. There were about ten dark-wood tables with chairs, their floral-patterned seat pads frayed. It was an amazing place, but it all looked rather unloved.

Even so, she could picture it there with the fire on, posies on the tables, the smell of home baking, friendly waitresses in black skirts, white blouses and frilly aprons, and herself cooking away in the kitchen, doing plenty of Nigella spoon-licking, having to test all the cakes personally, of course – Ellie's Teashop.

Back in the car a few minutes later, she realized she was trembling. Maybe it was just the Northumberland March chill. Or perhaps it was the fear that this was the last she might see of this place. She wanted this so much.

2

Ellie

She pulled up, finding a parking space four houses down from her family home in Heaton. Rows and rows of brick terraces crowded around her. It wasn't a bad place to live; the neighbours were friendly, there were coffee shops and takeaways around the corner, a park near by and a ten-minute metro ride and you were in the lively city centre of Newcastle-upon-Tyne. But today she'd had a taste of something different; a castle brimming with history in the middle of the most stunning countryside, big Northumbrian skies, open space, a taste of freedom. And she wanted to taste just a little more of it, to live it, breathe it, cook in it.

Today had given Ellie a sense of her future. Made her want the job all the more. Yet she wasn't at all sure how the interview with Lord Henry and Joe had gone. Her inner interview-ometer was registering pretty low.

She got out of the car, walked down to number five, and wandered in for what might have been the thousandth time. Smells of polish and vegetables filled the air. She found her mum, Sarah, in the kitchen, peeling carrots. Onions, parsnips and a hunk of marble-fatted beef sat on a chopping board ready for cubing.

'Hello, pet . . . *So*, how did it go?' She turned to her daughter with a cautious smile.

'Umn, I don't know, to be honest . . . It was an amazing place . . . proper castle . . . big grounds. The people seemed nice.' Well, Lord Henry seemed quietly intimidating, but he was the sort of person it might take a while to get to know. Deana, she was just lovely. And Joe, hmn, gorgeous Joe, something about him made her feel uneasy, yet he seemed okay, a bit aloof, maybe, but then it had been a formal interview. His questions had definitely been more searching than Lord Henry's. She'd need to be far more prepared, do some full costings, a business plan and book her health and hygiene course, if there was to be a second interview or anything. *If* . . . a small word, *massive* implications. She plastered on a hopeful smile as her mother looked across at her.

'Well,' her mother's tone dipped into school-marmish, 'It is a bit out of the way up there. I'm still not sure why you're looking that far out? Just think of all the fuel. How long did it take you to get there?'

'About an hour.' Due north up the A1, then a maze of winding lanes. She wasn't thinking about travelling every day, she wanted to live there – the ad said there might be accommodation with the lease. But she hadn't mentioned that yet. No point getting her mum all wound up if it wasn't going to happen.

'Are you *sure* about all this, Ellie? It does seem a bit of a whim. I still can't grasp why you're thinking about giving up a good office job with a reasonable salary. What if it all goes wrong? You won't be able to waltz back into the insurance job again, you know – what with the recession and everything.' Sarah looked up from chopping carrots, her blue-grey eyes shadowed with concern.

'Well, thanks for the vote of confidence.'

'Oh, pet. It's not that I don't want you to do well. I just don't want you to fall down with this. Get caught up in some dream and then realize it's not all it's supposed to be. I'd hate for you to end up with no job at all.' She wiped her hands on her floral apron and gave Ellie an affectionate pat on the shoulder. It was as near a hug as she was going to get.

Her mother was sensible, cautious; she liked order and stability. Sometimes it drove Ellie nuts. Yes, the concern was no doubt born of love, but lately the family safety net felt like it was strangling her. When were dreams so bad, so dangerous? The two of them got on alright, but often Ellie felt very different from her mother. They viewed the world through different eyes. Ellie felt that there was something more out there in the big wide world, something she hadn't found yet. And so what if it all went wrong? At least she'd have tried.

'It's not as though there are jobs on trees at the moment, Eleanor.' Jeez, her full name was coming into action now. Mum really was toeing the sensible line.

'I know that. But, I'd find something else if it came to it, Mum.' She'd waitress, clean loos or something if she had to, if it all went belly-up a few months down the line.

Sarah just raised her eyes to heaven and took the slab of meat to hand.

Ellie sighed. Nanna Beryl would have understood. But she wasn't here to back her up any more, bless her. A knot of loss tightened inside. She was such an amazing character, hard-working, fun, loving and wise. Nanna had inspired Ellie into this baking malarkey, many moons ago in her tiny kitchen flat – Ellie cleaning the mixing bowl out with big licks of the wooden spoon once the cake had gone into the oven. She had watched, she had learned, had her fill of sticky-sweet cake mix, and she had loved. She kept Nanna's battered old Be-Ro recipe book stashed in her bedroom, with Beryl's hand-written adaptations and extra recipes held within it. Her choffee cake was awesome – a coffee-chocolate dream: one bite and you felt you'd gone to heaven.

But bless her, she had died just over a year ago. Ellie still felt that awful pang of missing her. Hopefully she was up in heaven somewhere still cooking cakes and keeping all the angels cheery and plump. Yes, she was sure Nanna Beryl would have supported her in this, told her to go out there and give it a try. She could almost hear her voice, that golden-warm Geordie accent, 'Go on canny lass, diven' worry about your mam. She was born sensible, that one. It's *your* life, *your* dream.'

And she needed this change, especially with everything that happened six months ago with that tosser Gavin. Nah, she didn't want to even think about that. He wasn't worth spending thinking-time on.

Ellie popped her jacket in the understairs cupboard and came back to the kitchen offering to make the dumplings for the stew. She asked her mum about her day, glad to divert the attention and questions from herself. Sarah had a part-time job at the Co-op around the corner, as well as doing a couple of mornings' cleaning at the doctor's surgery. They chatted comfortably. Mixing the dumpling ingredients took Ellie's mind off things. She added dried herbs to the flour, then the suet and water, rolling the dough between her hands, circling broken-off lumps in her palms into neat balls ready to float on the stew.

Ten minutes later, the front door banged open and Keith, Ellie's father, appeared with a loud 'Hullo' and a broad grin, returning home after a day plumbing and handy-manning. He popped his head into the kitchen. 'Good day, girls! How did it go, then, our Ellie? Head chef already?'

'Not quite,' she smiled. 'There's a chance of a second interview. But I'll just have to wait and see.'

'Well, best of luck, bonny lass. Best of luck. Better go up and get myself changed out of these work things. Stew is it tonight, Mam?

'Ah-hah.'

'Great. I'm starving.'

Things had been slower for him these past few years with the recession biting hard in the building trade, but he'd do odd jobs as well as the plumbing, anything really. He had a trade – he was lucky, he often said. Ellie listened to his cheery whistle as he headed upstairs to change out of his navy boiler suit.

Jason, Ellie's brother, sauntered in soon after, dumping muddy football boots in the hall. He was nine years younger than Ellie, seventeen to her twenty-six, and still at sixth form. In the main he tried to avoid schoolwork as much as he could, filling the gap with sport, occasionally interrupted by a crush on a new girl. This month it was Kylie of the white-blonde hair and dark roots from down the road. She was still giving out confusing signals, apparently, one minute sitting next to him on the bus to town, full of chat, the next giggling with her friends and hardly giving him the time of day.

'Jason, boots out the back, please. *Not* the hall. The house'll be stinking. I don't know how many times I have to tell you,' Sarah shouted, catching him before he drifted off upstairs, and the aroma of sweaty teenage footwear permeated the house.

An hour and a half later, they were all assembled around the kitchen table. Jay was famished, as per usual, and shovelled his stew down like there was no tomorrow. Then a normal night in the Hall household followed: telly – sport or soaps, *Coronation Street* being Mum's favourite, the boys swapping channels to any footie that might be going, general chit-chat, cup of tea, off to bed.

Ellie opted for an early night. The trip up north, the interview, had drained her. Lying there under her single duvet, within the four pink-painted walls – one cerise, three blossom (she'd chosen the shades aged twelve) – of her small bedroom, she thought about her day at Claverham Castle. Was there any chance they might offer her the lease? If so – *wildest dreams* – would they also offer her a room there? What might it be like, working there, living there? Her dreams felt like bubbles, floating iridescent in a blue sky of hope. But, then, wasn't there always the inevitable pop, then plop, when you came splatting back down to earth?

Her thoughts spun on, sleep elusive. She should have been better prepared, done her homework, thought about it all more thoroughly. *And,* she hadn't even mentioned half the things in the interview that she'd mentally prepped in bed the night before. Maybe her mother *was* right; doing things on a whim was never the best option. But something inside told her she was right to try for that interview today. She'd been so excited reading the ad in the job pages of the *Journal,* then ringing up, actually getting an interview, taking those steps towards her dream. She *could* make a go of it, given half a chance. The *if* dangled before her, her dream on a very thin thread, making her feel queasy in the pit of her stomach.

Ellie's baking adventures continue in the second
Cosy Teashop novel

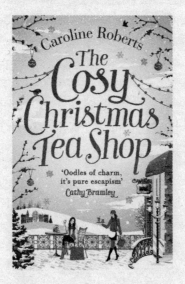

Also available to buy now